Dead Reckoning

Dead Reckoning

PATRICIA HALL

This edition published in Great Britain in 2004 by
Allison & Busby Limited
Bon Marche Centre
241-251 Ferndale Road
London SW9 8BJ
http://www.allisonandbusby.com

Copyright © 2003 by Patricia Hall

The moral right of the author has been asserted.

ISBN 0 7490 0674 9

Printed and bound in Spain by
Liberdúplex, s.l., Barcelona

Also by this author

In the Ackroyd & Thackeray series

Prologue

He twined his fingers in her long dark hair which she had loosened from its normal severity. But when he pulled her closer and tried to kiss her she pulled away and shuddered slightly.

"What if they find me?" she whispered.

"They won't find you," he said, with as much reassurance as he could muster.

"They will be so angry. My brothers..."

"Your brothers won't find you. Take the train. You'll be quite safe. And then as soon as I can get away I'll join you. We'll be together in another country. A new life. Away from all the nonsense that's going on here. You'll be fine, I promise."

"You can't come now?" Her voice trembled with an anxiety she tried hard to conceal.

"You know I can't," he said holding her close again. "I have to finish things here. I can't just walk out. In any case, it will be less obvious to your family if we leave separately. Much safer for you. I'll only be a few weeks behind you. Everything's finalised, official. You'll be fine. "

"Your family will hate me," she said.

"My mother will love you because I do," he said.

"It wouldn't work like that with my family," she said, and he could feel her trembling again through the soft silk of her dress. "They try so hard to be modern and sophisticated and European but deep down nothing changes. They'll try to find me."

"And they won't succeed. You'll be safe, I promise. And we'll be happy." And this time she let him kiss her, and all the anxieties about what they had planned so carefully seemed to melt away as passion took over.

The next day she took the train south.

Chapter One

In normal circumstances the body would have been found quite quickly. Broadley Crag was a local beauty spot, a ragged cliff of millstone grit which dropped from the dun-coloured winter expanse of Broadley Moor to a finger of sheltered green fields where the local farmers over-wintered their sheep and a few hardy ponies were left out to graze until snow or frost made it impossible. Normally, even in the most bitter weather, when sharp winds blasted unimpeded over the hundred miles of hill and heather that lay directly between this part of Yorkshire and Scotland, the rutted car-park, set well back from the edge of the crag, would have been busy most afternoons in anything less than a blizzard. But this winter a pocket of foot-and-mouth disease some five miles away had seen the car-park blocked off with a few well-placed boulders and stark red notices which had deterred most of the hikers, runners, model aeroplane enthusiasts and bird-watchers who normally frequented this wild green lung only ten miles from the industrial centre of Bradfield and Milford.

Which was why farmer Fred Stanley's first reaction was one of fury when he noticed a patch of something red lodged half inside a natural cave beneath one of the huge black boulders which littered the shallower part of the crag above his farm.

"Little bastards," he muttered. "Can't they bloody well be told?"

The cave, with its soft and usually dry sandy floor was a favourite hiding place for sheep seeking shelter from the wind and rain and for young boys playing along the crag's hidden paths and tumbling screes. It was one of the first

11

places he had looked when he discovered tell-tale scraps of wool where, overnight, one of his dry-stone walls around the sheep pastures had given up its hundred year struggle against gravity and the elements. He did not blame the sheep. The disease restrictions meant that they had remained in a pasture long after they had nibbled every scrap of goodness from the grass, and some of them found the hay he was providing a poor substitute. He did not know how long sheep could remember anything. They were stupid animals. But he guessed it was not impossible that some of the ewes could recall better commons up on the open moorland above the little valley, moorland where they normally roamed for most of the year, and that they had decided to take a look when the chance offered. After all, foot-and-mouth restrictions on grazing meant nothing to them, he thought. But kids? Kids from round Broadley especially? They should know better. Surely no one could have missed the rancorous debate about the disease, its origins, its wild-fire progress across the country and the best methods of dealing with it, which had raged across the newspapers and television screens all the previous year. He had been as bitterly disappointed as everyone else when another case had been confirmed so close to Broadley.

"Hey oop," he yelled towards the hiding place forty feet above him. "Get out of theer, you little beggar. Clear off!" But when there was no response from the intruder he began to clamber carefully up between the heather and bilberry tussocks which had almost overgrown the sheep-paths during the emergency. It was not until he had reached the boulders, which at some point, long before his or even his father's time, had tumbled from the top of the crag more than a hundred feet above the farm, that he could see that whoever was lying there was unnaturally still.

"Bloody hell," he muttered when he had scrambled closer, crouching over what was undoubtedly an adult, dressed in black sweat-pants and the red shirt which had first caught his attention from the farm track below. Tentatively he rolled the body towards him so that he could see the face and realised as soon as he saw the mess of blood and bone that he hardly needed to touch the ice cold skin to confirm that the man was dead.

All thought of his lost sheep disappeared as he turned away, unexpectedly queasy so close to a human death in a way he would not have been had the victim been an animal. Awkwardly he lumbered back down the slope, made slippery by a hard overnight frost, and ran back to the warmth of the farm kitchen where his wife was cooking breakfast. His hands were shaking as he dialled 999 for the police.

"Accident, was it?" DCI Michael Thackeray looked up from his paperwork as Sergeant Kevin Mower put his head round the door of his office later that morning. Mower had been the senior detective on duty when the body had been found at Broadley Crag and had followed the uniformed officers out to the scene.

"I reckon so, guv," he said. "Amos came out to have a look and will do a PM later, but there were no obvious signs of foul play. He was dressed for a run so it looks as if he slipped on the icy vegetation and went over the edge. Head-first by the look of it. Made a mess of his face."

"Do we know who he is?" Thackeray asked.

"He had no ID on him. He was in sports gear. But the local uniforms are looking for a car. He won't have got up there any other way unless he's very local but the car-park close to the crag is closed off because of foot-and-mouth so he'll have left it somewhere else. He shouldn't have been on that land,

13

by rights. The farmer who found him is doing his nut. More seriously, it could have been months before the body was found except for the fact that he was wearing a bright sweat-shirt and it stood out like a red rag to a farmer looking for a lost sheep, would you believe?"

It was not clear whether Mower, a sharp-suited, sharp-wit-ted and crop-haired urban man to his fingertips, had been more surprised to rediscover the existence of sheep or by the fact that even in the twenty-first century the Biblical creatures occasionally went astray. He looked more than slightly aggrieved at his unexpected early morning encounter with icy rocks that had threatened his stability, rough terrain that had scuffed his loafers, gorse bushes which had plucked viciously at his trousers and the monosyllabic outrage of a taciturn countryman whose pastoral calm had been invaded so brutally.

"Perhaps he didn't know about the foot-and-mouth restric-tions," Thackeray said.

"You'd have to be blind not to see the notices up there, guv," Mower said. "And a recluse not to have heard that the disease is back. The local bobby had us all trailing through disinfectant before he'd let us set foot off the main road. Bloody marvellous." He glanced down at his shoes with some anxiety. "Anyway, he reckons it couldn't be someone local. He must have come from further afield to be so pig ignorant, he reckons. But they'll ask around Broadley village if a car doesn't turn up soonish, just in case. Though he's not one of your locals who admits he could be wrong, isn't PC Moody. Typical bloody Yorkshireman."

"So everything's under control then?" Thackeray asked with only the faintest smile in acknowledgement of the criti-cism of his native heath from the Londoner. And Mower knew that it was not just the sudden death that he was referring to.

14

"Yes, guv," he said quietly. He knew that the DCI would not press the issue, but was aware of being on an unofficial and unspoken probation that he suspected might prove permanent. Well, he thought, if the trust Thackeray had placed in him had been shattered beyond repair he would have to manage without it. It would not be the first time in his career that senior officers had regarded him with suspicion. And if the worst came to the worst, his decision to come back to the job after three months' sick leave was not irrevocable and the prospect of moving on not unattractive. There must, he thought, be easier ways to earn a living than gazing into the remnants of a man's smashed and bloodied face before breakfast, as he had done that morning.

"Keep me up to speed, Kevin," Thackeray said.

"Guv," the sergeant muttered as he closed the office door behind him. Thackeray sighed. He had stuck his neck out for Mower when his superintendent, Jack Longley, would have sacked him, but with Mower apparently securely back in harness he knew he would get no thanks for his stand, either from above or below, if the sergeant's new-found stability proved to be an illusion. There were times, he thought, when the tightrope he negotiated at work and at home felt dangerously frayed. He glanced at the clock, closed the file in front of him and flung it into his out tray. His next appointment was with his solicitor.

Across town in the newsroom of the *Bradfield Gazette*, Thackeray's girlfriend Laura Ackroyd scowled at her own reflection in her blank computer screen and tried to control the fury which had overtaken her more than an hour ago as she had walked through the town centre on her way in to the office.

She had come hurriedly out of a coffee shop clutching a

polystyrene take-away, anxious to get to work before her irascible boss began hurling himself round the office like a rogue torpedo seeking a target, when she found herself surrounded by a group of young men who were milling about on the pavement laughing and shouting apparently amongst themselves. But when Laura had dodged to the other side of the group she realised that the object of their jeers was two Asian women in traditional dress who were hurrying along the pavement on the other side of the street. Before she could react, the youths had dodged through the traffic and surrounded their prey, while other shoppers edged away, doing nothing to deter them. The women, probably a mother and daughter, Laura thought, glanced around wildly for help and the younger of the two, a protective arm around her companion, caught Laura's eye with a desperate appeal as the boldest of the youths tweaked her headscarf off her sleek black hair and said something which made both women flinch.

Without thinking, Laura dodged the traffic herself and pushed her way through the laughing youths and grabbed the arm of the one who had been most prominent in the assault.

"What's your problem?" she yelled, to the evident amazement of both attackers and attacked. "Can't you think of anything better to do with your time than harass women?"

One or two of the youths backed away slightly at this unexpected attack but the ring-leader stood his ground, his grin of disbelief turning quickly to an angry snarl.

"Who've we got here then?" he asked his mates. "A bloody Paki-lover? Don't you read your papers, love? Don't you know they're all fucking terrorists and should be shipped back where they came from?" And with deliberate intent he turned back towards the gang's two victims and spat in the older woman's face.

16

"You pig," Laura said, her colour rising as she searched desperately for at least one friendly face amongst the scatter of onlookers who had stopped on the fringes of the group since she had intervened. "You disgusting racist pig. Can anyone see a policeman?"

"There's never one there when you need one is there?" her antagonist mocked amongst more raucous laughter from his mates, while behind her she could hear one of the women sobbing.

"It doesn't bloody matter," Laura said. "I'll take them to the police myself."

This threat did not seem to alarm the youths much but as the crowd of onlookers grew larger and one or two murmurs of disapproval seemed to reach them, they began to retreat.

"You want to watch it with that ginger hair, love," the ringleader flung over his shoulder as he moved off. "You'll catch fire and burn thi'sen if you're not careful. And you won't find a bloody Paki rushing to put t'fire out neither."

As the adrenaline drained away, Laura found herself shaking, and when she turned to the two women behind her, she met dark frightened eyes and near inarticulate thanks. But when she tried to persuade them to come with her to police headquarters they both shook their heads.

"No police," the younger woman said. "They won't do owt. Ever since New York this has been happening all t'time. T'police don't want to know."

"Of course they want to know. I'll make bloody sure they want to know," Laura had said recklessly. "There are witnesses. We can find those yobs again." But the women merely looked more frightened than ever and began to edge away along the pavement, watched impassively by the remaining onlookers who were quickly losing interest.

"No police," the younger woman said again. "You are

17

very kind, but we're all reet now." While her daughter spoke in the unmistakable accent of what was almost certainly her birthplace, the older woman nodded and said something voluble in what Laura guessed was Punjabi, the most common of the Asian languages used in Bradfield. She had wrapped her long lace-fringed head-scarf tightly around her head and face so that little was visible except her dark frightened eyes, still full of tears.

"I'm so sorry," Laura said, overwhelmed by a feeling of shame that an elderly woman should be so humiliated.

"We must go. Me mam's got an appointment at the Infirmary," the second woman said.

Laura watched them hurry to the traffic lights at the end of the street and then trudge up the hill towards Bradfield's main hospital.

"You want to watch yourself. Lads like that'll have a knife out before you know it." Laura turned to identify this unexpected voice and found a heavily built man with a florid complexion watching her from a shop doorway.

"Did you see what happened?" she asked quickly.

"Aye, well, I might have, and then again I might not," the man said. "I'm just sayin', that's all. You're taking a chance facing beggars like that down. And for Pakis, an'all."

"Well someone's got to," Laura said, turning on her heel and marching so angrily to the office that by the time she got there she found that most of her skinny latte had been shaken out of the loose top of her cup and splashed down her almost new black coat before she reached her desk. She drank the dregs, flung the cup into her waste bin with a thud, tried to scrub herself dry with a tissue and fastened back the strands of unruly red hair which had escaped from their anchors as she had hurried to the office. But the fury that had erupted in the street did not dissipate, it merely died into a glowing

18

ember of anger that she knew she had to do something about.

As soon as Ted Grant, the *Gazette's* editor, had settled himself into his glass-walled enclosure at one end of the newsroom – and before he had time to begin his morning prowl amongst the reporters' desks – Laura had tapped on his half-open door and dropped into the single hard chair which Grant reserved for visitors when it was not piled high with back-copies or the heaps of material which passed for in and out trays in his scheme of work. He glanced up from his close reading of the morning's *Globe*, on which he had once served what he claimed had been a triumphant stint before returning to his home town, and took in Laura's flushed face and still-dishevelled hair.

"What's rattled your cage so early?" he asked.

She told him what she had witnessed outside the coffee shop.

"We need to do something about this sort of thing," she said. "It's getting out of hand, getting the town a bad name, and anyway some of the Asians are our readers."

"Those that bother to learn English," Grant objected.

"This was in broad daylight in a main shopping street," Laura said. "Two women on the way to the Infirmary, for God's sake. Even if it won't stand up as a news story it's a good peg for a feature on race relations. There's going to be real trouble if someone doesn't stop these yobs."

"They're their own worst enemy some of the Asians. Young men threatening this and threatening that. They sound like terrorists even if it is all bravado."

"They'll fight back if this sort of harassment gets any worse," Laura said. "We'll have a war on our hands."

"Aye, well, that's your boyfriend's problem, not mine," Grant said, his eyes flicking back to the *Globe's* page three.

"We're reporters not bloody race relations experts. Why don't you do summat for your women's page about forced marriages, if you want an Asian subject? Find out how many girls they're shipping back to Paki-land every year to pick up a husband."

"That's..." Laura began but Grant's rising colour and bulging blue eyes stopped her completing her objection, which she knew was a waste of breath in any case. If Grant could not already see how fragile the peace was becoming in Bradfield she guessed that she lacked the powers to persuade him. His belief that the word of a woman was worth only a fraction of that of a man was almost Muslim in its intensity.

Back at her desk she gazed at her reflection for a long time before switching on her computer and reading through the features for the next day's paper. But before she felt calm enough to begin editing the fashion contributor's stilted prose, she pulled a carefully folded letter out of her handbag and scanned the contents again. Then she made a phone call.

"Kelly?" she said when she was connected. "I've been thinking about what we discussed last week. And yes, I'd like to stand in for you while you're away if your bosses are happy with that arrangement. Listen. What do you think of this for a theme?" She glanced around the newsroom as she put the receiver down, to make sure that she had not been overheard, and then gave her reflection its first smile of the day. Just possibly, she thought, she had found the escape tunnel from Ted Grant's Colditz that she had been seeking for so long.

Chapter Two

The message to call Amos Atherton, the pathologist, was on Michael Thackeray's desk when he arrived in the office after a canteen lunch.

"There's something not right about this lad they found up on Broadley Moor this morning," Atherton said bluntly when he took Thackeray's call. "My fault. It looked like an obvious accident to me but now I've got him stripped down I'm not so sure. I think the body's been moved around. D'you want to come down?"

Thackeray had little choice but to agree, in spite of his distaste for the cold intimacies of the post-mortem examination process, and within ten minutes he and sergeant Kevin Mower had walked the short distance from police headquarters to Bradfield Infirmary, where the pathology department was housed in the cavernous tiled basement of the Victorian hospital. In the fiercely lit morgue, Atherton and his assistant had stripped the clothes from the remains of the still unidentified jogger and were listing the head and neck injuries which had evidently killed him, and the bruises and abrasions on other parts of his body. To Thackeray's unskilled eye there seemed to be little on the slab which was not consistent with the theory so far accepted by the medics and the police who had attended the scene, that the jogger had slipped and crashed over the edge of the crag, falling some hundred feet to smash head-first onto the rocks below. Even in the bright mortuary lights, the man's own mother would have difficulty recognising what was left of his face.

Atherton ended his recitation into his tape-recorder and switched the machine off.

"It did strike me as a bit odd that rigor was so far advanced when I examined him," he said. "It was damn cold up there, well below freezing, which usually slows the stiffening down. Of course he could have been there all night but the farmer was adamant he wasn't there when he went to look at his animals at dusk, so the consensus seemed to be he'd been on an early morning run and lost his footing on the frosty surface."

"And now?" Thackeray prompted.

"You can be wrong about rigor, but not about hyperstasis. Look at him. He's like a bloody ghost."

The figure lying on its back on the slab was certainly pale but the police officers had not immediately grasped the significance of that.

"After death the blood pools in the lowest part of the body," Atherton explained with some impatience. "You should know that by now."

"And of course he was found face down," Mower said quickly. "Sorry guv, maybe I never mentioned that. The farmer had turned him over, actually, but he said he was definitely face down when he found him."

"It'd have helped if you'd shared that bit of information with me while we were up there," Atherton said sharply. "Any road, face down, the blood should have run to the chest and stomach. Instead of which it's very obviously run to the back, the buttocks and the back of the thighs and calves. Look." Atherton rolled the body, like a board with rigor mortis, to one side slightly to reveal the purplish underside. "He lay on his back for some time after death to arrive in that condition," he said. "You may have an accident here, but I wouldn't bank on it. I suspect he was dead when he went over the crag. And if he'd landed on his back instead of his front whoever chucked him over might have got away with it. If the hyperstasis had been in the right place I'd not have

22

been any more suspicious now than you lot were when you found him. Now…?"

He shrugged his broad shoulders and patted his green plastic apron over his belly.

"Now I think we'd better do a serious job on this young man, don't you? I take it you lads'll be stopping?"

Back in his office after two hours spent watching Atherton's detailed dissection of the body on his slab Thackeray wondered how many murders were written off as accidents – as this one had so nearly been. Kevin Mower, who had followed him into the room, tried to conceal the anxiety twisting his stomach in a way which took him back to places he did not wish to revisit.

"Sorry, guv," he said. "We nearly missed that one. It wasn't really Amos's fault. I'd already talked to the farmer and sent him back down. It was bloody dangerous up there."

"He should have checked whether the body had been moved," Thackeray said, without much sympathy for the heavyweight pathologist.

"Yeah, well, he was working crouched on a ledge on a bloody mini-precipice covered in ice. I had to hold him steady once or twice or he'd have slipped to the bottom himself. Let's face it: he's not built for that sort of work. He must have reckoned it would be better to get the body out and into the morgue sharpish rather than hang around there. No one suspected foul play. I've had the site taped off but I didn't think it was worth leaving anyone up there."

"Right," Thackeray said. "You're both lucky that bit of ground is off-limits to the public so it shouldn't have been touched since he was found."

"Except for the odd lost sheep," Mower muttered, with a sideways smile at the inimitable details of country life.

"The farmer will have safely corralled them by now," Thackeray said, with the certainty of one who had grown up on a farm. "It's illegal for them to be loose on the moors in restricted areas. And that goes for us too, but there'll have to be a way found round that so we can treat the area as a crime scene. Call the Ministry of Agriculture or whatever they call themselves now. Tell them we need to do a fingertip search of an area of Broadley Moor and the Crag and get whatever permission that takes. Disinfectant up to our eyebrows, I shouldn't wonder. And then get an incident room set up. First priority is to find out who he is, next how he got there. If he was dead before he went over the top, as Amos suggests, it sounds as if it would take a vehicle and at least two men to get him to where he was found."

"If the killer had known about hyperstasis he might have got away with it," Mower said.

"Maybe," Thackeray conceded. "Although Amos would probably have found the suspicious head wound anyway once he'd started looking closely at the skull. The cuts and bruises from the fall were obviously not enough to disguise the clean blow on the back of the head which probably killed him. Let's hope there's some forensic evidence as well when the lab results come back. And one thing we can be sure of. Nothing's going to get past Amos now. He's made a mistake and his pride's on the line. Did I hear an apology, by the way?"

"I wouldn't go quite as far as that, guv," Mower said with a grin. "But I reckon he'll be good for a drink at the end of the day." Thackeray's instant glower reminded him that he had not yet completely convinced his boss that the odd pint might not lead to far too many more, but the DCI made no comment. He glanced instead at the papers on his desk.

"Anyway, let's find out who our battered jogger is, shall

we? Get your idle local bobby off his backside and get some house to house inquiries launched in Broadley. At least the victim's white enough for race not to be an issue on this one."

"White, fair-haired, probably blue-eyed, though I wouldn't swear to it – apart from that his mum'd have trouble recognising him. It'll be a distinguishing marks job," Mower said. "Appendix scars and birthmarks in unusual places."

"It's possible, I suppose, that someone deliberately tried to make sure he was unrecognisable, but Amos seems to think most of the facial injuries came from the fall. Anyway, you may be surprised what a clever undertaker can do to his face when Amos has finished," Thackeray said. "But we'll not get any sort of picture for a while, that's true. So sift through the missing persons reports and see who fits what we do know about him. He's not your average missing teenager, is he? Or one of the great unwashed. Someone'll be going frantic for him somewhere, I'd guess. Wife, girlfriend, mother."

"Do you want to talk to the troops?".

"Two o'clock," Thackeray said. "In the meantime set up the search of the crime scene while there's still time for the forensic troops to do something useful in daylight. I'll fill Jack Longley in, and sort out what we're going to tell the Press."

But when Mower had closed the office door behind him, Thackeray felt disinclined to move upstairs to see his boss. He supposed there were detectives who felt the thrill of the hunt when a new murder inquiry started. He was not one of them. As the years went by the burden of anger and sorrow at each violent death he encountered seemed to make his limbs heavier and his mind slower as he contemplated the details of the inquiry ahead. The victims were seldom only the body or bodies on Amos Atherton's slab. The innocent were always hurt and often tainted by the remorseless nature of a murder investigation. The adrenaline, he knew from experience, would kick in eventually as evidence began to accumulate but on this chilly grey morning, with his own life on the brink of changes which he knew he should have concluded long ago, he felt nothing but a weary pity for the man whose violation he had so recently witnessed in the mortuary and for all those whose lives would be devastated by his death, even, he thought wryly, for the murderer himself. "You're going soft," he told himself as he picked up the phone. "Or maybe that's your trouble. You always have been when it comes to the crunch. Laura would be proud of you."

Laura Ackroyd had been at her own desk early that morning in spite of her encounter with the town's racist youth, and by dint of taking a sandwich lunch in front of her computer screen she felt able to slide out of the busy newsroom by four. Much of the day's news agenda had been taken up with rumours and counter-rumours that one of Bradfield's three remaining textile mills, Earnshaws, which had been weaving high quality worsted cloth for the tailoring trade for more than a hundred years, was to close. Time was when the wool correspondent of the Bradfield Gazette had been a power in the town, dividing his time between the gothic Exchange, now converted into a shopping precinct, and the bar of the Clarendon Hotel, where the mill owners traditionally took a three course lunch, smoked several cigars and routinely cut local politicians off at the knees if their policies did not suit. Those days were long gone and, on the day the once staple industry looked like taking its terminal plunge into oblivion, Ted Grant was hard pressed to find a single reporter who could even distinguish between combing, spinning and weaving let alone a top from a noil. But Ted did not expect female members of his staff to bother their pretty little heads about the local economy or industrial relations – which looked like becoming imminently stormy – and on this occasion Laura was keen to keep her head down. Fifteen minutes after leaving the office she was sitting with two young Asian women in dilapidated armchairs in a women's centre just off Aysgarth Lane.

"What I'd like to do in these radio interviews is give ordinary members of the Asian community space to tell people what it's like at the moment with the tension so high," Laura said. "I was horrified by what I saw this morning in town. This was an elderly woman being abused and no one took a blind bit of notice."

"Have you talked to councillor Khalid?" asked Amina Khan, a tall woman in dark shalwar kameez and severe white hijab covering every inch of her hair. But Laura shook her head quickly.

"I don't want to talk to the community leaders and politicians for this," she said. "They get plenty of opportunity to have their say. I want to talk to people, especially women, about their own experience day to day, going shopping, taking children to school, going to the hospital like the women who were being abused this morning in the town centre. It's not the politics that I want to talk about but the reality on the street."

Amina looked dubious and shook her head but her companion, Farida Achmed, fashionable in a black trouser suit, boots and a long silky scarf thrown back from her dark hair in defiance of tradition, nodded.

"The councillors are not always the best judges of that," she said. "I work in the town hall in the housing department and I must say that no one has bothered me in the street or anywhere else for that matter. Maybe it's because I look as

27

though I can stand up for myself. But the problems are getting worse. The men are starting to talk about taking women everywhere, which knocks us back a whole generation. And there are a lot of young men who are eager to meet violence with violence. You say you don't want to get involved in the politics but to some extent this is all about politics. It's about whether immigrant communities can live here without being harassed when things get nasty in the old country."

"It's not new," Laura said. "The Irish used to become very unpopular every time there was an outrage in Belfast or London."

"But there weren't many young Irishmen prepared to stand up publicly for the terrorists, were there?" Farida came back quickly. "We have these young idiots making martyrs out of murderers, growing their beards, ranting from the mosque. None of the rest of us believe that blowing people up solves anything but we get tarred with that brush. That's why your passers-by wouldn't help the old lady. They blame us all for New York, the Taliban, terrorism in Pakistan, and all the rest of it."

"Most of them hate us anyway," Amina said quietly. "They don't want us here. Never did. It's just that much worse now."

"Well, they'll have to put up with us," Farida said. "I was born here. I went to school and college here. I don't belong anywhere else."

"There's a lot of people who'd dispute that," Amina said, her face closed and cold. "You try to dress and behave like an English girl but they laugh at you behind your back. You're still a Paki and always will be."

In spite of her traditional dress it was clear that Amina was the more forceful of the two young women and Farida glanced away, evidently unwilling to argue with her any further in front of Laura.

28

"Will you come on the programme and talk about some of these issues?" she asked Amina specifically. "Especially about how they affect women."

But Amina looked cautious.

"I'll talk to my father about it," she said at last.

"You're a grown woman. You should make your own decisions," Farida said sharply, her dark eyes bright. "I'll do it. No one ever bothers to ask the women what they think. I'd love to be on your radio show."

"Give me your mobile numbers and I'll get back to you," Laura said and, to her surprise, both Amina and Farida wrote them down for her.

She walked back across the brightly lit town centre to the *Gazette* to pick up her car more aware than usual that the late shoppers did not include many Asian women and that the groups of men in traditional dress who chatted in the town hall square stared with more than usual suspicion at passers-by from other ethnic groups. As she walked past the straggling bus queues, especially those for the services which made their way up Aysgarth Lane, the Asian community's bustling, shabby heart, before heading to outlying suburbs, she thought she detected an electric tension in the air. She had occasionally wondered if it were true that animals could sense the approach of an earthquake or a volcanic eruption and was more inclined to believe it tonight. It felt as if the centre of Bradfield, enclosed between its seven encircling hills, was about to explode.

Laura drove home in a thoughtful mood and to her surprise she saw that the ground-floor lights of the large Victorian house of which she owned one floor were on, a sign that, unusually, Michael Thackeray had arrived home before her.

Dropping her coat in the hall of the flat and her shopping in the kitchen, she opened the door of the living room and found him watching the local television news. She stood for a moment with one hand on his shoulder as the presenter described the morning's discovery of an unidentified body over shots of an unseasonable Broadley Moor, with the gorse in its brilliant summer glory.

"Stock pictures," she said, with professional certainty. "There's cars in the car-park too, look. We had the same problem. I heard one of our photographers complaining he wasn't allowed anywhere near the site because of the foot-and-mouth restrictions. It looks as though the telly cameras couldn't get any closer. Have you no idea who he is yet?"

"No one's come forward to claim him," Thackeray said, taking Laura's hand in his and pulling her onto the sofa beside him.

"Was it an accident?" Laura asked. Thackeray shrugged, not wanting to spend time discussing death tonight.

"Probably not," he said. "Did you have a good day?"

"In parts," Laura said, willing enough to distract him. So often the nature of his work hovered like a dark cloud between them.

"Only in parts," Thackeray said wryly. "You talked to this Kelly Sullivan at the radio station?"

"I did, we had a chat this morning and discussed the technicalities and some ideas I've got for interviews. And I had a quick drink with her just now on the way home and that's the good part. Her boss, the station manager, is happy for me to do her segment of the early evening show for the three weeks she's away. I can choose the people I interview and it'll be recorded in advance so it's not as nerve-wracking as live radio. It sounds great."

"And the bad part?"

Laura shuddered and told him about seeing the Asian woman harassed on her way in to work.

"It was horrible, Michael. I thought you had people trying to stamp on that sort of thing. Those lads were just brazen about it, and no one did anything to help."

"Except you, I suppose," Thackeray said. "Rushing in where angels fear to tread again? I wish you'd be careful, Laura. Gangs of lads can be dangerous. You know that."

"There were masses of people about…"

"And not one of them would help you? Perhaps that's a topic you should explore on your radio show?"

"That is a good idea, chief inspector," Laura said, taking what might had an offhand remark more seriously than Thackeray expected. "But one I've already had, as it happens. Kelly thinks it's a good idea too."

"What's Ted Grant going to make of this new career move?"

"I'm looking forward to seeing his face when I tell him," Laura said delightedly. "He can't stop me. I've done it before. There's nothing in my contract says I can't do freelance work so he'll have to lump it. Kelly says we can do the recordings to suit me so it won't interfere with what I do at the *Gazette*. Anyway, apart from picking up dead joggers on Broadley Moor, what have the forces of law and order been doing today?"

Thackeray hesitated for a moment before he spoke, choosing his quiet words with care.

"I went to see Victor Mendelson this afternoon and signed the divorce papers."

Laura turned to Thackeray in surprise, her heart thudding and her green eyes bright with expectation. This was a subject which had been flung back and forth between the two of them for so long that she had almost despaired of Thackeray's

31

ever making the vital first move towards the marriage they had discussed so often and so inconclusively that it seemed unlikely ever to become a reality.

"You really did it?"

He nodded, although she could see from his eyes that even this first step had hurt him in some way which she could only dimly understand.

"What can I say?" she said softly. "Thank you, I suppose. I know it's hard for you."

"It feels like…" Thackeray shrugged wearily. "Abandoning the two of them again, I suppose. It was never their fault. This just compounds it."

"You can't hurt them any more. It was all over long ago."

"I don't think it will ever be over," he said, and she turned away, her eyes clouding again, knowing that might be only too true.

She left him watching television and went into the bedroom to tidy up. She had been more deeply moved than she had allowed Thackeray to realise by his decision to process his divorce at last. The marriage had effectively ended more than twelve years before when Aileen had been brain-damaged by an overdose but she knew that Thackeray's sense of responsibility for the shell of a woman who had lived on in an institution ever since was profound. He blamed himself for her condition and for the death of their baby son which had preceded and provoked her suicide attempt. She knew that breaking the agonising link between them would be as hard now as it had ever been. As she brushed her deep copper curls and tied them back with a deep green ribbon which matched the silk of her shirt, she wondered whether this was something he could do without tearing himself apart all over again. He had promised to marry her, but maybe she was wrong to force the issue. And even if she eventually got him to the registry office, she wondered if he could ever satisfy what she felt as an increasingly urgent yearning to have children. Might that, even now, be a step too far?

Life was never simple, she thought with a sigh, and hers seemed to become even more complicated as she got older. She turned out the light in the bedroom, went into the kitchen, put on a butcher's apron and began to slice onions for their evening meal, though not all the tears which sprang to her eyes were caused by the fumes. Half an hour later, with a slow-cooking casserole in the oven filling the flat with its aroma, and a Billie Holiday CD on the player, and her head on Thackeray's shoulder, she was irritated when her phone rang and surprised when she recognised her father's voice at the other end.

"Dad! Is Mum all right?" she asked sharply. Her parents had retired to a villa on the Portuguese coast near Lisbon when her father had sold out his business for more millions than he was ever prepared to admit, and relations between father and daughter had passed from chilly to almost frozen over the years.

"I'm at Heathrow, love," Jack Ackroyd said. "I'm stopping at the Dorchester tonight but I'll be up in Bradfield lunchtime tomorrow. Couldn't get a flight any sooner. Booked up, they were. Things looking up in Bradfield at last, are they?"

"You must be joking. Leeds maybe, but not here. Do you want to stay with us?" Laura said, feeling stupid as her brain refused to assimilate this unexpected information. "Is Mum with you?"

"Don't be daft," her father said. "You know how she hates flying. No this is just a business trip. I've a project locally that I want to check out myself, that's all." Laura knew that her father still had business connections in Yorkshire although

33

he played his cards so close to his chest that she had no idea what they were.

"I've booked into the Clarendon," Ackroyd said. "Come and have tea with me tomorrow about four. I should have finished my first round of meetings by then. And get your gran down, an'all. She's still in that poky little place up on the Heights, is she? She'll never learn."

"I'll have to go and fetch her. Her hip's not getting any better," Laura said. "Better make it five o'clock, not four."

"Aye, right you are," Jack Ackroyd said. "I've offered to pay for a new hip if the bloody NHS can't do anything for her but you know what she's like. You'd think I'd suggested robbing a bloody starving child the way she carried on. So I'll see you both tomorrow then. I'll not be stopping long if I can avoid it."

"Right," Laura said, slightly bemused, as the line went dead.

"A visitor?" Thackeray asked wryly as she hung up.

"Not here, thank God," Laura said. "Just my father making one of his flying visits. He'll stay at the Clarendon."

"Good," Thackeray said, pulling her back onto the sofa. "I'm not in the mood to share you."

Chapter Three

To her surprise, Laura found herself summoned, along with all the rest of the more senior journalists on the *Gazette*, into the dusty, seldom-used "conference room" by a flustered looking Ted Grant almost as soon as she arrived at the office next morning.

"The chief executive has arranged for us to have a briefing from Frank Earnshaw himself about the troubles at t'mill," he said, with enough self-awareness to appreciate at least some of the ironies of such a meeting with a grim smile.

"You don't need me then, do you?" Laura asked, irritated both by the compromising situation the offer put the *Gazette* in and the unlikelihood of her being asked to write anything about what looked like becoming a major confrontation as the mill's unions worked themselves up for a strike ballot. However hard the workers fought, she thought, they were unlikely to save this struggling remnant of a once great industry.

"We might need a backup feature," Ted said grudgingly. "You'd best hang on." Laura shrugged and doodled idly on the pad of paper in front of her. She let her mind wander back to the previous evening when she had found herself facing a Thackeray distracted by thoughts of work and his divorce and at his most morose. She had eventually persuaded him early to bed where they had made love with a passion which seemed unaffected by their anxieties. Her mouth still felt bruised and the echo of her response lingered and she hoped none of her colleagues could guess what she was looking so pleased about. Like the cat who got the cream, she thought, and struggled to suppress a broad grin. But she straightened her face quickly as the conference room door opened to admit Richard Babbage, the expensively suited and optionally bald local executive and representative of the media company which owned the *Gazette* and scores of newspapers like it around the country. He was followed by an older man, smartly dressed but with a face creased by anxiety beneath the thinning grey hair.

"G'morning guys," Babbage said briskly. "You're lucky this morning to get a word with Frank Earnshaw, chairman of a company which I'm sure you all know. He's anxious to have the opportunity to tell you a little about what's going on with Earnshaws, which has been a world textile leader for a hundred years or more, and is hoping to continue – in some form at least – for another century to come."

He chivvied Earnshaw into the waiting seat next to Ted Grant and then bustled back to the door.

"Sorry I can't stop myself, people. I've a meeting in five minutes – but Frank, do drop by when you've finished here. I've a nice malt in the drinks cupboard you might appreciate." And with that he was gone leaving an unusually awkward Grant to introduce his "top staff" around the table and then give his guest the floor.

"We don't go in for posh public relations advisers at Earnshaws," Frank Earnshaw began with an unexpected glare at the assembled journalists. "As you probably know, we're a private company with most of the shares still in family hands and the quality of what we produce has always been able to speak for itself – till now, apparently." Earnshaw shuffled the papers he had placed on the table in front of him. "Well," he resumed, with slightly less bravado. "Now we've run into a few little difficulties, but I'd rather deal with the media myself than hand the firm over to some flash company from Leeds who wouldn't know a wool mill from a bloody call centre."

Laura smiled faintly. The old rivalry between big brash commercial Leeds and small, inward-looking manufacturing Bradfield had been multiplied many times in the nineties as the textile industry's sickness became near terminal and the larger city flourished on a boom in financial services. The southerners' old jibe that travelling to Yorkshire meant venturing to the Third World could now be heard amongst travellers making the twenty minute trip on the train from Leeds to Bradfield. The words *knives* and *twisting* sprang to mind, Laura thought, and Earnshaw was obviously not a man who liked to be on the losing side in any competition. A bit like my father, she thought, reminded of her teatime engagement at the Clarendon. But one of her colleagues had asked the mill boss to outline his company's problems and in spite of her initial lack of interest she found her attention seized.

"We're not bust," Earnshaw was saying combatively. "But as you know the economic climate's tight for manufacturing and we need to put together a refinancing package to keep going until sales look up again. That's all in hand, with meetings set up this week and next with people who are considering our position. In the meantime we've had to go to our workforce and ask for some sacrifices from them. We need to cut costs and there's not much chance of that on the raw materials side so it has to be the workforce. I don't like it, I won't pretend I do, but we need to cut wages, cut overtime, retrench now in the hope of bouncing back in a year-or-so's time when the climate improves."

"D'you really think it will improve?" put in Bill Wrigley, who wrote most of the industrial and transport stories for the *Gazette*. "I mean, the market may not bounce back this time, not for high quality stuff like you produce."

Earnshaw looked at him for a long time before he replied.

"To be honest, there's no telling," he said. "All I can say is that I'm determined to keep this business going if I can and I know that in the present circumstances, if the workers vote for a strike, that will upset the customers we do still have. I'm trying to persuade them that what they're planning is suicide for them as well as the company. And that's the point I want you to get across in your coverage of the dispute. The union'll tell you different of course. But it could be the end of us if they strike."

"You say it's a family company still. Exactly how does that work now, Mr. Earnshaw?" Wrigley pressed.

"The mill was built in 1872 by my great-grandfather," Earnshaw said. "It was a model of its kind at the time. It's always been a family firm and that's the way I want it to stay. At present the shareholding is divided between my father George, myself and my two sons, Matthew and Simon. A four way split."

"Wouldn't floating the company help you at this juncture?" Wrigley asked. "If you need extra capital to streamline your operation…"

"Not if it meant we lost control," Earnshaw said flatly. "You'd not find outside finance that gave a monkey's for Bradfield worsted cloth."

"And your father's still fit, is he?" Wrigley asked. "He must be knocking on a bit."

"He's fighting fit," Earnshaw said. "Still a working director at 78, and shows no signs of tiring."

"But…" Wrigley began again but Ted Grant intervened.

"I don't think that's really relevant to our coverage of the labour dispute, is it Mr. Earnshaw, if you're not thinking of selling out. So give us a run-down on what happens next?"

Laura let her mind wander again as Earnshaw went into details of how he planned to reduce the pay of the mill's 600 workers and how long a strike ballot would take if the union pushed the dispute that far. Personally she doubted that it would ever come to that. She suspected that enough pressure would be brought to bear to persuade the workers to vote for their own pay cuts in the perhaps vain hope that better times would return to the massive mill which dominated the southernmost of Bradfield's seven hills. Nothing in the recent history of the textile industry persuaded her that such sacrifices saved mills in the long run. She had no doubt that Earnshaws mill would join the long roll of derelict Victorian structures which had gradually been demolished or occasionally refurbished into something entirely different as the long decline of the English textile industry came to its dispiriting close.

When the *Gazette's* first edition came out later that day Laura was not surprised to find a picture of Earnshaws massive neoclassical building on the front page with a sympathetic interview with Frank Earnshaw beside it. It was not until she turned to the continuation of Wrigley's story on an inside page that she found anything to surprise her slightly. There a picture of a union meeting outside the mill's massive iron gates revealed that most of the workers were Asian, something which had not been alluded to even in passing at that morning's meeting. There might, she thought, be good reasons for hoping that a strike ballot at Earnshaws failed in the current climate. A bruising dispute there involving the descendants of the Pakistani immigrants who had first been encouraged to come to Bradfield in the 1960s and 70s to work in the town's then flourishing mills would do little for race relations in an area which was stubbornly failing to flourish in the bright new millennium.

DCI Michael Thackeray leaned back in his chair, ran his hands through his unruly dark hair and sighed. They said that if a murder inquiry did not make significant progress in the first twenty-four hours then the police were in for a hard slog. This one had not even succeeded in identifying the victim in the first twenty-four hours. Progress had been limited to a fingertip search of Broadley Moor, which had turned up little of significance, in spite of the fact that it had been out of bounds to the public for so long, and to an appeal in the previous afternoon's *Gazette* for help from the public in identifying the unknown man who still lay in the mortuary, now in the care of an undertaker's technician who had been contracted to rebuild his shattered face in the hope of obtaining a reasonable likeness for publication. But that could take some time.

Thackeray glanced at Kevin Mower, who had just delivered the latest sheaf of negative reports to his office: no identification in the jogger's clothing, no signs of a struggle or identifiable footprints at the top of the crag where the early mornings' hard frost had now melted twice and refrozen again since the man's likely time of death, no unidentified cars left in Broadley village, and no obvious candidates on the missing person's register.

"So what have we got, Kevin? Anything at all that's useful?" Thackeray asked.

"Male, white, around twenty-five to thirty, fit and healthy and keen to stay that way, not poor – his hair was well cut, nails trimmed, no nicotine stains, jogging gear was common enough designer kit – not cheap, pretty untraceable though – underwear from M & S. Probably lives alone…"

"Why do you say that?"

"Because if he didn't someone would have been on to us by now to report him missing," Mower said. "Wife, mother, girlfriend, boyfriend, whoever. We've had no new missing person reports in the last thirty-six hours so we can only assume that no one realises he's missing. We've got another paragraph in the *Gazette* tonight saying he's still not been identified, but yesterday's story only brought in half a dozen calls and five of those were from the usual nutters. The other was from a woman whose son went missing six years ago and hasn't been seen since."

"And?"

"Right age group, but he was black. Poor cow."

"Tonight's *Gazette*'ll be dropping through letter-boxes by now, commuters will be buying it. No calls so far?"

"Not yet, guv, no," Mower said. "We've got two people manning the phones all evening but I wouldn't hold your breath."

"An employer might take a few days to register that someone was missing, I suppose," Thackeray said but Mower just smiled grimly.

"These days they want a sick note if you spend too long on the bog," he said. "Mind, if he didn't work in Bradfield an employer might not have seen our appeal. I didn't see the story in any of the national rags. Perhaps we should ask the papers in Leeds and Sheffield to do something. It's possible he's some way from home."

"Talk to the Press office about circulating the appeal right across the county," Thackeray said. "And if we get no leads by the weekend, we'd best go for radio, TV, the national papers – someone must know who he is, and by then we should have some sort of picture to give them. Have we checked his fingerprints?"

"Yep," Mower said. "No match found so he seems to have been a good lad, whoever he was. Amos is keeping DNA samples, of course, but if his prints aren't on record there's no chance his DNA is."

Thackeray sighed again in frustration.

"It's more than twenty-four hours since he was found, probably thirty-six since he died, according to Amos, so why has nobody missed him? Even if he lives alone, he has to go out to work, he can't live in total isolation." And yet, he thought, there had been a time years ago when he had spent bank holiday weekends, and even whole weeks of official leave locked in a bleak flat on his own, deep in a black depression, speaking to no one, his only companion the plaintive voice of Billie Holiday, and as far as he knew, in nobody's thoughts until he chose to emerge again when the duty roster demanded. Perhaps the dead man had his own reasons for living a solitary and isolated life. Perhaps there really was no one who cared enough to miss him now he was gone. He shivered slightly as if a ghost had walked through the door, and got to his feet, anxious to be away. He suddenly felt urgently in need of Laura's company.

Laura helped her grandmother up the stone steps and through the lobby of the Clarendon Hotel, where the heavy swing doors were held open for them by the uniformed porter. Joyce had looked pale and stressed, Laura thought, when she had collected her from the tiny bungalow in the shadow of Bradfield's most notorious tower blocks, officially named the Heights but since as long as Laura could remember, jeeringly and not inaccurately, dubbed Wuthering both by the locals who lived there and the majority who were thankful they didn't. Joyce had dressed carefully in her smartest navy blue suit but her efforts could not disguise her increasing frailty and the massive effort she had to make to walk with her single stick.

Laura spotted her father as soon as they entered the lobby. Under cover of helping Joyce off with her coat, she assessed the short, dapper, smartly suited man standing by the bar, drumming his fingers impatiently on the dark mahogany and chatting to the motherly woman on the other side of the counter. It was almost two years since she had seen Jack Ackroyd and he had put on a little weight in the meantime. Life in the sun evidently suited him: his hair had thinned and the family red had turned to silver but his skin was tanned and glowing and his smile as self-satisfied as she remembered it. He had survived one heart-attack, which had provoked the sale of his business and his retirement to the golf courses of Portugal, but today at least he appeared to be rejuvenated, excitement in every inch of him.

Laura had never been able to pin down the precise point at which she and her father had found themselves on opposing sides in the family war but it was almost as far back as she could remember. He had appeared to treat her mother, a kindly woman who hated conflict, abominably from as long ago as Laura could recall and by the time she had been sent away to boarding school to, in her father's words, knock the rough edges off her, she had already been telling her mother, in a tight angry whisper, to leave him. But that was something her mother would never contemplate and in some ways Laura had been relieved to find herself removed from the battlefield at the age of eleven, at least during term-time.

The person she had missed most when she left home, of course, was the grandmother she so resembled both physically and in temperament, and she realised now that her banishment to blandest southern England for her schooling was as much a ploy to remove her from Joyce's influence as to curb her increasing involvement in the conflict at home. She had infuriated her father further by insisting on returning to Bradfield to go to the local university, instead of trying for the Oxford place that her father coveted for her. She had not followed Joyce as far down the socialist road as her combative grandmother had wished, but nor had she been overwhelmed with enthusiasm for her father's ruthless business instincts. Both accused her of fence-sitting even now, and she had to acknowledge her own scepticism, uncomfortable at times, but an attribute quite useful for a journalist. But every time she saw Jack again she knew that her heart, if not her head, was still with Joyce who had marched her unprotesting as a child to stuff leaflets through the letterboxes of Bradfield's grimmest estates. Nothing much had changed out there, she thought, except that the warriors ready to do battle for the dispossessed seemed thinner on the ground these days and their voices muffled by the greater contentment which had swept the country. Which did not mean that the warriors did not have a point.

"Dad," she said, advancing across the bar's thick carpet and leaning down slightly to peck him on the cheek. He had bitterly resented the moment when his daughter had grown taller than he was. "How are you? How's Mum?" Laura asked.

"In fine fettle, as it goes, both of us," Jack said. "The old ticker seems to be bearing up whatever that expensive quack at the Infirmary predicted. He'd have had me six foot under by now."

He looked past his daughter, who as usual had turned every other male head in the bar, to where his mother was approaching more slowly, leaning heavily on her stick.

"Now then, Mother?" he said. "Still not ready to move out to warmer climes?"

"Jack," Joyce said, without much warmth. "They'll put me in a box first."

"Aye, I reckon they will that," her son said, his smile freezing and bright blue eyes turning cold. He turned to Laura. "She'll still not be helped, then?"

44

"Not a lot," Laura said with a wicked smile. Her grandmother's fierce independence was something she could understand even if, on occasion, it gave her sleepless nights.

"Pot of tea do you then?" Jack asked. "You'll not be wanting anything stronger just yet, will you?" Without waiting for an answer he led the way to the adjoining lounge where a congregation of Bradfield's decreasing band of blue rinse matrons who had resisted white flight to Harrogate were indulging in tea and cream cakes. An empty table set with tea-cups and a plate of sandwiches had evidently been reserved for Jack but as the waiter bustled up and the two women made themselves comfortable Jack glanced at his watch.

"I've an unexpected meeting at five thirty," he said. "But we're time for a chat."

"This is just a business trip, then?" Laura asked.

"Aye, just a couple of days, all being well. You know one of the big mills is in trouble, terminal trouble from what I hear, if some beggar doesn't put a rescue package together."

"And you're involved in the rescue package? For Earnshaws?" Laura said incredulously.

"Aye, well, summat like that," Jack said, tapping the side of his nose ostentatiously. "And don't you go mentioning that to anyone at that rag of yours either. That's strictly confidential, that is."

"There's hundreds of jobs threatened if they close that mill," Joyce said sharply.

"I dare say," Jack said. "But that goes for you too, Mother. I don't want you tipping off your union mates that summat's in the wind. Not a word to anyone, right?"

"Most of my union mates are long dead," Joyce said bitterly. "And the young ones don't seem to have the faintest idea how to take the bosses on and win."

45

"That's not what I hear about Earnshaws," Jack said. "Any road, never mind about business for now. If anything comes of what I'm here to talk about you'll be the first to know, Laura. How'll that do?"

"Fine," she said without much enthusiasm. Like her grand-mother, she seriously doubted that anything Jack would be associated with was likely to benefit the workers even frac-tionally more than it would benefit Jack Ackroyd.

"You and Frank Earnshaw go way back, don't you?" Joyce said, still prickly with suspicion.

"I rented space from him in that white elephant of a mill years ago, when I was getting started." Jack said. "It's been on its last legs for as long as I can remember."

"How's that wife of yours?" Joyce said, changing the sub-ject and shifting her position awkwardly in her chair. Laura guessed that her arthritis was painful but knew she would never complain. She had also suspected for years that Joyce had never fully approved of her daughter-in-law, a woman who seldom answered back and the last person to cope with a man as overbearing as Jack Ackroyd.

"She's very fit," Jack said. "She sent her love to you both and wants to know when you're coming out to see us. A trip would do you the world of good, Mother. It's still in the sixties in the afternoons, at this time of the year, and a nice breeze off the Atlantic. And what about you Laura? Still seeing that cop-per of yours, are you? Bring him with you, if you like. "

Laura nodded, bending to sip her tea to hide her annoy-ance.

"Anything in it, then?" Jack persisted, oblivious to the ris-ing tension around the tea table. "Is he going to wed you, or not? He seems to be taking his time about it."

"I'll send you an invitation to the wedding, if and when," Laura said through gritted teeth, her cheeks flaming.

"Like that is it?" Jack blundered on, with a meaningful look in Joyce's direction. "I've said before you could do better for yourself than a bloody detective. After all the money I laid out on your posh education."

Laura got to her feet abruptly, almost spilling her tea.

"He's an Oxford graduate, you idiot," she hissed as she made her way to the cloakroom, watched by a dozen pairs of censorious eyes as the duennas of the Clarendon lounge paused to take in the scene, forks of creamy confections halfway to their pursed crimson lips. With the heavy door shut behind her, Laura splashed her face with cold water and attempted a smile at her reflection in the mirror. Why do I let him wind me up like that? she wondered. She combed her unruly curls and more coolly contemplated the undoubted fact that Michael Thackeray was taking an unconscionable time to marry her. His moves towards a divorce at last gave her grounds for hope, but that was not something she intended to share with Jack. The irony was, she thought ruefully, that when Michael had met her father the two men had got on quite amicably, had possibly even liked each other. She was probably, an impediment to a beautiful friendship.

"Bloody men," she said, not realising that she had spoken aloud until someone emerging from a cubicle behind her spoke.

"Bloody right," the woman said, manoeuvring her endowments more comfortably inside her skin-tight Lycra dress and moving to the mirror to effect repairs to an already camouflage-thick maquillage. She seemed as out of place as a clown at a funeral in the rather stuffy environs of the Clarendon but by no means fazed by her surroundings. "Never give 'em an inch without t'cash up front, I say," this unexpected adviser offered.

47

"A wedding ring would be nice," Laura said, throwing caution to the winds.

"Oh, that," the primping woman said, fluffing out her big blonde hair and contorting herself to inspect her stocking seams. "Not worth the paper they're written on these days, marriage lines. A pre-nuptial contract's worth having though. Pins the beggars down, that does."

"I'll bear it in mind," Laura said with a grin, quite cheered at the thought of persuading Michael to sign away half his worldly goods, which consisted largely of a collection of jazz and blues recordings, and some scruffy furniture which she would not give house-room to, before she consented to become his wife.

"Must dash," her companion said, cramming her make-up back into her tiny black handbag. "It does no harm to keep them waiting, but not so's they get bored." And with that she swept out of the cloakroom in a haze of a heavy perfume that Laura knew Michael would hate.

When she went slowly back to the lounge, she found Jack and Joyce chatting reasonably amiably over their buttered scones. Joyce glanced at Laura, sharp-eyed, but relaxed when she saw that her granddaughter had evidently calmed down.

"Jack wants to take us both out for a meal tomorrow night," Joyce said. "That'd be nice."

"Bring your copper along, an'all," Jack said magnanimously.

"I'll call you," Laura said noncommittally.

Her father shrugged and glanced at the door.

"I can see the colleagues I'm meeting, so I'll love you and leave you. Give us a bell in the morning and I'll book us a table in the carvery," he said, getting to his feet. Laura and Joyce watched him thread his way through the tea tables and join two smartly dressed men in the lobby, one white and one Asian.

"What's he up to?" Joyce asked.

"I've no idea, but I shouldn't think it'll necessarily do Earnshaws mill any good," Laura said. "Come on, have another cup of tea as he's paying. And then I'll run you home."

Chapter Four

While the Ackroyd family was taking tea in the Clarendon lounge, a fair-haired young man with the beginnings of a paunch and an air of sleepy superiority was downing his third consecutive double malt and leaning against the mahogany and brass bar next door at an increasingly acute angle.

"I mean, it's obvious that these people won't move into the twenty-first century, isn't it?" Matthew Earnshaw asked the comfortable woman in a black dress who was carefully polishing already gleaming glasses on the other side of the counter. "They're hardly out of the bloody middle ages, are they?"

"I wouldn't know about that, sir," the barmaid said with well-rehearsed neutrality. "I take people as I find them. You have to, in this job."

"I know, but let's say someone wanted to modernise the Clarendon, and let's face it, it could do with a make-over. Wouldn't you be pleased about that?"

"I suppose it would depend on whether I'd still have a job or not, sir, wouldn't it. They don't vote for Christmas, don't turkeys, do they?"

"God, I despair of this bloody country," Earnshaw muttered pushing his empty glass over the counter. "Give me another, will you? I don't know where my bloody brother is. He promised he'd be here at four and it's twenty-five past bloody five now. I'm going to be driving home through the blasted rush hour."

"Do you think you should, sir? If you're driving, I mean?" The barmaid's voice was as deferential as ever as she stood with the bottle of Glenmorangie poised and made her point, but the young man flushed with anger.

"Are you fucking refusing to serve me?" he asked.

"No sir, just wondering…"

"The same again," Earnshaw said flatly, looking round the bar where the scattering of customers were glancing curiously in his direction. He drained his fresh drink quickly.

"If my brother Simon comes in looking for me tell him to call me on my mobile," he said to the barmaid. "He's had his switched off all day, the silly bastard. Can't contact him."

Concentrating hard to keep his gait steady he made his way to the door, where he passed a group of three men coming the other way. He nodded vaguely at the one who gave him a nod of recognition as they passed. In his present state he could not for the life of him recall who the tall grey-haired man in the designer suit was, still less his companions, a heavily built Asian and a small silver-haired man with acute blue eyes.

"Who's that?" Jack Ackroyd asked when they were out of earshot.

"That's Matthew Earnshaw, Frank's younger lad, pissed as usual," the tall man said. "He's one of the problems that company's up against. I tell you, if it weren't for him they might not be in the terminal mess they're in. Still it's no skin off our nose."

Matthew Earnshaw arrived at his father's house unscathed more than an hour later, the erratic driving of his BMW safely masked by the heavy traffic which had kept his speed down to a crawl for most of the ten mile journey to Broadley. He pulled up in a scatter of gravel on the drive outside the heavy stone Victorian mansion where he and his brother had been brought up. He pressed the doorbell persistently and pushed past the Phillipina housekeeper who opened it for him without a word, storming into the sitting room where his parents were drinking sherry.

"He didn't fucking turn up," he announced with a scowl.

"Language, Matthew," his mother said reprovingly but his father, grey-suited and showing signs of the anxiety which seemed to have creased his face deeply around the eyes and forehead was more interested in his son's message than the manner of its delivery.

"Didn't he call you?" he asked sharply.

"His mobile's switched off. I haven't heard from him since we made the arrangement to meet on Sunday. I know he's got some girl he's not letting on about, but this is ridiculous." Matthew crossed to the sideboard on the far side of the room and poured himself a large Scotch without ice or water. "You get the feeling he enjoys buggering us about," he said, lowering himself carefully onto the sofa beside his mother. "Making us sweat."

"I'm sure that's not true," Christine Earnshaw said placatingly. "He must be busy."

"The bloody university's on vacation. Why should he be busy?" her husband asked. "He knows what we're trying to do and how important his input is. He knows we need to talk to him."

"You should have bought him out when he decided to go all eco…eco…fucking green on us," Matthew said. "You can bet your life he'll be as obstructive as he can as long as he can and then where will we be? This week's bloody crucial and he knows that. But if he really wants to get up our noses, he and Grandad between them can stop us dead, you know that. It'd be just like the pair of them to do it deliberately, out of spite."

"I'm sure Simon can be persuaded to go along with our

52

plans, or at the very least sell us his shares so that we can outvote your grandfather," Frank said, though without total conviction. "Even now he doesn't want to be involved directly in the company any more he'll not want to see it wrecked. He'll lose as heavily as the rest of us if we go belly up."

"I wouldn't put it past him," Matthew mumbled, "Though last time I saw him he seemed to be worried about money, and that was a bloody first for him." His words were beginning to slur now. His mother looked at him anxiously.

"You'll stay for a meal?" she asked.

"I suppose so," Matthew said ungraciously. He lived another ten miles out of industrial Yorkshire in the rolling Dales, where he and his now divorced wife had bought and renovated an old stone farmhouse. Since Lizzie's precipitate and acrimonious departure he had lived there alone.

"I'll tell Juanita," Christine said, leaving the room to discuss the meal with the housekeeper.

When she had gone, Frank Earnshaw looked angrily at his older son.

"Where the hell is he?" he asked. "Did he say he was going away when you spoke to him on Sunday?"

"Nope," Matthew said, his eyes heavy with sleep now. "I told you, he's being very mysterious about some woman he's taken up with. Perhaps he's with her. He doesn't confide. You know that."

With good reason, Frank Earnshaw thought. Not only had Simon given up his management role at the mill to go back to university to study for a postgraduate degree in environmental science, but he had made it very clear on more than one occasion that one of the reasons for his change of direction was the increasing impossibility of working with his older, more volatile and increasingly drunken brother.

"I wouldn't put it past your grandfather to try to collar him to put his side of the argument before we talk to him," Frank said, but his son's eyes were shut now and before long he was snoring softly in the comfortable sofa across which he could now sprawl, mouth open and a thin trickle of saliva running from one corner and down his chin.

It was more than two hours later, after an uncomfortable meal at which both parents had attempted unsuccessfully to limit the amount of wine Matthew consumed, that Frank Earnshaw was surprised to pick up the phone and hear a female voice asking for his younger son.

"Simon doesn't live here," Frank said, a shade more sharply than he intended. "I've not seen him for weeks."

"He was supposed to call me yesterday," the woman said. "I've been trying to get him ever since."

"Who is this?" Frank said. "Do I know you."

"No. It doesn't matter. I'll keep trying his mobile."

"Who was that?" Matthew asked.

"Some woman trying to find Simon," Frank said. "The girlfriend, d'you think?"

Matthew took the portable receiver out of his hand and quickly punched in 1471 but he soon switched off again with a shrug.

"Number withheld," he said. "Where the hell is Simon?" he asked no one in particular. "It's bloody typical of him to go missing just when he's actually needed for once."

"Missing?" his mother said sharply. "Do you really think he's missing? Could he have had an accident, do you think?" She hesitated. " He gave me a key to his flat, in case of emergencies…"

Frank Earnshaw stood up as if he had made a decision to take charge of the situation.

"In that case, I think I'll go down to his flat and have a look round," he said. "I reckon this might be an emergency. You'd better come with me, Matthew. I'll drive. You're in no fit state."

Within the hour the two men were standing in the small flat Simon Earnshaw now called home. It was the bottom half of a Victorian terrace house, close to the university where he was now studying.

"How can he go back to living like this?" Matthew said disgustedly, drawing a toe across the worn carpet which looked none too clean. "A bloody student hovel all over again."

"You both made your own decisions," Frank said mildly, privately thinking that Simon's choices, disappointing as he had found them at first, were in many ways preferable to the fast-lane lifestyle Matthew attempted to sustain. "If he wants to live on his savings, that's his business. He earned his money while he was at the mill. I've no complaints."

"What you mean is, I don't," Matthew muttered angrily. "Earn it, I mean."

"You can work that one out for yourself, Matthew," his father said. He crossed the room to where an answerphone was winking. There were three messages, all from the same young woman he had spoken to earlier in the evening, each sounding more anxious than the one before. She had not identified herself, but the soft and intimate "It's me" told Simon Earnshaw's father and brother clearly enough that this was someone special in his life.

"There's something not right," Frank Earnshaw said, as he switched off the woman's voice, which by that morning had been pleading for Simon to get in touch. "I'm going to call the police."

Laura Ackroyd picked at a couple of lettuce leaves and

watched Michael Thackeray tuck with gusto into the steak and chips she had just cooked him. It was the sort of food she suspected he still preferred in spite of her long-standing efforts to tempt him with all sorts of dishes from the Mediterranean, India and points south, east and west. After sandwiches and scones with her father, she was not hungry and had made herself a salad which the good Yorkshireman across the table from her would have dismissed as rabbit food if she had offered him the same.

"So what's he up to then, your dad?" Thackeray asked through a mouthful of chips and brown sauce.

"Some money-making scheme," Laura said, not wanting to break Jack's confidence and mention Earnshaws. "He kept various interests here when he went abroad. I'm not sure how he fixes it with the Inland Revenue, but I know every time I go and visit he's poring over his investment portfolio."

"He can only spend a limited amount of time in the UK if he wants to avoid tax," Thackeray said.

"Oh, knowing my father, I'm sure he wants to do that," Laura said wryly. "He's one of those Tories always ready to moan about the quality of public services but never prepared to pay his whack to fund them. He drives Joyce crazy."

"You must drive him crazy too," Thackeray said mildly. "I've never known such an ill-matched family in some ways, but you're all Ackroyds to the tips of your fingers – pig-headed through three generations. Do you think if we…"

Laura's heart lurched uncomfortably.

"If we what?"

"Oh, nothing," Thackeray said quickly. He finished his steak thoughtfully and pushed the plate away with a satisfied grunt.

"That was good," he said.

"How did I get involved with a man who doesn't know his

mozzarella from his focaccia?" Laura asked. "Do you want anything else? Apple pie and custard or jam rolypoly?" For a second Thackeray's eyes lit up until he realised she was teasing.

"You know that wouldn't do my waistline any good," he admitted reluctantly. "Your trouble is, you spent too long down in the effete south."

"Ha, you've obviously never experienced boarding school food or you wouldn't say that," she said. "Funnily enough, it was my father who got me interested in good food. He tried to seduce me away from Joyce's puritan habits by taking me to good restaurants when I was home for the holidays. And I have to confess, I loved it. Will you come to dinner with him tomorrow? I can guarantee the food'll be good, and if it's the Clarendon, pretty traditional too."

"If I can get away in time," Thackeray said. "I like your father. Which reminds me, I must go and see mine." He was suddenly sombre.

"Ah," Laura said softly. "About the divorce? Will he be very opposed, after all this time?"

"Resigned, I think," Thackeray said. "He's not a fool. He knows what's going on. But I owe him an explanation, not just a wedding invitation. Not that he'll come, of course. He's about as dyed in the wool as you can get without actually being the Pope."

"Michael, you mustn't tear yourself apart over this," she said. "We can go on as we are…"

"No," he said. "That's not an option is it? I see you with Vicky and David's children and I know very well what you want. You're going to get fed up with the way we are. And I couldn't bear to lose you."

"Maybe I can't have children, after… you know…"

"We won't know till we try, will we," he said, as lightly as

57

he could, although he felt breathless with panic at the thought. "Come here," he said, and took her in his arms and kissed her so fiercely that she had to pull away, laughing, for breath.

"Shall we leave the washing up?" she asked, pulling him back towards her and feeling his hardness against her thigh and opening her mouth for his next kiss. But before they could reach the bedroom, locked in a close embrace, his phone rang loudly and long enough to split them reluctantly apart.

"Damm" Laura said as she watched Thackeray flick on the mobile and listen impassively to the voice at the other end.

"I'll be right there," he said at length and she flung herself onto the sofa, feeling defeated.

"It looks as if we may have identified our jogger," he said, pushing her hair away from her brow and kissing her on the cheek. "I'm sorry, Laura. Really sorry. You know what it's like."

She shrugged, trying to conceal her disappointment.

"I'll see you later then," she said. "I'll keep the bed warm." But she knew that he would come back exhausted and fall instantly into a deep sleep in her arms as he had done so many nights before.

Thackeray sat across an interview room table from Frank and Matthew Earnshaw as Sergeant Mower eased his way through the door with two brimming polystyrene cups of grey-looking coffee in his hands. He placed them in front of the visitors and sat down beside Thackeray. Everyone in the room looked pale and haggard in the harsh lighting but Frank Earnshaw in particular seemed to be finding it difficult both to sit still for long and to frame his words carefully enough for coherence.

"Sergeant Mower tells me that you didn't know that a body had been found on Broadley Moor," Thackeray said at length.

"We don't see the local rag," the younger Earnshaw said dismissively.

"The village has been full of police…" Mower objected mildly.

"We'd not noticed," the older Earnshaw added. "We're a bit preoccupied at the minute. We've other problems to worry about. You'll have heard about the financial difficulties we've run into. Simon's whereabouts were the last thing on my mind this week, till he failed to turn up to meet his brother this evening."

"So when did you last see Simon?" Thackeray asked.

We've not seen him since Christmas, but I spoke to him on the phone on Sunday to arrange a meeting at the Clarendon today. There was some business stuff we needed to discuss," Matthew said. The crisis appeared to have sobered him up.

"Simon is a major shareholder in the company," his father added dully.

"But he doesn't work for you?" Thackeray asked.

"No, he used to, but not now. He did a management degree and I put him in charge of marketing and administration when he finished. He was very good. But then a year or so ago he had some sort of conversion to green politics and decided to go back to university to do a postgraduate degree. He said he wanted nothing to do with the company any more. Or the family, it seems. He's kept himself very much to himself since."

"He kept his bloody shares, though," Matthew said. "He wasn't so converted he didn't know which side his bread was buttered."

59

"So you wouldn't have expected to see him regularly?"

"We speak to him on the phone if we need to. His mother meets him in town for lunch now and again, though she doesn't think I know that," Frank Earnshaw said, his bitterness overcoming the anxiety in his faded blues eyes.

"He knew how important it was to talk about the problems at the mill," Matthew said. "We told him it was urgent and he didn't object, just said he wasn't keen to come up to the mill or out to Broadley. He suggested the Clarendon. I think he thought it was some sort of joke. It's not the sort of place he goes these days."

"So you wouldn't normally expect him to be jogging on Broadley Moor?" Thackeray said. "Too close to home, maybe?"

"I wouldn't expect him to be jogging anywhere," Matthew said sourly. "He's not the type. Unless that's another sort of conversion he's gone through that we don't know about."

"Do you happen to have a photograph of Simon with you?" Thackeray asked. "We could possibly eliminate this body quite quickly without any more distress…"

"I brought this one from his flat," Frank Earnshaw said. "I thought if we reported him missing you'd want one."

He reached into an inside pocket and pulled out a snapshot of a young man standing outside a substantial Victorian house beside Frank himself and a woman Thackeray guessed must be his wife.

"It was taken about three years ago, but he's not changed much. Hair's a bit longer, maybe."

Thackeray looked at the photograph carefully but his hopes of finding some distinguishing characteristic, such as dark hair or unusual stature, which could make it impossible that the body in the Infirmary freezer could be Simon Earnshaw, faded almost at once. Simon was about the right height, and as fair-haired as the unknown victim, and allowing for three years, of around the same build. He sighed and handed the photograph back to Frank Earnshaw.

"I'm sorry," he said. "It's impossible to rule him out. I think you'd better have a look at the man who was found the other morning."

As the quartet walked the short distance across the city centre to the Infirmary and down into the basement where it had been arranged that a technician would retrieve the remains of the unknown jogger, Thackeray explained as gently as he could the nature of the injuries that had been inflicted on the corpse and the efforts which had already been made to repair the damage in the hope that by the following morning a suitably cosmetic photograph could be issued to the media. But as it turned out the undertaker's efforts were enough.

Frank Earnshaw and his son stood pale-faced and rigid beside the gurney as the technician pulled back the sheet covering the corpse but their reaction was instant. The older man choked slightly and then nodded, jaw clenched, while Mower moved quickly to provide a steadying arm to his son, Matthew, who was visibly swaying.

"You're sure that is your other son, Simon Earnshaw?" Thackeray asked, his own face rigid with tension.

"It's Simon," Earnshaw said, his voice hoarse. "How the hell did he come to fall down the Crag?"

"He didn't fall, Mr. Earnshaw," Thackeray said. "We have good reason to believe he was murdered."

"Oh my God," Earnshaw said, while his other son slumped against Mower, who grabbed him in a bear hug, before he vomited all over the floor and the sergeant's shoes.

Chapter Five

Sergeant Mower seized his companion's arm fiercely as he came out of the main entrance to Bradfield Infirmary and pushed him to a stop against the wall at the bottom of the broad stone steps, holding his elbow across the younger man's chest.

"Don't ever, ever, let your personal feelings go like that again," he said. "It's not helpful, it's not professional, it's not even safe. You were winding that girl's father up, you idiot. Trying to get him to commit himself to something he can't possibly judge at this stage. As if they haven't got enough to cope with."

DC Mohammed Sharif, commonly known in CID as Omar, a name he accepted so amiably that Mower suspected that the joke was his own idea, pushed the sergeant's arm away irritably.

"You can't treat that sort of shit as if the girl's grazed her knee," he said angrily. "She'll possibly lose the sight of that eye. Someone's got to deal with these fucking racists. She's going to be scarred for life, she'll never marry…"

"And how do you know that it's not the work of a gang of Asians pissed off because she's got a white boyfriend?" Mower snapped.

"What?" Sharif said, his angry eyes suddenly uncertain. "Is that what they're saying? Is that what she said?"

"She didn't get a look at whoever threw the stuff," Mower said, more quietly, aware that they were attracting curious glances from passers-by making their way in and out of the busy hospital. "You're assuming it was a racist attack. You're pushing her father into claiming it was a racist attack. And you may well be right and of course we have to take that possibility on board. That's the way it works. But we don't know for certain. Not yet. So calm down and let's try to behave like bloody detectives instead of emotional schoolboys, shall we? That's what they pay us for."

Sharif pulled himself away from Mower's restraining arm and walked ahead of the sergeant, back towards police headquarters. Mower caught up with him quickly.

"When I talked to her father initially he was evasive, evidently not sure of what was going on with the girl," Mower said in a fierce whisper, one cautious eye on a couple of Asian youths leaning against a wall. "I want you to talk to him and the mother, calmly and rationally. I'll come with you but my Punjabi's not up to it if she doesn't speak much English. You know the rules. This is a racist incident if they say it's a racist incident, but so far I'm not getting that message clearly enough. The girl can't be sure. I'll talk to the guv'nor when we get back because in the present state of tension we don't want to go winding anyone up if we don't have to. We need to be sure. Do you understand?"

"Yes, sarge," Sharif said, his plump boyish face still betraying signs of sulkiness as they made their way up to the CID office and Mower went to report to DCI Thackeray on what he had learned so far about an attack with corrosive liquid on a fourteen-year-old girl, which had shaken even an old hand like Mower who reckoned he had seen everything that human beings could inflict on one another.

Thackeray listened to Mower's report with a deepening anger of his own.

"This one will make it into the *Gazette*," he said. "Laura was complaining that Ted Grant seems to be ignoring the attacks and harassment that have been going on, but he won't be able to ignore this. So we need our facts straight. I'll

63

talk to the Super and he'll want to brief the Press Office, so can you get the family's complaint clear by lunchtime. Where was she going, this kid?"

"To school," Mower said. "She's at that Muslim girls' school near Aysgarth Lane."

"On her own, was she?"

"With her two younger sisters. It's not far from where she lives, but she says that there was no one around in that little alleyway that goes up between the Lane and Alma Street at the back of Earnshaws mill. They take that route every day, apparently. Then these lads appeared, hoods up, running, and as they went past she felt this liquid hit her. It was acid of some sort, the hospital's analysing it. Burnt her scalp and cheek badly and splashed into one eye."

"What do the doctors say?"

"Bloody equivocal, as usual, but the burns will probably leave scars and the eye damage could go either way. Too soon to tell."

"Is the girl sure her attackers were white?"

Mower shrugged.

"She says she didn't get a good look. It's a bit of a bastard this one."

"And one we need to sort out sharpish," Thackeray said. "It's not what we needed with the Broadley murder investigation set to go now we've got an identification, but of the two it could be the more tricky to handle. So watch it."

"I'm taking Omar with me to see the family," Mower said.

"Makes sense," Thackeray said. "Make sure he doesn't get too emotionally involved."

"I'll watch him, guv," Mower said, his smile grim. "Like his guardian angel."

Thackeray got to his feet slowly and made his way upstairs to Superintendent Longley's office. His boss was leaning back in his swivel chair, his fingers tented in front of him and his usually jovial features sombre.

"This is a beggar we could have done without, Michael," he said, without preamble. "Who've you put in charge?"

"Mower," Thackeray said. "With Sharif in tow. They'll not put size ten boots where they shouldn't, with the family at least."

"We're sure it's racist, are we?"

"No, not yet," Thackeray said. "But I'd put money on it. And Mower knows the local Nazis as well as anyone. He knows which stones to turn over and which slimy bastards' tails to salt."

"Are they getting any reinforcements from outside, d'you reckon?" Longley asked. Thackeray shrugged.

"We'll check that out when Mower's made sure that there aren't any other reasons why this girl might have been attacked…"

"Family reasons, you mean?"

"Exactly. We'll check that out first – carefully – and then consult Special Branch about extremist movements. We've not had serious attacks on women before but this may not be the first. There's been a lot of low-level harassment going on in the streets for a while, and a few gangs of lads facing off. But it's not as if people always rush to report things to us. I'd like to think they did but…" He shrugged. They both knew that some of the Asian community were as suspicious of the police force as they were of the extreme right wing youths who stoked up violence on the streets from day to day.

"Right, keep me up to speed on this one. It could turn nasty. And what about the Earnshaw murder? As if one politically sensitive case isn't enough we get landed with two. I take it you've told the Press who the victim is?"

"The Press Office have issued a statement," Thackeray said.

65

"I used to play golf with Frank Earnshaw until he transferred his affections to that new country club out at Arnedale. Along with the bloody Assistant Chief Constable, no less. We could do without that beggar Ellison watching our every move in a murder investigation. How the hell did this lad come to get pushed off a cliff?"

"Amos Atherton says that's not the way it happened," Thackeray said mildly. He was determined not to let the Earnshaw family's local status cloud his judgement now or later. "We were supposed to think he slipped over the crag, but Amos says he was already dead when he fell or, more accurately, his body was dropped over the edge. He died somewhere else. God knows where. Given the time scale it could be anywhere in the county, or even further away. He'd been dead at least twelve hours by the time he was found and the cold is making an accurate timing difficult."

"Leads?" Longley asked.

"Not yet, it's early days. I've got a team searching his flat. There's supposed to be a girlfriend, but apart from messages on the answerphone there's no sign of her yet. The victim's car is missing, so we've got a call out for that. His university colleagues aren't due back in Bradfield until tomorrow but we've located his tutor and will interview him later today and then chase up his mates. And I'm going to talk to the family myself this afternoon, parents and brother – and there's a grandfather still around too."

"Old George Earnshaw, aye, I remember him," Longley said. "I didn't know he was still alive. A big noise, he was, in the wool trade, when there was a wool trade. Still, give him his due, he kept that mill alive when most of them were going spectacularly bust. This could be something as simple as a robbery that went wrong, presumably? Someone mugged him and chucked his body somewhere they hoped it wouldn't be found for a while?"

"He was dressed in jogging gear. It's unlikely he'd be carrying anything of value, except perhaps a Walkman or a mobile phone," Thackeray said.

"Or his car keys," Longley said. "Perhaps he was mugged for his car keys, he was hit too hard, his body dumped and chummie escaped in the car? A car-jacking? Feasible?"

"Certainly feasible," Thackeray said evenly, refusing to allow himself to be irritated by Longley's persistence which he knew only too well arose from the fact that the superintendent already felt assistant chief constable Peter Ellison's hot breath down his neck. "I've got the lads looking for tyre tracks right across the top of the crag. It's been out of bounds for months so if there's anything fresh up there they'll certainly find it. I'm ruling nothing in and nothing out at this stage."

"Of course not," Longley said quickly. "There's the trouble at the mill to bear in mind, too. I suppose it's feasible someone there's got it in for the family. Worth a look, maybe?"

"As I understand it Simon Earnshaw has nothing to do with the business any more. He bailed out some time ago."

"Could be a way of getting at his father," Longley suggested.

"I gather industrial relations are pretty ropey there but surely not bad enough to provoke murder," Thackeray said, trying to keep the incredulity out of his voice. Longley, he thought, was letting his anxieties get to him. "I'll bear it in mind as another lead anyway."

"Aye, do that," Longley said heavily. "It looks like we're in for a messy few weeks one way and another. Keep me up to date, Michael. I don't want to be caught on the wrong foot and end up in the sticky stuff with either of these cases."

"Sir," Thackeray said.

It was mid-morning before DCI Thackeray and DC Val Ridley parked on the gravel drive outside the Earnshaw family's substantial house on the outskirts of Broadley.

"Not short of a bob or two, then, boss," Val said, pulling a wry face as she glanced at a gleaming Jag and a muddy Range Rover parked outside and gazed up at the dark stone façade and tall windows each side of the heavy front door. As they stared, a thick curtain at one of the downstairs bays swayed slightly as if someone had been pulling it aside to look out and had then let it fall again.

"One of the great wool families, when that meant anything," Thackeray said. "But from what I hear that mill is a white elephant now. One of the things I want to get out of this is some idea of just how much financial trouble the Earnshaws are in. But I guess they won't be keen to tell us."

The front door was opened almost as soon as Thackeray touched the bell and the small plump housekeeper showed them into the main sitting room at the front of the house: a large, opulently furnished, immaculately tidy room where the only items that appeared out of place were the three people who inhabited it. Matthew Earnshaw, dressed in navy tracksuit bottoms and a green polo shirt, was sprawled on a pale cream sofa with a glass of what looked like whisky in his hand. He looked pale and drawn. His father and mother were sitting in armchairs, one on each side of the fireplace like a pair of porcelain ornaments, both dressed in black, both pale-faced and red-eyed, both apparently uninterested in the visitors who hovered for a moment awkwardly by the double doors from the hall.

"I'm sorry to intrude," Thackeray said. "But you do understand that we need to talk to you about Simon's death?"

This elicited a flicker of reaction from Frank Earnshaw who turned his head slowly in Thackeray's direction. Matthew Earnshaw ignored them, taking another gulp of his drink and turning his head away while his mother did not stir at all.

"Mr. Earnshaw?" Thackeray persisted. "This is DC Val Ridley. Today we merely need to establish some of the basic facts about Simon so that we can start the investigation into his death as quickly as possible. The first twenty-four hours of an inquiry is reckoned to be vital and a lot of time has already been wasted in this case because we didn't know who our victim was."

With what appeared to be an enormous effort Frank Earnshaw forced himself to sit up and take notice and waved the two officers to sit down, Thackeray taking the end of the sofa on which the surviving Earnshaw son was slumped and Val Ridley selecting a seat close to the door from which she could observe everyone else in the room. As she pulled out her notebook she felt she could almost touch the brittle tension which surrounded the bereaved family. Any of them might shatter, she thought, at the slightest touch.

"We've had the Press and TV onto us already, bloody vultures," Earnshaw complained.

"We need their help to trace witnesses, find Simon's car, all of that," Thackeray said quietly. "These first hours of an inquiry are vital."

"Aye, I suppose so," Earnshaw conceded. "So what do you want to know, Chief Inspector? I thought we dealt with a lot of this last night."

"Only in outline, Mr.. Earnshaw," Thackeray said. "You and your son were too shocked last night for a lengthy interview." He glanced at Matthew Earnshaw who had also been far too drunk to be coherent when he had recovered from his brief collapse at the mortuary but who did not appear to be in much better condition this morning. He wondered whether he had slept at all or whether he had kept on drinking all night. It was impossible to tell. It was odd, he thought, how deep his revulsion was these days for the weakness which had once threatened to destroy his own life. There's no one so fierce as a convert, he thought.

"Let's start with your son Simon's recent activities, shall we?" Thackeray said. "And then work as far back as seems sensible. You said he was studying for a post-graduate degree. Do you know the names of any of his friends at the university? Or enemies, for that matter? We will need to talk to as many people he was in contact with as possible."

"He kept his new life very separate," the dead man's father said. "He's brought nobody here from the university on the odd occasions he's come up to Broadley since. Never talked about it much, to me, anyway. Knew I didn't approve, I suppose. Thought it was all a bloody waste of time. What about you, Christine? I know you have sneaky lunches with Simon when you think I won't notice. Was he any more forthcoming with you?"

Christine Earnshaw turned her gaze very slowly from the elaborate flower arrangement in the stone fireplace and looked at her husband and then at Thackeray with heavy, dazed blue eyes, puffy with crying.

"He talked about his new life to me," she said, so quietly that Val Ridley, on the other side of the room, had to strain to catch what she was saying. "He loved his course. It was what he had decided to do, decided for himself I mean, not something Frank pushed him into." She flashed another glance at her husband and Thackeray was surprised at the venom in it. There was some history there, he thought, and it might be necessary to tease it out.

"Did he mention friends and fellow students at the university, Mrs. Earnshaw?" he asked quietly. "A lot of them are still on vacation and we need to trace them as quickly as we can."

"He talked a lot about someone called Steve. He was working on some project with Steve, something about regeneration? Would that be right? I never totally understood what his course was all about. It seemed to cover so much."

A snort of derision from the other end of the sofa distracted them briefly, in time to notice Matthew Earnshaw refilling his glass from a bottle which he had evidently tucked out of sight into the cushions of the sofa behind him.

"No other name? Just Steve?" Thackeray persisted.

"Just Steve," Simon's mother said. "I'm not sure whether he was another student or a teacher."

"I'm sure we'll be able to trace him," Thackeray said reassuringly. "Any other names?" But Christine Earnshaw shook her head.

"Now the other point Matthew raised last night was Simon's girlfriend. Did you know anything about her?"

"He had a lovely girlfriend called Julie before he gave up work at the mill," Mrs. Earnshaw said. "They'd been going out for years but he broke up with her. I don't think she understood what he was doing going back to college."

"Did any of us?" Matthew Earnshaw asked the room at large.

"But a current girlfriend? You said last night, Mr. Earnshaw, that there were messages on the answerphone. Do any of you know who those could be from?"

"She rang here an'all," Frank Earnshaw said. "Said she was supposed to be meeting him. But she didn't say who she was. It wasn't Julie. I'd have recognised her voice."

"Do you know, sir?" Thackeray asked, turning to the

71

semi-recumbent figure at the other end of the sofa. The younger man looked at him with something close to contempt in his eyes.

"I know nothing about Simon's hippy friends," he said. "I never met any and he certainly never told me about any of them. As far as I can see they want us all back in the bloody stone age, growing veg on the back lawn and walking everywhere. It's all bollocks, as far as I'm concerned."

"He did have a new girlfriend," his mother said suddenly. "I could tell someone was making him happy. But he never told me her name. And I never asked. This falling out with his father and his grandfather has made us all suspicious. I hated it, every minute of it." And Christine Earnshaw began to cry quietly.

The husband and son exchanged glances, half embarrassed and half guilty.

"It must be the girl who called here," Frank Earnshaw said. "But she wouldn't leave her name, or a message. It was the same one on the answerphone at the flat. The voices were the same."

"There was a woman he was involved with," his son added sulkily. "Something serious was going on. Last time I spoke to him on the phone he said something about not asking me to be his best man. I never thought any more about it. It was just a crack about my divorce I thought. Him being as snotty as he always is…was…these days. Oh, hell, I don't know who killed him. If I had any idea I'd tell you. We fell out lately but he was my brother, for God's sake. I still cared about him in spite of the bloody hippies he was hanging out with at the uni."

"Let's move on, then, from friends to enemies," Thackeray said carefully. "Do any of you know anyone who disliked Simon, hated him, even – enough to want him dead?"

But the three members of the family looked horrified at the idea and shook their heads.

"Simon was a popular lad," his father said eventually. "Always had lots of friends at school and at college the first time he went. I've never heard anyone say a harsh word about Simon. Of course I was disappointed when he decided to leave the business and we had rows about that, but in the end we accepted it. If anyone bore a grudge it was him. He stayed away from us, not the other way round."

"What about the difficulties your business is having, Mr. Earnshaw," Thackeray persisted. "Could that have impinged on Simon in any way, even though he'd stopped working for the company?"

"It's two years, nearly, since Simon walked out, resigned, whatever you want to call it," Earnshaw said, angry now. "He's not been involved since. I don't think he's been near the place even. What's going off there now is nothing to do with him."

"He has no financial interest? I thought from what Mr. Matthew Earnshaw here said that's what he was meeting him to discuss?"

Earnshaw hesitated.

"He has a shareholding," he said reluctantly. "We did talk to him about the future of the company. We needed to make sure he knew what was going on and agreed with it, that's all, with redundancies and strike threats and everything else that's blowing up. And that's why Matthew was expecting to see him on Wednesday evening. Simon's not given up his shares, or sold them, I'd know if he had, so he's still involved in that sense but I don't see what that's got to do with someone mugging him."

"It's not an obvious motive," Thackeray said mildly. "Was

Simon's shareholding a large one? Could it interfere with any plans you might have to sell out."

"What plans to sell out? We don't intend to sell out," Earnshaw said angrily. "We're talking a rescue plan here."

"But the shares will come back to you now?"

"As far as I know, yes. Unless Simon's left them elsewhere. But I don't see where this line of questioning is taking us, Inspector. I really don't."

"Was Mr. George Earnshaw in touch with your son, do you know?" Thackeray changed tack suddenly.

"Grandad loved both the boys," Christine Earnshaw broke in. "He was heartbroken when Simon left the mill, absolutely heartbroken. I don't think he's seen him since."

"We have an address in Farmoor Lane for Mr. George Earnshaw. Is that right?"

"Do you really need to question him?" Frank Earnshaw asked, his face flushed. "He's an old man, and seriously ill. He doesn't need to be bothered with all this."

"I'll have to be the judge of that," Thackeray said. "But I'll bear what you say in mind. Now, just one last thing. According to the DVLC in Swansea, Simon Earnshaw was the owner of a 1992 Volvo estate, colour red. Is that right?"

"Clapped-out old heap of junk," Matthew Earnshaw muttered into his full-again glass. "Bought it when he went hippy on us. Used to drive quite a decent Beamer before that."

"So the Volvo is definitely the car we're looking for?"

"He must have used it to get up to Broadley. There's no bus service to speak of except at peak times," Frank Earnshaw said.

"That's assuming he drove himself up here," Thackeray said quietly and the dead man's family stared at him speechlessly for a moment as the implications of that remark sank in. "But if he did, where's the car now?"

"Nicked," Matthew Earnshaw said flatly. "You can't leave anything unattended for ten seconds these days."

"Maybe," Thackeray said although he knew very well that the dead man did not have his car keys with him when he was found. But that was not a fact he wanted known at this stage, even by Simon Earnshaw's family.

"We'll put out a call for the car," he said. "It'll turn up, I'm sure. The trouble was until we identified the body we didn't know what we should be looking for."

"It's not worth anything, that car," Frank Earnshaw said. "If someone stole it they'll probably have dumped it by now."

"Torched it, more like," Matthew Earnshaw said, refilling his glass yet again.

"Yes, well, we'll keep you in touch with developments. We're planning to tell the media who the victim is this afternoon, and seek help from the public to put us in touch with his friends and find the car. If you need any help, or think of anything else that may help our inquiries, DC Ridley here is the person to contact. She's your liaison officer." Val Ridley smiled faintly in the direction of the Earnshaw family who were not, in her judgement, the sort of people who would seek out her, or anyone else's, shoulder to cry on.

"I'll leave you the numbers you need," she said as, following Thackeray's lead, she got up to go.

Back outside in the car she glanced at Thackeray, who sat for a moment in silence before switching on the engine.

"I wonder why the son who was evidently well-trained and effective left the business while the one who's obviously drinking himself to an early grave stayed on," Thackeray said at last.

"Perhaps because his brother was so useless," Val suggested. "They're certainly an odd lot. There doesn't seem to be

75

much love lost, does there? Why the hell does the mother have to meet Simon in secret. It's not as if changing your career is such a big deal. It happens all the time and most families live with it."

"I don't think she's telling us everything she knows. And I will go and see the old man, whatever they say," Thackeray said. "He might be more forthcoming about what makes that lot tick. But not yet. First I think we need to know more about Simon's current relationships. And find his car. It's not impossible that some yob hit him over the head for his car keys and then dumped the body. Let's not invent a complicated explanation when a very simple one might do."

Chapter Six

Soraya Malik lived with her family in one of the narrow terraced streets in the shadows cast by Earnshaws mill on the hill half a mile or so from the bustling thoroughfare of Aysgarth Lane with its curry houses, Asian grocers and a mosque converted from a Wesleyan chapel. The Maliks were a devout family, and had decided to send their daughters to the small Muslim school for girls being run a few streets away rather than to the local comprehensive. The women and girls wore hijab, the austere head-covering of the strict Muslim, rather than the more revealing, and in Bradfield far more common, loose Pakistani headscarf. Even so, the girls' father had felt it safe enough for his daughters to walk the half mile or so to school on their own and for several years Soraya and her sisters had walked there through the almost traffic-free streets of this poor, mainly Asian neighbourhood and arrived home again safely. But not that morning.

Laura Ackroyd stood for a moment outside number 17 Blenheim Street and gazed up at the towering smokestack of the mill which dwarfed the rows of houses beneath and wondered at a family history which had moved in a downward spiral from the building of this commercial monument to the younger Earnshaw's murder, the sensational story of which had been working its way onto the *Gazette*'s front page when she had left the office. Like Titus Salt at Saltaire, the original George Earnshaw had recognised the need to house his labourers close to their workplace, though not nearly as generously. These had been small, cramped and strictly utilitarian dwellings when they were new: more than a hundred years later roofs sagged, window frames rotted and families of Victorian proportions packed themselves into the single living room and kitchen with at most three small bedrooms above and a bathroom tacked on in the back yard, just as their predecessors had done in the nineteenth century. Only the colour of their skin was different.

It was a townscape Laura felt she was barely familiar with. Earnshaws mill loomed over this side of the town just as the blank slabs of the Heights dominated the hill to the west, and both were neighbourhoods where Bradfield's more affluent citizens seldom ventured. Laura watched an elderly man in khaki shalwar kameez under a thick black overcoat walking slowly down the deserted street, his white lace cap offering little protection from the chilly drizzle. He glanced at her car and then at her, his eyes full of suspicion. White faces were probably rare in Blenheim Street, and white people arriving in cars even more unusual. More often than not, she thought, such an incursion meant trouble. After the last bout of violence on the streets of Bradfield the powers-that-be who inquired into such things had concluded that the town's various communities were leading parallel lives and Laura, whose profession brought her into contact with politically and socially active Asians in all walks of life, had thought that an exaggeration. Here she was not so sure.

Soraya must have walked the length of the street, Laura thought, before turning into the narrow alleyway which linked Blenheim with the parallel Alma Street. It was there that a former Labour club housed the Muslim school. Somewhere down that alley the girls had met a group of boys running in the opposite direction and, after they had passed, Soraya had fallen to the ground screaming in agony and trying to rub the liquid one of the boys had hurled at her from her face and eyes.

Laura felt slightly sick when she contemplated what had

happened, and she had to steel herself to knock at the Malik family's front door to seek the interview with the family Ted Grant had sent her to find, though years of experience had taught her that surprisingly often the victims of tragedy were comforted rather than repelled by the chance to talk about what had happened, even to a stranger. After a long silence the door was opened by a short, stocky Asian man in traditional Pakistani dress. His eyes were not friendly and Laura hurried to explain who she was and what she wanted. Eventually he turned back into the house and shouted something in Punjabi to those inside. He was quickly joined by a taller, younger man, dark and bearded but in a smart western suit and tie and with an equally unfriendly expression.

"I am Sayeed Khan," the newcomer said. "I'm a lawyer and I'm advising the Maliks. I'm not sure that giving interviews to the Press is what they need to be doing just now."

"If you want to catch the thugs did this terrible thing you need publicity," Laura said bluntly. "There may be people who saw them running away and who don't realise what happened. If Soraya's parents will talk to me, I can give a better picture of the girl and her sisters, and perhaps give the readers some information that someone may need to persuade them to help."

"I doubt many of your readers will be much interested in helping," Khan said curtly. "We're getting racist abuse and attacks almost every day of the week and the *Gazette*'s not shown a scrap of interest up to now."

Laura nodded, knowing how much truth there was in that allegation and cursing Ted Grant under her breath for his casual prejudice.

"Of course we'll publish what the police tell us about the attack," she said. "But an interview with Soraya's family, perhaps pictures of her sisters, would put a human face on it,

79

get more space in the paper even. I'm also going to be doing some interviews on Radio Bradfield soon and I wanted to talk about race problems in those. But of course it's up to Mr. Malik…"

She glanced at the older man who had been listening to her exchange with Khan intently. He in turn glanced at Khan. It was clear that it was the lawyer who would be making the decision for the family. He seemed to consider for a moment and then nodded.

"You may be right," he said. "But I'll stay while you talk to them, and if Soraya's mother is distressed, then you must leave. Her English is not good, but I, or one of the girls, will translate."

Laura followed the two men into the cramped living room where a woman and two young girls of ten or eleven were sitting together on a shabby sofa, their eyes red with crying. Khan explained in Punjabi who Laura was and then waved her into a chair. She took out her tape-recorder cautiously, watching Mrs. Malik carefully. Sometimes the technology frightened reluctant interviewees and a notebook and pen were less threatening.

"Is this OK?" she asked, and reassured by the nods from the woman and girls, she switched on.

She asked Soraya's sisters first to tell her exactly what had happened that morning, a story which became even more upsetting, Laura thought, as the two girls, their eyes bright and troubled under the severe hijab, explained how they too had been pushed to the ground in the narrow alleyway by three or four boys or young men running at full pelt towards them with their hoods pulled tights around their faces so that only their eyes were visible.

"And you really couldn't see if they were Asian or white?" Laura asked.

"Asian boys wouldn't do that to girls," the older of Soraya's two young sisters said firmly in her broad local accent, and Laura was inclined to agree with her. Asian young men were not necessarily angels and many were increasingly involved in crime, but attacking young female children, and these were children, seemed an unlikely transgression for that culture.

"How old is Soraya?" Laura asked her mother, but in fact it was her father who answered.

"She is fourteen," he said.

"And before you ask the insulting question I can see on your lips," Sayeed Khan broke in angrily. "I can tell you this is a very devout Muslim family and that Soraya has had nothing to do with boys. If that suggestion appears in your newspaper, that this is some sort of attack launched from within the community, the family will regard it as deeply insulting."

He spoke quickly, and Laura guessed deliberately so, so that the girls' mother would not be able to follow what he was saying, but his tone annoyed her.

"It is not so outrageous a question with a girl of her age," she said. "You know the cases which spring to mind." The previous year two young Muslim girls had fled Bradfield in fear of their lives after being discovered with boys their families disapproved of. "Izzat", or dishonour, was still a very real concept for many of the families who had come to Bradfield from the rural heart of the Punjab only a generation or so ago, and some fathers and sons still policed their daughters and sisters fiercely. Rumour had it that there were young men in the community who would hunt down and even kill a young woman who defied tradition too blatantly. Laura knew it had happened elsewhere and she knew that Sayeed Khan knew it too.

81

"Could you really not see whether these boys were Asian or white?" she asked the girls again. "It could be very important to help the police catch them if they knew the answer to that." But the two girls shook their heads.

"It was so quick," the older girl said. "They came round the corner, and we were all pushed and then they were gone. We thought they had stabbed Soraya but it was her face…" The girl turned to her mother and began to sob quietly.

"I'm sorry," Laura said. "You've been very patient. I think you've told me enough now to give people an idea of how dreadful this is for you." She switched off her tape recorder. She could, she thought, concoct enough paragraphs from this brief encounter to satisfy Ted Grant's passion for personal detail without being too intrusive, although in his book there was no such thing as intrusive when someone was catapulted into the public eye, for whatever reason. She glanced at Sayeed Khan and smiled her thanks but he did not respond. As she closed the front door behind her she heard him begin to speak angrily in Punjabi again and wished that she could understand the language. She hoped that her visit had not caused the family too much distress, but she was sure it had not brought much comfort either.

As she turned back to her car, her stomach lurched as someone grabbed her arm from behind. She spun round and found herself face to face with two Asian boys of fourteen or fifteen. They made no further attempt to molest her but their eyes were unfriendly.

"Round here women cover up their hair," one of them said.

"If you want to visit round here, you cover up," the other added.

Half a dozen objections to these instructions sprang to Laura's lips but she bit them back. Discretion might be safer, she thought as she unlocked the car with careful deliberation and slipped into the driver's seat. Only as she started the engine did she lower the window.

"You'll do no one any good if you try to set up a no-go area," she said then.

"Just an Islamic area," the older of the two boys said. "You don't have to come back if you don't like it."

"They've taken the place apart, guv," Sergeant Kevin Mower said, dropping a thick file onto Michael Thackeray's desk later that afternoon. "You say his father says he was paying his way from his savings. Well, according to his bank statements that's exactly what he was doing. No problem there. He's got almost a hundred thousand in a deposit account and he's been taking a monthly amount out and obviously using it to live on. Nothing odd going into and out of his current account: rent, utility bills, smallish amounts of cash, that sort of thing. But then there's this." He opened the file and pulled out a travel agents' folder and opened it wide.

"Two air tickets from Heathrow to Marseilles in France for a date in April."

"In whose names?" Thackeray asked.

"Mr. S and Mrs. S Earnshaw."

Thackeray took hold of the tickets and flicked through them.

"No return date," he said. "Open tickets."

"Yep," Mower agreed. "And who the hell is Mrs. Earnshaw?"

"Whoever she is, no one in his family seems to know that he was married," Thackeray said. "They're aware of a girl-friend, but no more than that."

"Perhaps he wasn't married," Mower said. "Perhaps he was just planning to be and these are the tickets for his honeymoon. But that's not the only French connection. Look, I found these." He pulled a couple of brochures from the file, closely typed and with photographs of several red pantiled cottages amongst the text.

"My French is even worse than my Punjabi but if these aren't estate agents' details I'll eat the *chapeau de ma tante*."

Thackeray flicked through the brochures quickly.

"No sign that he's actually purchased a property in southern France?"

"No. Maybe he was just going to look."

"Well, find someone who does speak reasonable French and get them to call these people and see if Earnshaw made any arrangements with them, will you? They're all close to Marseilles, in Provence anyway, so it seems a reasonable bet that the flights were linked with this. Perhaps he wanted to buy a holiday home. It's not unusual these days. And check with the Registrar's office and see if he is married – or about to be. They may have booked the tickets to follow the wedding. Are his phone bills here?"

"Only up to December last year," Mower said.

"Get a more recent one from his phone company. We need to know who he's been calling regularly and who's been calling him. We should be able to trace the girlfriend, wife, whatever she is, that way."

"There is one mobile number which keeps cropping up but it's a bloody pay-as-you-go so no joy there. Could be anyone but I'd guess that's the girlfriend's. And there are bills for a mobile as well as his land-line," Mower said. "Though there's no mobile around, and he didn't have one on him when he was found, which is odd. You'd think if he was going running he'd have it in his pocket."

"Maybe it's in the missing car," Thackeray said. "No joy on that, I suppose."

"Not yet," Mower said. "Maybe Matthew Earnshaw's right and it's a burnt-out wreck somewhere."

"I don't think this is a mugging gone wrong," Thackeray said sombrely. "There's too many anomalies around this young man. Has anyone been to the university yet to talk to his tutor?"

"I was going up there next, guv."

"I'll come with you," Thackeray said. "This isn't an eighteen-year-old we're talking about here. He's a mature student, a post-graduate with plenty of cash and one apparently successful career behind him. I reckon his tutor will be more of a friend than a teacher. He may well have a lot of the answers we're looking for."

Bradfield University had grown from its original technical college roots in a sprawl of Victorian college buildings and modern slab-like blocks on the lower slopes of the town's most westerly hill. It reminded Mower of the polytechnic in south London where he had taken his degree when he and his teachers had finally discovered that his wits could carve him a way out of his teenaged semi-delinquency. It could not have been more unlike the Oxford college of St. Frideswide where Thackeray had found to his deep disillusionment that a sharp mind was not a sufficient passport to acceptance amongst mores that were almost as foreign to him as they would have been to a Pakistani, and about as unacceptable. Both men had found a sort of ethical haven in the police force, where even if the ground occasionally shifted beneath their feet, they could rely most of the time on a system which distinguished firmly enough between right and wrong to keep them upright.

"Seems an odd place to be doing environmental stuff," Mower remarked as they made their way into one of the university's more dilapidated blocks, which were generally the most recently constructed.

85

"Once the bottom fell out of the old industries they had to diversify, just like everyone else," Thackeray said. "I knew a lad at school who came here to study textile engineering when it was the best place in the country for that sort of thing. And if you think about it, this part of the world needs an environmental leg-up more than most. Maybe that's what Earnshaw reckoned."

Mower punched the lift button for the fourth floor where Simon Earnshaw's tutor was waiting for them.

"So why was he apparently heading for Provence?" he asked, as the lift struggled upwards.

"Maybe Dr. Stephen McKenna can tell us," Thackeray said as the doors creaked reluctantly open and they found themselves face-to-face with a stocky man with a neat red beard and mournful brown eyes. He held out a hand, first to Thackeray and then Mower, and his grip was firm and dry.

"Gentlemen," he said. "Tell me what I can do to help. Anything. I just can't believe that Simon is dead."

When they had squeezed themselves into his tiny office, which involved much shuffling of chairs and piles of books and files, McKenna inserted himself behind his cluttered desk and repeated his offer.

"What can I say," he said. "Simon was a good friend as well as a post-graduate student. I'm simply devastated."

"How much longer did he have to go to gain his master's?" Thackeray asked.

"Not long. He's – he had, I mean – completed the examined part of the course and was half way through his project and dissertation. It was going well, I thought. Some more research to do here and there, and some tidying up of the arguments, but he was well on his way. He just needed to settle down and write for another few weeks, a month maybe…He was looking at problems of urban regeneration, obviously close to his heart and just the sort of study this area needs. Such a bloody waste," McKenna concluded sombrely.

"So you would be the Steve his family had heard him talk about, the Steve he was working with?"

"Well, yes, I suppose so," McKenna said. "As I say, I regarded him as a friend as much as a student."

"He was actually studying local problems?" Mower broke in. "Relevant to the redevelopment of the family mill, for instance?"

"Well, as part of a theoretical study, of course, but yes, there are plenty of examples of successful and unsuccessful regeneration projects in this part of Yorkshire as you probably know. Look at the redevelopment of Leeds. And Salts Mill and the Hockney gallery and the success they've made of that. Once or twice he said he wished his father would consider something similar for the family mill – you know about Earnshaws, of course?" When the two police officers nodded, McKenna rushed on, as if he feared the emotion which would overwhelm him if he dared to pause.

"Of course, he played no part in the running of the business any more. I got the impression that he and his father had fallen out over ecological issues. I don't think the family had any time for his change of direction."

"How seriously had they quarrelled?" Thackeray asked.

McKenna hesitated.

"I regarded Simon as a friend, as I say, but he never confided much about his family. He simply said he had got out when it seemed to him that the company was heading in the wrong direction, that it was missing opportunities, I think was the way he put it. I got the feeling that he had cut himself off from all that when he came back here to study."

"But the mill's problems might have appeared in his dissertation? They were relevant?"

87

"Well, I got the impression that he thought so. He seemed to be keeping in touch with what was going on there, though not through his family I suspect. More likely through the trade union."

"The people who are threatening to strike?" Thackeray asked.

"Well, I guess so. He never said, but I think he was far more sympathetic to the workers at the mill than he was to the management," McKenna said. "I'm not trying to make him out to be some sort of revolutionary, Chief Inspector. Don't get me wrong. But he was deeply concerned about how a place like Bradfield can survive in the twenty-first century, and he seemed quite convinced, as I am, that it won't be through hanging on to industries which are essentially moribund."

"Did he say what he wanted to do when he finished his dissertation?" Thackeray asked.

"Not really," McKenna said. "I think he wanted to travel. He once said that he regretted not taking time off the first time he graduated. He missed his 'gap year' he said, because his father wanted him to go straight into the business. But, no, he never mentioned anything specific."

"Would it surprise you that he seemed to be planning to buy a house in France?"

"In France? Yes, that would surprise me. I got the feeling he wanted to go further afield than that."

"And did he tell you he was planning to get married?"

"Ah," McKenna said, making a steeple of his fingers in front of his face. "That might explain the house in France."

Thackeray waited while McKenna evidently had an internal argument with himself.

"We're dealing with a murder, sir," he prompted at last, battening down his impatience with difficulty.

"I know. I'm sorry," McKenna said. "Of course, I must tell you everything I know but as you'll realise when I tell you, there are other people involved here – and possibly at risk."

"At risk?" Thackeray said and Mower glanced sharply at the academic, wondering what was coming next.

"I said Simon was a friend," McKenna said. "And in a sense he was, but when I think about it I realise what a shallow sort of friendship it really was. We were intensely interested in our subject, both of us were, and we followed up our tutorials very often in the pub, long evenings talking, but talking professionally, you understand. In some ways Simon was an intensely private person. He talked very little about his family, and not at all about his love life, if he had one. And I think he had. I heard from other sources that he had acquired a girlfriend this year, this academic year I mean, and that she was a student here and...and this is where it gets difficult...that she was Asian – Pakistani, I assumed."

"You don't know who she was?" Thackeray asked sharply.

"I think Simon took care that no one knew that."

"So she was someone whose family might not have welcomed the relationship?"

"That's what I assumed," McKenna said. "I never asked. Perhaps I should have done. Perhaps if I had, Simon would still be alive."

Chapter Seven

Laura fastened Naomi's nappy and slipped chubby legs, pink from her bath, into pyjama bottoms before picking the child up and burying herself in the sweet smell of her.

"Let's go and find your mummy now, sweetheart," she said and carried the little girl carefully downstairs to the kitchen where Vicky Mendelson, Laura's closest friend since they had been students together at Bradfield University, was tending a large and aromatic pot over the stove. Vicky's enthusiastic adoption of an earth mother role had initially startled Laura and now occasionally caused her to wonder what she was missing.

"There, I told you I could bath a baby if pushed," she said triumphantly, putting Naomi down on the floor where she tottered delightedly towards her mother. "It's not some arcane skill you need a degree in, is it."

"Well done," Vicky said noncommittally. She wiped a smear of bubble bath foam from the shoulder of Laura's deep fuschia shirt before picking Naomi up and putting her in her high chair. "You're all dressed up too. I just wonder how long you can go on borrowing my kids when you so obviously want your own."

"Ouch," Laura said. "Is it so obvious?"

"Of course it is, you idiot."

"Well, a wedding looks as if it may be on the cards this year," she said. "As for the rest, we'll have to wait and see."

Vicky parked her wooden spoon carefully and gave Laura a hug.

"That's great news," she said. "We did introduce you so I feel some responsibility when he makes you miserable. I like

Michael, though he's obviously not the easiest man in the world."

"You could say that," Laura said with a wry grin. She glanced at her watch slightly anxiously. "Will David be long? I'm supposed to be fetching Joyce from the Heights and then having dinner with my father at the Clarendon. He's on a flying visit – for some mysterious purposes of his own, of course, not simply to see me."

"He's here, I think," Vicky said. "I just heard the car." And even as she spoke the front door opened and David Mendelson, preceded by two excited sons, came down the hall and into the kitchen. David kissed his wife, his baby daughter and then Laura while Daniel and Nathan milled about both telling anyone who would listen what they had done at their after-school computer club.

"Whoa, whoa," David said at last, pushing the boys towards the table which was set for their tea. "Laura, you said on the mobile you wanted to talk to me. Shall we have a drink in the other room and leave this gang to eat?"

Laura shot an apologetic glance at Vicky, contentedly surrounded by the family she envied, and followed David into the calm of the sitting room where he poured her a vodka and tonic without being asked, and a Scotch for himself.

"Problems?" he asked. David too was an old student friend and now used his legal training as a member of the Crown Prosecution Service where his work had often brought him into contact with Michael Thackeray. The two men had formed a firm friendship, something both David and Laura knew was an unusual event in Thackeray's life, and it was round the dinner table in the next room that Laura had first set instantly interested eyes on her lover.

"Just an informal query really," Laura said. "I've been covering this attack today on the young Asian girls, and it's only a day or so since I witnessed a really nasty bit of harassment in the street – two Asian woman minding their own business and a gang of lads making their lives a misery. I want to write a piece about it all tomorrow and I wondered whether the CPS had any policy on prosecuting these racists. They seem to be getting away with it to me."

"You've talked to Michael about this, presumably?" David said cautiously.

"He just says that the minor stuff is left to the uniformed police. It's not CID's concern unless a serious crime's been committed – like the acid attack, presumably. Or unless there's some concerted campaign going on. And I'm beginning to wonder about that."

"Yes, that attack on the young girl was pretty horrific," David said. "It's not just the Asian community that's being threatened either. My father tells me that there's been an outbreak of swastika graffiti around the synagogue. Of course, they tend to keep quiet about it, though I'm really not sure they should." As a not-very-observant Jew married to a gentile, David was not a very frequent visitor to Bradfield's small synagogue.

"So there's a nasty racist group taking on anyone and everyone they don't like?"

"I think so, yes. But as far as prosecutions are concerned, we rely on the police to bring us the suspects. You know that. And so far they've not come up with anyone much, as far as I know."

"You can't make it any sort of priority?"

"That would be down to the Chief Constable. Or some sort of national initiative. We can only take action on what the police bring us," David said.

"Do you get the impression that the police aren't very interested? The top brass I mean, at county?" Laura asked carefully.

"I don't think it's a priority," David said. "But for Christ's sake don't quote me on that. My boss would go bananas." He hesitated for a moment then seemed to come to a decision.

"I shouldn't really be telling you this, so you'd better protect your sources or I'll be out of a job."

Laura sat very still, her face serious.

"You know me well enough," she said. David nodded.

"Last year we initiated a police investigation into a man called Ricky Pickles. CID were pretty sure that he was behind a pretty obnoxious letter campaign to ethnic community leaders, including the Jewish community, which is how I came to hear of it."

"Michael was involved in this?" Laura asked.

"No, it was organised from county HQ. But he probably knew it was going on. Anyway, a lot of evidence was accumulated about Pickles and his friends. They were running some sort of far right splinter group and we were pretty sure they were behind the threatening letters. But in the end the whole thing collapsed. You know we have to reckon that there's a fifty per cent chance of a prosecution succeeding and in this case it was decided there wasn't enough evidence for that. So it's not as if the authorities haven't been trying. But it's hard to pin down, this sort of crime. Conspiracy always is."

"Pickles," Laura said. "Where does this splinter group hang out then?"

"Laura, you mustn't go anywhere near these people. They say they're only involved in legitimate political activity but I think they're very dangerous," David said, his face instantly anxious. "I shouldn't have mentioned it..."

"They'll wreck this town if they get away with chucking acid at schoolchildren," Laura said, her expression closed and angry.

"You've no evidence that they were involved," David protested.

"No, it just gives me an idea where to direct my questions, that's all," Laura said. "Tomorrow I'll go right to the top and ask the Chief Constable what the hell he's going to do about acid attacks on little girls on the way to school. And whether or not Pickles and his friends are still being investigated."

"He won't like that," David said.

"I don't suppose he will. But it's a fair question. And I'll talk to the police locally about what they're doing to protect vulnerable groups, including people who go to the synagogue." She drained her glass quickly as David smiled faintly in a way which, she thought, could just have been encouraging. "I must go or else Joyce will be rampaging around the Heights looking for me and Dad will be knocking back far too many G and Ts in the Clarendon bar. Say my farewells to your gang for me, will you?"

David saw his guest out of the house and into her Golf which was parked under the trees in the leafy street outside. He watched the car thoughtfully until the lights disappeared down a bend on the hill in the direction of the town centre. A beam of light directed at the murky underworld of extremist groups might be just what Bradfield needed, he thought. On the other hand, it might provide the spark for the explosion that a lot of people dreaded but half expected.

Sergeant Kevin Mower was definitely a believer in shining the brightest possible searchlights into murky corners of society. He had grown up on a south London high-rise estate where he had lived and gone to school with children from a rainbow of different nationalities and ethnic identities. When his mother had regularly retreated into a surreal world of her own, some stability had been brought to his chaotic life by a motherly Indian neighbour. He had never known his father who, his mother had told him when she mentioned him at all, had been Greek or possibly Turkish Cypriot. He had loved and lusted after and invariably lost women of every shade of skin-colour and when – very rarely – he considered the prospect of having children of his own he fully expected that they would be a shade or two darker than he was. He was not by nature a crusader, he had simply accepted from an early age what his experience had taught him: that human beings come in a variety of shades and with a variety of traditions as well as personalities and had lived his life without letting that bother him in any way. Now he found himself, somewhat to his consternation, in a small town where two different cultures appeared to live parallel lives without many people remarking that this was in any way peculiar let alone undesirable. And he found himself disoriented by it.

DC Mohammed Sharif, who called himself Omar, was different, Mower thought, as he trawled with the junior officer through computer details on local extremists, and he did not just mean because his skin was several shades darker than Mower's own. Omar thought that a slight difference in skin colour was not just important but crucial in all sorts of ways. Omar was not in any sense colourblind. He was acutely colour sensitive, and religion and ethnicity sensitive too. He was too intelligent not to realise that the police force was bound not, discriminate in any way, but he did discriminate personally if not officially, minutely and, he no doubt hoped, invisibly. But it was not invisible to Mower. He knew from experience that Omar did not like people of African descent and that he distrusted Hindus and Sikhs on the rare occasions that he came across them in Bradfield. He knew that Omar did not like women in positions of any authority and was not even quite comfortable with women officers of equal rank. And he knew that Omar was pretty happy with some of what Mower regarded as the local Muslim community's more deeply sexist traditions. All this Mower knew by instinct as much as observation because Omar was very careful to hide his prejudices and beliefs and it took antennae as sensitive as Mower's to probe beneath the young Muslim officer's smoothly cheerful and apparently modern exterior.

Looking over his shoulder at the computer screen, Mower sighed heavily.

"They're getting bloody professional these days," he said. "Reading some of this stuff you'd think butter wouldn't melt. In reality they've about as much commitment to using the ballot-box to get what they want as President bloody Mugabe."

"This lot don't seem to be arguing for much more than separate communities staying separate," DC Sharif said doubtfully. "Most Asians I know can live with that."

"You've not read enough history, my son," Mower said. "The phrase 'separate but equal' has a long and murky history in South Africa and the USA. Anyway, this lot, as you call them, the British Patriotic Party, happen to have a young man called Ricky Pickles as their general secretary, or whatever title he chooses to use – general officer commanding, probably – and he's a thoroughly nasty piece of work. A thug in a designer suit, maybe, but a thug all the same."

"Any previous?" Sharif said, flicking the computer keys to log onto the Police National Computer.

"Not recently, I don't think," Mower said. "He's too careful to get involved in the street violence himself these days. But look at that. ABH, GBH, racially motivated assault, probation, community punishment, three years in a young offenders' institution…a lovely lad. I think maybe it's time to pay Ricky another call."

"And what about the other stuff you were on about, sarge," Sharif asked, just the faintest signs of mutiny in his dark eyes. "Do you really want me going up to Aysgarth Lane to find out if Asians chucked acid at Asian schoolgirls? It's bizarre, if you don't mind me saying so."

"Look, you don't have to make a big deal out of this," Mower said, slightly wearily. "But you know as well as I do that there are a few self-appointed enforcers up there who'll take on girls who step out of line. Just go up and keep your ears open. Have a chat at the mosque. See if the gossip suggests that there might be anything in that line of enquiry. My guess is that you won't find anything, but if we don't check it out and then it turns out that this was a family affair we're the ones who'll have egg all over our faces."

"Yeah, right," Sharif said. "You won't be coming with me then?"

"No, but you can come with me to see Pickles. If I recall that young man correctly, seeing you will really annoy him, maybe even rattle him, and that's all to the good. Not that I think he'll give us a convenient membership list of all the racist yobs in Bradfield, but he might let something slip. This shiny new political façade can't be more than skin-deep with him, can it?"

The façade was shiny enough when they ran Pickles to earth behind a glossily painted shop front with opaque and, Mower thought, significantly reinforced windows on the outskirts of the town centre. The BPP logo was discreetly displayed but the doors were locked and it took someone inside some time to manipulate several keys and bolts in response to Mower's peremptory knocking. The two officers found themselves facing a tall, heavy, shaven-headed gorilla of a man in jeans and a sweat-top adorned with the same logo as the windows, who scowled at Mower and almost snarled when he took in Sharif, darkly good-looking in leather jacket and designer jeans. Mower flashed a warrant card at him quickly.

"We're here to see Ricky Pickles," he said. "He's expecting us."

The doorkeeper nodded, although his eyes remained mutinous.

"Yeah," he said, allowing them into the building and ostentatiously locking the door behind them again. What had obviously been the shop part of the premises was divided by a counter piled high with boxes of what looked like leaflets, and the posters on the walls advertised Pickles' most recent attempts, so far unsuccessful, but only just, to gain election to the local council.

"Through there." The taciturn doorkeeper waved a hand towards a door marked office at the back of the shop area and Mower tapped and went in without waiting for a response. Pickles was sitting behind a large executive desk with a telephone to his ear and waved benignly at his two visitors as he wound up his call.

"Sorry about that, Sergeant Mower," he said. "Craig's here for security not his social skills." He had stood up and held out his hand as his visitors came in but Mower ignored the gesture and Pickles sat down again with a shrug, without acknowledging Sharif's presence at all.

"What can I do for you?" he asked curtly, his enthusiasm for the visit evidently waning within seconds.

"We just wondered if you knew anyone who might have been throwing acid around in the Aysgarth Lane area," Mower said, his face bland and his voice mild in spite of the bluntness of his assault.

"And why would I know anyone like that, sergeant?" Pickles countered airily. "This is the office of a political party

98

not a hangout for yobs. We've espoused the ballot box rather than the acid bullet, as you might say, just like our Fenian friends. Not that I've ever waged war on little girls, you understand, unlike the fucking IRA. A bit OTT that, don't you reckon?" He flashed a triumphant glance at Sharif, who was simmering beside Mower but who had learned the hard way not to rise to the racist bait.

"However legitimate your own ambitions are, I'm sure you know a few people who are less – shall we say? – scrupulous," Mower said. "DC Sharif here certainly knows that there are plenty of white lads willing to raise hell round Aysgarth Lane when the mood takes them. Are none of them your supporters, then?"

"What folk do in their spare time is nowt to do with me or the Party," Pickles said, the smooth façade beginning to look a little strained. "I've told you. I've gone legit. I know you know I were a bit of a wild lad once but I've put violence behind me. I know I can get where I want to get in this town through the political system."

"You're sure of that, are you?" Sharif asked suddenly.

"Oh aye, I'm sure of that," Pickles said. "You'll see, all your lot'll see, and sooner than you think an'all. There's more people don't like your lot than you can ever imagine. More and more since New York."

"And what exactly's your platform for the white voters?" Mower asked. "I'm assuming no one of Asian descent will want to vote for you."

"No, well, they wouldn't would they? Knowing that they'll lose all the favours they're getting from t'council now. Special this and special that and let's not upset the minorities. Fair shares of what's going for white folk is all I'm saying. Nowt wrong wi'that, is there?"

"It depends what you think's fair, I suppose," Mower said.

99

"But we're getting away from the point. I'm looking for three or four lads, young lads probably, prepared to run around the streets close to Earnshaws mill looking for trouble. Any ideas?"

"No ideas at all," Pickles said, regaining his ruffled composure. "Why should I have?"

"And if you had you wouldn't tell us?" Sharif asked.

"Did I hear summat then?" Pickles asked Mower. "Sort of chattering noise, like a monkey or summat?

Mower felt Sharif tense beside him and put a restraining hand on his arm.

"I think at the very least you need to pass on a message to your supporters, Ricky," he said. "I think you need to let them know that we're going to get whoever did this acid throwing. It was a disgusting attack on innocent kids and they won't get away with it. Nasty, vicious, child abuse I suppose. Let them know it's me they need to contact if they've got any information. And tell them that this is the sort of crime I don't forget and I don't let up on – ever. Pass it on, will you?"

When the shop door eventually closed behind them, Mower glanced at Sharif who banged his fist so hard against the wall that it skinned his knuckles, although he did not wince.

"Leave it, Omar," he said. "You can't let it get to you. You won't survive in this job if you do."

"Sarge," Sharif agreed, his dark eyes blazing. "So maybe I won't survive in this job if I come up against that scum one dark night. Might be worth taking a chance on."

* * *

Jack Ackroyd was late for his dinner engagement. Laura and her grandmother had arrived at the Clarendon just before

100

seven thirty and settled themselves in the bar where Joyce, in a blue dress that was beginning to seem loose on a frame that was thinner and more stooped than it used to be, sipped a sherry with an air of faint disapproval as a noisy group of young people in dinner jackets and revealing dresses milled about prior to what looked like an office dinner dance. For her part, Laura gazed at her vodka and tonic and wondered if she was too old for anything quite as revealing as one of the little slinky numbers being thrust in her face. She glanced down at her own black silk dress, low enough at the neck she had thought until she had seen tonight's competition, and wondered how had she managed to fall in love with a man ten years her senior and a not-so-closet puritan to boot.

"We'd have been locked up if we'd gone out looking like that," Joyce whispered fiercely.

"Come on, Nan," Laura remonstrated. "You're not telling me you never showed a bit of bosom in your salad days, are you? It's not what I heard. I've seen the photographs. You were a stunner. Good enough for Page 3."

"We knew what to keep for the bedroom, any road," Joyce said tartly. "You can see up to that lass's knickers."

"If she's wearing any," Laura said doubtfully. "I don't see how she can be." At which both she and Joyce both collapsed into delighted giggles.

"What's so funny, then?" Jack Ackroyd asked. He had pushed through the crowd to their corner table without their being aware of his approach.

"Tell you later, Dad," Laura said. "Have you got a drink or do you want to eat straight away? I'm starving. I didn't have time for much lunch."

"Aye, let's eat. I can have a Scotch at the table while they're bring the food. Is Michael coming, then?"

"He can't. The old story, working late," Laura said, pulling a face, although in some ways she was relieved that Thackeray had eventually declined the invitation. She thought she might get more out of her father about his mysterious plans if she was not accompanied by a detective chief inspector this evening.

In the restaurant the head waiter evidently recognised Jack, even though it was more than six years since he had lived and worked in Bradfield, and he ushered them to a table in the large bay window which overlooked Exchange Square and its cluster of statues of local worthies, mainly those who had transformed an early nineteenth century village into a bustling manufacturing town in the space of less than fifty years, making themselves millionaires in the process.

"Still got your finger on the pulse then, Jack?" Joyce said as she sat down and accepted the large leather-bound menu as if it might explode in her hand.

"Oh aye, here and there, Mother, here and there," Jack said. "Now as I recollect they always had a good roast here. I do hope they've not mucked the menu up with olive oil mash and onion marmalade and towers of roast cod on spinach. I just fancy a traditional English meal tonight. Can't get that easily in Portugal. It's all bloody cod there, an'all."

"That's the price you pay for the sunshine and the golf," Laura said unsympathetically.

"Your mother still likes fish," Jack muttered, as if this were a character defect in his wife he should have eliminated by now. He ordered their meal and a bottle of Bordeaux old enough to impress although Laura knew it would suit her father's roast beef much better than her chicken. Jack was not a person who would willingly put his pleasures second to anyone else's. Joyce declined wine and sipped mineral water with her asparagus and herb omelette, seeming subdued although Laura could not tell whether it was by her surroundings or a more general depression which she thought she had noticed before. Joyce was not taking kindly to the frustrations of old age.

Laura had to admit that Jack was never less than generous with his treats and she felt the wine going to her head as it met the vodka and tonic which she had drunk with David Mendelson and followed up with Joyce in the bar while they were waiting for Jack. It would have to be a taxi home tonight, she thought wryly, or a frosty reception from Thackeray if she arrived in her own car after drinking. But if anything the wine emboldened her and, as she nibbled a trio of miniature chocolate puddings which she knew she would regret ordering next time she got on her bathroom scales, she tackled the subject which had been simmering at the back of her mind during the family small-talk which Jack had masterminded throughout the rest of the meal.

"So come on, Dad," she said. "How's this rescue plan for Earnshaws you're being so mysterious about going? What are you going to do, take them over, or what? That would be a shock to the local system."

"Aye well, it might be no more than they deserve," Jack said. "But it's not as simple as that. It never is in business. No, a take-over's not on the cards. I told you. I'll let you be the first to know when there's owt to tell."

"I met one of the younger Earnshaws once at a party when I was a student," Laura said. "But the awful thing is that I can't remember if it was the son who's been killed or the other one, what's he called? Matthew is it?"

"Bumped off the wrong one if you ask me," Jack said unsympathetically. "Matthew's bloody useless, by all accounts. Booze, cocaine, you name it, he does it, apparently."

"Will it muck up your plans then, this murder?" Joyce

103

asked sharply, evidently deeply suspicious of Jack's interest in Earnshaws.

"I'd not think so, no. He was out of the loop, was Simon," Jack said. "It's Frank I'm dealing with, any road. I've known him from way back. He'll not muck me about, won't Frank. A sight different from his father. Now he's a cantankerous old beggar, is George. I met him a couple of times years ago and he could teach me a thing or two about keeping a work-force in order."

"And that'd be difficult," Joyce said, her voice sharp.

"He knew a trick or two, did George," Jack said with a gleeful glance at his mother.

"Surely he's long retired?" Joyce asked. "He must be as old as me, must George Earnshaw. I remember him an' all. Nearly got taken to the Race Relations people for refusing to employ Asian workers when all the other mills were bringing them over here in their thousands. Had to back off in the end, of course, when he found that no one else would work for him for the wages he was prepared to offer. Now of course a lot of those poor devils are unemployed, and their children and grandchildren as well."

"Aye, well, I don't think old George's got much to do with the business now," Jack said. "I've no doubt he'd like to keep the place going until it goes spectacularly bust, but I reckon we can do better than that. You should be grateful, Mother, if we can keep Earnshaws viable and employing a few folk."

"A few?" Joyce said. "Time was it were thousands. It was the biggest mill in the town in its day, was Earnshaws."

"Time was no one in the third bloody world knew what a loom looked like," Jack said without sympathy. "Times change and you've got to change with them, or go under. Your Mr. Blair knows that."

"He's not my Mr. Blair," Joyce objected, her lips pursed.

"Come on, Dad," Laura said. "Let's not have a political row now. But I'll hold you to your promise, you know. I want this story, when there's something to print. It'll earn me a few brownies points with Ted Grant and I'm short of those at the moment."

Laura was aware of Thackeray watching her from the bay window of their sitting room as she paid off the cab and she felt that lurch in her stomach which still hit her every time she caught sight of him unexpectedly. Damn you, she thought. It's time you exorcised your ghosts and made an honest woman of me before I go chasing some delicious hunk somewhere else. Thackeray, she thought, might have been reading her mind as he helped her off with her coat with unusual solicitude and sat beside her on the sofa with an arm around her. She pecked him on the cheek and lay back and closed her eyes.

"Bad day?" Thackeray asked. She nodded.

"How's your father?" he continued.

"Some things never change," Laura said. "And my father's devious financial schemes are one of them. It must be something pretty lucrative to have brought him running all the way back from Portugal."

"I should let him get on with it," Thackeray said. "If he's thinking of investing in Bradfield again that can't be bad."

"I suppose not," Laura said. "But what, exactly, is he proposing to invest in, that's what I'd like to know? I can't imagine he's going to prop up what's left of the wool trade single-handed."

"People have made a lot of money out of redundant mills and warehouses in Leeds and Manchester," Thackeray said. "Luxury flats, art galleries, you name it. Maybe that's what they've got in mind for Earnshaws."

"Not in an area as run down as Aysgarth," Laura said grimly. "You'd have to pay yuppies to live up there. One of my calls today was on the family of this girl who was attacked. I've never felt worried going anywhere in Bradfield before, but it felt a bit creepy up there today."

Thackeray's lips tightened.

"They're bound to be uptight. That was a particularly vicious attack."

"Yes, I know, and today I felt distinctly unwelcome." She hesitated, not wanting to spell out the details of her encounter with the Islamic youths. But Thackeray was there before her.

"There are a few hotheads up there who seem determined to set up a no-go area for the police – and for white people generally, I suspect. Some old boy was walking his dog in Aysgarth Park a week or so ago and a couple of youths told him to get out, dogs are unclean, apparently, in Islamic law. We're keeping an eye on the situation. I think the mosque is keeping the lid on it most of the time but there are a few who'd like nothing better than another riot. So be careful, Laura. Please."

"You know I am careful," Laura said. "But I have to do my job. We can't ignore the Muslim community in the *Gazette* just because there's a few fundamentalist idiots around. Anyway, I want to talk about these issues in the radio interviews. It's worse if it's all covered up, isn't it?"

"The whole town is like a pent-up volcano," Thackeray said. "It means policing's like walking on egg-shells. We really need to catch the yobs who attacked the Malik girl, but so far we haven't a clue where to look. And you never heard me say that, Ms. Ackroyd." Thackeray concluded by pulling Laura closer. "Come on," he said softly in her ear. "I've got to work this weekend and we've better things to do than try to sort out Bradfield's race relations at this time of night. Much better."

Chapter Eight

George Earnshaw himself opened the door to his visitors from police headquarters that Saturday morning himself. He was a tall man, but painfully stooped, and his clothes – baggy twill slacks and a blue-grey tweed sports jacket of antique cut – hung off a frame so gaunt that he could have been a starving refugee from some cataclysmic war. The old man stood for a moment with the door held half open as if sizing DCI Thackeray and Sergeant Mower up carefully with sharp, pale eyes before allowing them over his threshold. It was a smaller house than Thackeray had expected, a modern 'executive' style dwelling down a narrow lane which had once led only to a couple of farms on the edge of Broadley Moor, but which was now lined on each side by an anonymous development of marginally individual detached houses faced with an approximation of Yorkshire stone.

"You'd best come in, Mr. Thackeray," Earnshaw said. "Although I'm not at all sure I can tell you anything useful. I haven't seen my grandson Simon for a long while. As I'm sure you've discovered by now, there was a family falling out and Simon went his own way."

He showed them into a sitting room with French windows leading onto a well-stocked but tiny garden. It was comfortably, though not luxuriously, furnished every flat surface cluttered with books and pictures, photographs and nick-nacks, in no apparent order. The atmosphere was warm and stuffy and Earnshaw waved them into armchairs next to a flickering gas 'coal fire'. Mower chose instead to take a chair further away next to the window and Earnshaw raised an eyebrow at this show of independence before lowering himself carefully into what was obviously his own favourite well-cushioned chair close to the source of heat. He was deathly pale and his limbs trembled slightly as he moved around to find the most comfortable position.

"It's good of you to see us, Mr. Earnshaw," Thackeray said, waving away the offer of a drink. Earnshaw poured himself a large whiskey from a decanter strategically placed at his elbow, stretching long legs awkwardly from his low chair. "Do you live here alone?"

"My wife died some years back," Earnshaw said dismissively. "I've a woman who comes in to tidy up for me." It was as if his deceased wife had served no more useful purpose than the cleaning woman, Thackeray thought.

"I decided then that Frank should have the family home and I'd move to somewhere smaller. The grandsons were still teenagers then and needed the space. These places had just been built and seemed big enough for what I needed." The old man gazed for a moment at the flickering blue and yellow flames in the fireplace. "You can never tell how things will turn out, can you?" he murmured. "I had hoped that eventually Simon would marry and take on that house in turn from his father…and eventually run the mill." Earnshaw's voice drifted away.

"But Simon went his own way?" Thackeray prompted. "Were you disappointed about that?"

"Oh, yes, I was disappointed," Simon's grandfather said, his voice bitter and Thackeray gathered that disappointment was probably an inadequate word to describe Earnshaw's feelings. "Matthew never had the same staying power. Full of big schemes but never able to see them through. Failed his degree, you know. Frittered his time away at college, I dare say. He wasn't what Earnshaws Mill needed and he fell apart when his wife left him and I can't say I was surprised."

"When did you last see Simon, Mr. Earnshaw?" Thackeray asked carefully, conscious of Jack Longley's insistence that he conduct the interview with the old man in person. Even approaching his eighties, Longley had said, no doubt repeating the assistant chief constable's injunctions, the elder Earnshaw was a name to be conjured with in Bradfield and the time a sensitive one with the mill apparently in serious trouble.

"I was trying to think before you came," Earnshaw said, glancing at a side table where a series of photographs of two fair-haired young men were displayed. "It's not since he packed the job in and signed on for this daft course at the university. How long's that? Two years or so? You lose track of time at my age."

"His tutor told us that he would be finishing his course this summer," Thackeray said.

"Yes, well, we had a right old set-to when he came to tell me what he was planning," Earnshaw said. "I'll not pretend I was best pleased because I wasn't. I could see that without Simon young Matthew would run out of control and the business would suffer." The old man's creased face closed and his eyes were cold. "I told Simon to bugger off, if you want the truth," he said.

"And you've not seen him since?"

"No." Earnshaw spoke flatly, his face like stone. "He's not been round and I've not invited him."

"Or heard from him – by phone, letter, anything?"

"No, not a word."

"Not even a birthday card? From your favourite grandson?" Mower put in from the far side of the room where he was conscientiously taking notes.

Earnshaw flashed him a furious look.

"He did once send me a card," he said. "I sent it back. He never bothered me again."

"So you wouldn't know anything about his private life, a girlfriend for instance? We think he may have been planning to marry."

"I wouldn't know," Earnshaw said, with a finality which indicated that he would not care either. Thackeray sighed as another avenue of inquiry seemed to close.

"But as I understand it Simon maintained his shareholding in the firm?" he eventually suggested carefully. "Surely you, or your son, would need to consult Simon in present circumstances."

"I leave the day-to-day running of the business to my son Frank now," Earnshaw said sharply. "He consults me when he chooses to. Nothing more."

"But Matthew was planning to meet Simon apparently to discuss business on the day he died, or just after…"

"I have no idea what they arranged. No one told me about it. There was no reason why they should. Simon hasn't been to company meetings since he gave up his working directorship. The rest of us have taken the decisions. There's no reason why anything should change now. Frank has everything in hand."

"I thought…" Thackeray began, but injudiciously as it turned out.

"There's no reason for anything to change now," Earnshaw said again with a passion bordering on venom. "Simon let us all down and I've not regarded him as my grandson since he gave up his job. I had high hopes of that young man, but he flung it all back in our faces. As far as I'm concerned, he's already been dead for years."

"Whew," Mower said as the two police-officers settled themselves back in the car for the ten mile drive back into town. "What did you make of that, guv?"

"He's a man who can hate," Thackeray said. "I'd like to

111

have been a fly on the wall when he broke with Simon. But unless he's a lot stronger than he looks I can't see any way he could have dumped his grandson over a cliff, even if he had some motive we don't know about. He looks seriously unwell to me."

"Odd man," Mower said. "It looks as though he's got mementos of his entire life stuffed into that house. Did you see the photograph of him in RAF uniform? Must have been during the war, I suppose, a man that age."

"Or national service," Thackeray said absently.

"He had some Indian bits and pieces too." Mower had reasons of his own for noticing Indian arts and crafts and Thackeray merely nodded.

"What I'd like to know," he said slowly. "What I'd really like to know is how well the two brothers got on after Simon dropped out. You'd imagine Matthew would be quite pleased to be left as the heir apparent in spite of his evident handicaps as a businessman, but when I talked to him and his parents he seemed to resent the fact that Simon had left the firm. I think we need to do a bit more sniffing around the family, just in case. You know the statistics. Ninety per cent of murder victims are bumped off by their own nearest and dearest."

"Money, jealousy or revenge?" Mower asked. "Or any combination of the above?"

"What's the alternative?" Thackeray asked, as Mower negotiated the steep hill down from the centre of Broadley village to the valley below. "Random violence over a clapped out old Volvo? It doesn't make sense."

"Random violence seldom does," Mower said.

That lunchtime Laura grabbed a salad and a yoghurt in the town centre and walked slowly up the hill towards the university. A dozen years had altered the institution she had known well: the students were more diverse, the buildings shabbier and the sense of overcrowding more oppressive as she pushed her way through the bustling students' union to the women's office at the back of the building. She was expected. She was planning a Saturday afternoon shopping trip but agreed to spare an hour on a trip up the hill in response to a call on her mobile the previous afternoon from a young women who said she was the sister of Farida Achmed.

"Farida?" Laura had said stupidly, her meeting at the women's centre to talk about street harassment slipping her mind for a moment in the busy newsroom. "Oh, yes, Farida. Of course…"

"I'm her sister, Fatima," the voice said. "She gave me your number. I'm a student at the university. Farida said you were nice and wanted to write about the problems of Asian girls, and I couldn't think who else to call. Can we meet? I've got something you might be interested in. I need to tell someone…" She had broken off, her voice full of anxiety and Laura had not had the heart to turn her down. She had arranged to meet her the next day.

The girl was waiting for her, slumped in a chair in the women's room, her white scarf draped around her shoulders above jeans and a loose yellow shirt.

"Thank you for coming," she said.

"So what can I do for you?" Laura asked, settling herself down next to the girl and accepting a cup of weak coffee from a machine in the corner of the room.

"I'm sorry," Farida said. "I know you must be very busy. It may be nothing, but one of my friends on the pharmacy course, someone I've known since school, hasn't come back this term and no one seems to have seen her for nearly a

113

week. I'm worried about her. I can't get any reply from her mobile phone."

"Have you asked her family where she is?" Laura said, thinking that this was probably a wasted journey.

"Of course I have. She moved to Eckersley with her family and I went out there to call on her, to see if she was ill or something. But her brother came to the door and more or less told me to go away and mind my own business. Saira would be back soon, he said."

"In other words she wasn't at home? Is that how you took it?"

"I can't see why he wouldn't let me see her if she was there," Fatima said, looking miserable. "We've been friends for so long."

"What do you think has happened? What are you afraid of?" Laura asked.

"What we're all afraid of," Fatima said. "That she's been sent back to Pakistan to be married off to someone she hasn't met."

Laura swallowed her mouthful of coffee too quickly and nearly choked.

"Sorry," she said. "Are we talking about forced marriage here?"

"Not necessarily forced," Fatima said. "Saira said there's been talk at home about her marrying a cousin who lives near Lahore. She's never met him of course, and apparently he speaks no English, but they wanted her to go out and meet him. She was saying she must finish her course and get her degree before she even thinks about marriage. And she's afraid that even if she didn't like this cousin there'd be a lot of pressure on her to say yes so that he could come to this country. I told you, it's what we're all scared of, especially if we get to university and have that freedom and the chance of a profession. We want to live our own lives just like everyone else in this country."

"But your parents still want to arrange your marriages?"

"Arrange, force? What's the difference. In the end we get very little choice, especially if we agree to go back to Pakistan for the arranging to be done there," Fatima said, her eyes filling with tears, and Laura guessed that she might be under similar pressure to Saira herself.

"Have the tutors here noticed Saira's absence?" Laura asked.

"I don't know. Term's only just started. The classes are very big. They may not notice until she fails to hand some work in."

"I think you'd better talk to the university people and get them to make some inquiries," Laura said. "She may simply be ill or away from home for some very innocent reason."

"So why isn't she answering her mobile?"

"Perhaps it's been stolen, or she's lost it. It happens."

"It's only a pay as you talk one," Fatima said. "We buy those so we don't get bills going home." She grinned slightly shamefacedly at this admission of deceit.

"Did Saira have a boyfriend?" Laura asked. Fatima looked down for a moment at her hands and shrugged. When she looked up again Laura saw the fear in her eyes.

"I don't think so," she said. "I think she'd have told me if she had. She comes from an educated family. Her sister is a teacher and her brother is a lawyer..."

"Not Sayeed Khan?" Laura said. "I met him the other day at the home of that young girl who was attacked in Aysgarth Lane."

"Yes, that would be Sayeed. He does a lot of work around there. But that's the point. This is a family which wants their daughters to get a good education. They were really pleased

115

when Saira came to university, she said. You'd think they could cope with these things, but you never know. The mosque is very powerful. And there are risks…"

"What sort of risks?" Laura asked sharply.

"Girls who step out of line are hunted down," Fatima whispered. "It's all about family honour, *izzat*."

"So you think not a boyfriend?"

"She might not have told even me if there was," Fatima said. "It can be dangerous."

Laura sighed, seeing no way to resolve the girl's fears.

"If you like I could ask her family where she is, but there's no guarantee they'd tell me. Unless you have a really strong reason for thinking she may be in some sort of danger, it's up to her family to report her missing to the police if she really is missing."

"Would you do that?" Fatima asked, her eyes full of tears. She wrote down the address of the Khan family in Eckersley and passed the sheet of paper to Laura. "Her sister, Amina, works at the Muslim school in Aysgarth. I don't know her myself."

"Amina Khan?" Laura said, glancing at the paper Fatima had given her. "Yes, of course, I met her when I met your sister. We were talking about harassment – and that was before this girl got acid thrown at her in the street. I'm doing some radio programmes soon and want to talk about some of these issues. Perhaps you'd like to come on and talk about arranged marriages?"

Fatima shook her head vigorously.

"Oh, no, you've no idea how angry that would make the community. They don't want to talk about anything like that in public."

"Which leaves you caught between the two cultures."

"Oh, yes," Fatima said bitterly. "Trapped. But no one, and I

116

mean no one, is allowed to talk about that. And if you, as a white person, tried, they'd just accuse you of being racist and not understanding Muslim culture."

"I'd take a chance if young women like you want the issue discussed," Laura said angrily. "We wouldn't need to use your real name."

"It's too risky. You don't have to live with our fathers and the men at the mosque," Fatima said flatly.

As Sergeant Mower drove him up the hill towards Earnshaws mill, Michael Thackeray was thinking how much he hated cases where someone in the hierarchy above him seemed to expect him to tiptoe around on egg-shells. He could see no reason for treating Simon Earnshaw's family with any more or less deference than was due to the family of any murder victim. A certain respect for the bereaved was fine. But in the light of the fact that most murder victims were killed by their own relatives, anything more than that verged, in his view, on neglect of duty. And if Frank Earnshaw was over reticent about his business affairs and Simon's involvement in them, then he would not scruple to try to find out what he wanted to know by other means.

Which was why he had decided to take time out of the office and accompany Mower on his proposed visit to the shop-front office of the mill-workers union, which stood less than a hundred yards from the monumental entrance to the mill yard itself. Mower pulled up to the kerb, and eyed the crowd of mainly Asian workers who, although it was Saturday, were gathered on the pavement outside the office.

"I reckon the Earnshaws have got serious bother here," he said, with a grin. "Trubble at'mill and all that. I thought we'd moved on a bit from all that."

"Maybe not," Thackeray said. "Though it could be all froth and no substance."

"The *Gazette* says they want to cut wages. I can't see that going down a treat."

"Closing the mill won't go down a treat either," Thackeray said. "Unemployment round here's bad enough already, particularly amongst the Asians."

They got out of the car and pushed their way to the office door through a murmur of suspicion if not outright hostility which made the hair on the back of Thackeray's neck bristle. The mood of the men milling about on the pavement was volatile and he was sure that it would only take a single spark for the tension to flare into violence.

Inside the office a young Asian man and an older, grey-haired, bull-necked white man, both in crumpled suits, glanced up at the new arrivals from a desk where they were poring over what appeared to be lists of names.

"Bloomin' heck, I didn't know planning a strike ballot were a hanging offence," the white man said, the belligerence in his voice almost mocking, but not quite. "What can we do for you, Chief Inspector?"

"You have the advantage, Mr....?" Thackeray said.

"Jim Watson, regional organiser. We met at your nick once when I came in to complain about a bloody silly arrest one of your colleagues had made down in Arnedale. Some conspiracy theory or other, when Queen Maggie were on t'throne. You were nobbut a sergeant then as I recall."

"Yes, that's right, I do remember you now," Thackeray conceded. It had been a brief encounter about an arrest which had certainly been overzealous, but Thackeray also recalled his failure to warm to Watson then any more than he did now.

"This is Mohammed Iqbal, the convenor at Earnshaws,"

Watson went on, waving to his colleague who nodded to the two officers without any welcome in his dark eyes. "So what can we do for CID now then? Nowt to do with industrial relations, I hope."

"Not directly, Mr. Watson," Thackeray said. "And I think it's Mr. Iqbal we need to talk to anyway." Did he imagine a flash of anxiety cross the younger man's face, Thackeray wondered, although the convenor's response was bland enough.

"If I can help..." Iqbal said, hands in a gesture of openness.

Thackeray glanced behind him at the door which had just been pushed open by a couple of the men outside who obviously sought attention.

"Is there anywhere quiet we can talk?" he asked.

Iqbal shrugged slightly.

"There's only a little kitchen and a toilet out back," he said uncertainly.

"Oh, don't mind me," Watson said expansively. "I'll go an' put t'kettle on, if you're not going to be long. Tea wi'milk an'sugar all round do you?" He lumbered to his feet and pushed past Iqbal towards the back door without waiting for an answer.

"Give us a shout, lad, if they get too heavy for you," he said to Iqbal as he closed the kitchen door behind him, leaving Thackeray to speculate on how well their voices would be heard through the woodwork. Pretty clearly he guessed, feeling irritated and outmanoeuvred.

"Have you worked at Earnshaws long, Mr. Iqbal?" he asked, deliberately keeping his voice as low as he dared.

"Since I left school," Iqbal said. "Fifteen years now, I suppose."

"And in the union all that time?"

Iqbal nodded again.

"Earnshaws didn't recognise us then but, wi't'new law, they have to if we can get t'vote out. We got it out all right, no problem. Overwhelming support, we got." He shuffled his papers into a neat pile as if to give Thackeray his whole attention. "So are you going to tell me what all this is about?"

"It's about the death of Mr. Simon Earnshaw – indirectly at least," Thackeray said. "You've no doubt heard about his murder." There was no mistaking the fear in Iqbal's eyes now, and Thackeray wondered what was causing it. They had not come to see Iqbal with any idea that he might be a suspect.

"I heard about it," Iqbal said quietly.

"Did you know Simon Earnshaw when he was working at the mill?"

"Oh, aye, we used to see him about. He weren't involved in production so we didn't see him day to day, like, but I'd know him to look at if not to speak to. All t' family for that matter. Even t'old begger."

"George Earnshaw, you mean."

"Aye, him. Bill can tell you some tales about him."

"He doesn't like old George?" Thackeray asked, not greatly surprised that George Earnshaw might have disliked trades union activity in his mill.

"No one round here liked George Earnshaw," Iqbal said with complete certainty.

"Anti-union, then, was he?"

"Anti-union, anti-negotiations, but most of all anti-Asian, as I hear it. I'm told it weren't until the old boy retired that Earnshaws employed a single Asian worker. And even then it were only because t'union threatened legal action, and there were a spell of full employment making it hard to recruit anyone at all, that his son began to take some Asians

on – for t'night shift, of course. Nowt else at first. Now, of
course, we're in t'majority here, because no one else is fool
enough to work for Earnshaws' wages, day or night, are
they? You've got to be that desperate."

Iqbal's voice was full of bitterness and behind them
Thackeray heard the door from the kitchen open and an
ostentatious clink of cups as Jim Watson edged his way back
into the room with a tin tray loaded with mugs and swimming in milky tea.

"Racist beggars, all the Earnshaws," Watson offered. "But
we sorted them out in the end. Wi't'mill right here, surrounded by Asian families, they didn't have a bloody leg to
stand on, did they?"

"Simon Earnshaw wasn't a racist," Iqbal said unexpectedly.

"How do you make that out?" Watson asked. "He were no
different from t'rest o't'beggers in that family, as far as I
know."

"Yes, he was," Iqbal said. "After he left the mill, he was,
any road."

"You had contact with him after he left the mill?"
Thackeray asked quickly.

"He came to see me a couple o'months ago," Iqbal said,
aware that the eyes of all three men were fixed on him in
varying degrees of surprise. "If I don't tell you, you'll find
out some other way, I dare say. It were nowt bad, but he
wanted it kept quiet around here, especially in t'mill. He
were right scared his father would find out."

"Find out what?" Thackeray persisted.

"He were doing some research on regeneration," Iqbal
said. "Taking mills over, doing them up for other things, like
they've done wi'some o't'old warehouses an'that. He wanted ideas for Earnshaws if it ever closed down, wanted to

121

know what the local community would think about different uses for t'building, putting in workshops and space for small businesses, community space, that sort of thing. He wanted me to help him talk to people round here, introduce him to folk, make contacts and all that."

"And did you?" Watson interrupted angrily. "Did you go round talking about that sort of stuff while we're still fighting to keep the lads' jobs?"

"No, I didn't," Iqbal said fiercely. "He were going to contact me again, but he never did. I never heard from him again. Next thing I know, he's dead, isn't he? Murdered. And now I don't know what to think."

Chapter Nine

A dozen solemn little girls with large dark eyes under their severe white hijab looked curiously at Laura as they filed from their prayers to their classroom the next morning. Laura was waiting for Amina Khan in the cramped hallway of the Muslim girls' school which had been converted from a former political club in one of the bleak terraced streets close to Earnshaws mill. Amina, dressed in a long grey coat and hijab, looked harassed.

"I don't have much time," she said. "I have to take a class in fifteen minutes. They come in on Sunday mornings for religious studies."

"It's good of you to see me. I won't keep you long," Laura promised. She had been surprised when Amina had suggested meeting at the school that morning, but sufficiently worried by what Fatima Achmed had told her to spend an hour of her precious Sunday following up the disappearance of Saira Khan. Thackeray had come home the previous night so late and so tired that she had not yet told him about the apparently missing student, preferring to check it out thoroughly herself before presenting him with what would inevitably prove to be another sensitive police investigation if what Fatima feared proved to be well founded.

Amina glanced at the small group of girls of about ten years old who were evidently waiting for her.

"Go to your room and read quietly until I come," she said, and the girls trooped off dutifully, although not without the odd curious backward glance which Laura guessed was directed at her uncovered and glowing red hair. "Come in here," Amina said, waving her guest into a small office where the desk and computer were unattended.

"Our secretary doesn't come in today, when we're just here for the religious classes," she said. "So what can I do to help you?"

"Your friend Farida's sister contacted me," Laura said. "She's worried about an Asian friend who is on her course at the university. Her name's Saira Khan and she seems to have disappeared. Obviously as the name's the same I thought she might be a relation of yours..." Amina nodded, her face strangely impassive and nun-like beneath the hijab.

"She's my younger sister," she said. "I think if this friend of Saira's had contacted her family instead of the Press it would have been better."

"She said she tried that," Laura said quickly. "She said she went to your parents' home in Eckersley, is it? But she was still worried about Saira."

"Saira's fine," Amina said. "Saira's gone on a family visit. She'll be home soon and back at her studies. There's no problem."

"Has she gone to Pakistan?" Laura asked bluntly. "That's really what Fatima seemed to be worried about, and as I'm doing these programmes for Radio Bradfield, the ones I told you about, I was interested too."

"I suppose you think she has been sent to Pakistan to marry against her will," Amina said angrily. "That's the stereotype you all have of us, isn't it? Well, if you just thought about what you're saying for a moment you'd realise what nonsense that is. My parents have encouraged us all to get an education in this country, my sisters as well as my brother. It isn't cheap putting children through university these days, as you know. Why would they interrupt Saira's course in her final year, do you think? Just as she is coming up to her final exams? Wouldn't that be a very stupid thing to do? Or do you think that because we're Muslims we are by definition stupid?"

"Of course not," Laura said, irritated herself by Amina's outburst. "But you give the impression of belonging to a very traditional family…"

Amina laughed.

"I'm afraid you are not quite right there either," she said. "My parents are about as Westernised as you'll find in our community. Even my grandparents speak English. I chose to go down a different road and they dislike it very much. They are not very observant Muslims and they are the last people who would force me to dress like this. This is my choice. I do have the freedom to choose, you know, and this gives me lots of freedoms you don't have – to be taken seriously without men constantly being distracted by my attractions, for a start. And though in my family our marriages may be arranged they certainly won't be forced. We will have the right to say no to any man our father proposes for us. Why else do you think I'm still unmarried at twenty-five? I haven't met the right man yet. My father would be the last man to send Saira anywhere against her will. He's very keen for her to qualify and have her profession, just as he was for me when I chose to become a teacher."

"So she's quite safe, and her friends don't need to worry? Is that what you're saying," Laura pressed, not totally convinced by this fierce defence.

"Of course she is," Amina said.

"Is she in this country? Fatima says she's not answering her mobile."

"I didn't know she had a mobile," Amina said quickly with, Laura thought, just the faintest flicker of doubt in her eyes. "Maybe she's switched it off?"

125

"Maybe," Laura said. "Is it possible to contact her by phone, wherever she is? Fatima is very anxious about her. It would be a good idea to reassure her, if you can."

"I'll talk to my father, tell him that Saira's friends are concerned," Amina said.

"Does Saira share your religious views?" Laura asked. "Does she wear hijab?" Amina's eyes clouded for a moment.

"She's a Muslim, of course she is," she said. "But no, she doesn't wear traditional dress at all. She prefers designer clothes. That concerns my father a bit, but he accepts her choices so long as they are modest."

So there are tensions, Laura thought to herself and it was as if Amina had read her mind.

"Saira will be home soon," she said. "I must go now, Miss Ackroyd. I have children waiting for me."

"Are you still considering the radio interviews I'm planning?" Laura asked as she got to her feet. "I'm hoping to start doing the recordings in the next week or so if I can."

Amina shook her head.

"I don't think so," she said.

There were parts of Bradfield where white faces were not welcome, "no go areas", enforced by defensive and defiant young Asian men, which the *Gazette's* editor Ted Grant fulminated against regularly in his columns. It was equally true that there were pubs on the mainly white housing estates like Wuthering where Asians would not venture. DC Sharif was well aware of this and fumed quietly in his car that lunchtime as he watched Ricky Pickles park outside the Grenadier and disappear inside.

Omar Sharif was on a freelance expedition of his own, driven by the carefully concealed anger which consumed him. On the pretext of "sussing out" Asian views about the acid attack on Soraya Malik, which he knew without a scintilla of a doubt was a particularly vicious skirmish in the race war he believed was being waged in parts of Bradfield, he had taken his own car to the British Patriotic Party's offices, which were open and seemed unusually busy for a Sunday morning, to conduct a bit of informal surveillance on his own account. He was rewarded when Pickles had emerged and driven off in the direction of the Heights, ten minutes up the steep hill to the west of the town, and had parked his Escort outside a pub well known for its extravagant display of union flags and its clientele of football hooligans and assorted criminal thugs. Omar knew better than to go inside alone. His warrant card would not protect him at the Grenadier if he ventured in without backup, especially after a Saturday when United had played at home and lost five-nil. Tempers would be running high. So he discreetly parked fifty yards away, with his mobile phone switched off, and waited and watched.

It was more than an hour before his vigil was rewarded. Just before two o'clock Ricky Pickles emerged from the pub again, deep in conversation with three other men. Sharif regretted not bringing a camera with him but he concentrated on memorising Pickles' companions' faces and making a note of the registration number of the silver Mondeo they all piled into after taking an obviously friendly farewell of the BPP official. For a moment Sharif thought of following the Ford, but knew he was already pushing his luck with sergeant Kevin Mower so he contented himself with following Pickles back to his office at a discreet distance and then returning quickly to police headquarters to report back in for his overtime shift.

Mower seemed happy enough with Sharif's conclusion that there was no evidence Soraya Malik was anything other than a devout and obedient young Muslim girl who had run foul of racist thugs, unaware that this was a conclusion Sharif had reached on the basis of chatting to his own younger brothers.

"Yes, well, I thought it was a long shot," Mower said. "You'd better report back to the murder room now. We've wasted enough time on that line of inquiry."

"Right, sarge," Sharif said. But before obeying Mower he took a detour by way of the books of mugshots where the photographs of known criminals were stored. One of the men he had seen with Pickles at the Grenadier had looked vaguely familiar but in the end it was the other two he identified quite quickly, checking on the computer database for their personal details and extensive, violent and frequently racist criminal histories. He had never believed Pickles' claim that he was nothing more now than a legitimate politician and given the company he had been keeping that lunchtime Sharif felt more than justified in his scepticism. A check on the car registration number he had noted down gave him a name and address and an equally lurid criminal record for the third man. He took this information back to a surprised Kevin Mower and, by the end of the afternoon, Sharif's freelance endeavours had filtered up to the office of Superintendent Longley who had foregone a round of golf to check up on the murder inquiries.

"He says he was driving past the Grenadier when he noticed Pickles coming out," Michael Thackeray told his boss non-commitally, knowing as well as Kevin Mower did that driving past the Grenadier on the way to anywhere required a detour half way round the Heights estate. Longley was not slow to pick up the hint.

"But you think he was watching him as part of some agenda of his own?" Longley said.

"Mower thinks it's possible."

"You want to watch that young man," Longley said.

"He's not been here long enough to get to know well, but he seems to be a good enough officer," Thackeray said.

"But not a team player, evidently? And his loyalties may be getting stretched in this case. Any road, what do you want to do about Pickles? Sharif's not suggesting that these thugs are the ones who chucked acid at the Asian lass, is he?"

"No, the Malik sisters are adamant it was 'boys' who ran past them. There's no way you could mistake these three for boys, or Pickles for that matter. Jackson is at least six foot tall and Smith must be about twenty stone."

"A full surveillance on Pickles is an expensive option. Do you really think it's necessary?" Longley asked.

"I've got no evidence to justify it except this one sighting of Pickles with known violent associates. There's no crime they're immediate suspects for, except in the sense that all four of them are top of the list of the usual suspects for anything racially motivated," Thackeray said cautiously.

"But with an Asian neighbourhood likely to go off like Bonfire Plot if there was any more racist violence?"

"Oh yes, that's certainly a consideration," Thackeray said. "If you think that's justification enough."

Longley leaned back in his chair, his normally bland face creased in thought.

"Damn and blast," the superintendent said at last. "This is the last thing we need with this bloody sensitive murder inquiry going on at the same time. And likely a strike at Earnshaws to give the family even more grief."

"You realise that the majority of workers at the mill are Asian too, don't you?" Thackeray said.

"Terrific," Longley said. "Still, public order's uniform's

129

bag not CID's so leave me to handle that. What do you really want to do about Pickles and his undesirable friends?"

"Personally I wish we had enough officers to watch every move they make, from the time they get up in the morning to the time they get back into bed again," Thackeray said. "But we haven't and I can't see that keeping half an eye on them will do us much good. I think the only option is to watch and wait. I'll brief everyone to talk to their informants and be ready to jump in hard if we get anything solid to go on."

"I don't want this town going up in bloody flames like Oldham," Longley said. "So far we've avoided that."

"Right," Thackeray said, though he was sure that Bradfield's escape from major riots was more a result of luck than the good judgement of any sector of the community. And the omens for the town remaining immune did not look good.

"And the Earnshaw killing?" Longley asked. "That's what I really came in for. Any progress there?"

"Not a lot," Thackeray said. "Forensics we're waiting on, and we won't hear today of course. We've not found his Volvo estate. We've not found any witnesses to the murder itself. And we've not found his girlfriend, although everyone seems convinced he had one and his tutor thinks she's Asian, which is another complication we could do without. What no one seems to know is who the hell she actually is and why she hasn't come forward."

"Your prime suspect, then, is she?"

"I suppose she has to be, for lack of any alternative," Thackeray said. "If there really is a girlfriend and she knows he's dead, what innocent reason is there for not getting in touch?"

"Perhaps she doesn't know he's dead yet," Longley said. "Perhaps she's away somewhere. The university's only just started up after the holidays, hasn't it?"

"Maybe, though judging by the phone messages some young woman seems to have been getting very anxious to contact him. Anyway, today we're working our way round everyone at the university who knew Simon Earnshaw and we're launching another appeal in the *Gazette* and on local radio tomorrow for any friends of his who haven't been interviewed to come forward. Something has to flush this woman out, unless she's out of the country. I suppose she could have been trying to contact him by phone from abroad. We've not heard from the phone company yet about tracing the calls a woman made to Earnshaw's flat or his parents' place, and I don't suppose we will now till next week. But if they come from the pay-as-you-go phone that appears on his statements we'll be no further forward anyway."

"Keep me informed, Michael," Longley said. "I've still got Ellison breathing down my neck on this one."

"Sir," Thackeray said without enthusiasm.

Back in his own office he finished off some paperwork, which had begun to pile up since the murder inquiry had been launched, called Laura to say that he would not be home until late and then set off on a journey which he had been anticipating through a dark cloud all day. He retrieved his car from the car-park and joined the stream of Sunday shopping traffic which was heading north out of Bradfield to the suburbs and commuter villages in the Dales. Once past the bustling Asian shops of Aysgarth Lane and the quieter suburbs beyond, the road to Arnedale followed the twisting river valley and driving nose-to-tail took concentration which all but blotted out thought. But once on the dual carriageway which ate up the last ten miles of the journey Thackeray let his mind wander. He had not told Laura that he was going to see his father, and was not even sure that he would tell her he had been. It depended, he thought, on the old man's reaction to the news he was bringing him, although he could not imagine that there would be any surprise there. This was not by any stretch of the imagination a visit to seek a father's blessing, rather an attempt to blunt the edge of a father's anger.

Joe Thackeray was a survivor from another world, Thackeray thought grimly. He had spent a life-time farming sheep on the bleak hills above Arnedale, only to find himself driven out by modern economics from the holding where he had thought he would end his days. Retirement was too bland a word for the bitter enforced idleness Joe experienced in his small retirement home in the market town at the head of the Maze valley. And Thackeray knew that his uncompromising Catholicism would make it impossible for Joe to take any pleasure in the news that his son planned to remarry. In Joe's book, while Michael had a first wife living, no one could take her place in the eyes of God or her father-in-law. And Aileen, locked by brain damage into a world of unknowing, sometimes seemed to Thackeray physically fit enough to outlast them all. If there was a sin involved in all this, he thought bitterly, it was not his wish to free himself legally from Aileen but his desire of a dozen years' duration to see her as dead as the baby son she had drowned.

"Damnation," he muttered as he finally pulled up outside his father's bungalow and found himself parking behind another car he recognised. For a second he considered driving away again but then he shrugged wearily. He might as well be hung for a sheep, he thought, and got out, raising a hand in greeting to the parish priest who had watched his arrival from his father's front window.

The two older men quickly settled themselves back into their armchairs, one on each side of the flickering gas fire, like two prosecuting lawyers, and he guessed they both knew very well why he had come. Joe was an increasingly wizened figure, his face grey and lined under what remained of iron hair, one hand on the head of the elderly sheep dog who now kept as close to her master as she had once kept close to his flock. Father Frank Rafferty was an altogether bigger character, running to fat beneath his extensive cassock, and with a shock of white hair above a face veined with red. But both men were sharp enough of eye, both held glasses of amber whisky in their hands, and both watched expectantly as Thackeray made himself a cup of tea in his father's tiny kitchen and returned slowly, mug in hand, to take the third chair and face the jury in the chilly living room again.

"How are you, Michael?" Rafferty asked. "Policing still suiting you, is it?" Rafferty had never lost his Irish brogue although his ministry in Arnedale went back to Thackeray's boyhood when his father had woken him at dawn on a Sunday morning and driven him down to the town, fasting, to serve Mass.

"Crime shows no sign of going away," Thackeray said sharply. "Nor sin either, I guess." Rafferty nodded, with a faint smile.

"Sure, I suppose you could say we're in a similar line of business," he said.

"But my lot get no absolution from me," Thackeray said.

"Nor many excuses made, I dare say," Rafferty said, who knew his man.

Thackeray glanced away for a moment before turning to his father.

"How are you?" he asked quietly. "I see you've still got this old girl with you." He reached forward to fondle the dog's ears and avoid his father's accusing eyes.

"How's Aileen?" Joe Thackeray asked, as he always did,

133

almost giving the impression that Thackeray's wife might be sitting contentedly at home after washing up the supper dishes.

"She's the same, Dad," Thackeray said irritably. "She's always the same. She's never going to be any different."

"I remember you both in my prayers," Joe said. "And your mother. It's her anniversary next month. We'll be having a Mass said." Thackeray's mother had died of MS several years before, after decades of declining health. He nodded dumbly, his mind whirling between anger and humiliation at being assailed by this tidal wave of emotion. Perhaps recognising his distress, Rafferty put a hand on Thackeray's knee as if to calm him. Thackeray shook him off.

"Joe still finds it hard to accept everything that happened," the priest said.

"D'you think I don't?" Thackeray muttered between gritted teeth.

"But you were good enough to come up to see him after a long time," Rafferty said, a half question that Thackeray knew he could no longer avoid.

"I've begun divorce proceedings," he said. "Laura and I are hoping to marry later this year – perhaps in the summer…"

Joe contented himself with a snort of disgust but Thackeray was surprised to find a hint of sympathy in the priest's eyes.

"I recall the young woman. Haven't you met her yourself, Joe? Is she not a fine girl, with the red hair and the green eyes? She puts me in mind of a girl I used to know in Dublin."

"I'll not come to a register office," Joe said.

Rafferty smiled faintly.

"If you're going to cause a commotion, Joe, chance of an

invitation would be a fine thing," he said. "Which is a pity. You know as well as I do that Michael and his young woman are doing the right thing, whatever my lords and masters say about it. There's enough anguish in the world without creating more where none's required. Aileen's long past being hurt any more. Why should Michael go on paying for what's finished? D'you not think he's been punished enough?"

"The Church..." Joe began, but Rafferty would not let him finish.

"The Church makes general rules," he said. "Just as Parliament makes general laws. But hard cases make bad law. There are always exceptions. I dare say this will be a wedding Our Lord will smile on, whatever the Pope thinks."

"You'll be getting yourself defrocked, Frank, or whatever it is they do to renegade priests these days," Thackeray said, feeling some of the weight lifting from his shoulders. "But thank you, anyway." He glanced at his father, who was staring stubbornly into the flickering gas.

"They've left it a bit late," Rafferty said comfortably. "They keep trying to retire me but so far I've stalled the bastards." He glanced at Joe. "I can't say I'd relish retirement much."

"A registry office, then, is it? Not a Protestant church?" Joe asked, as if every word was being wrung from his lips by the inquisition.

"Not a church of any kind," Thackeray said, trying to hide his distaste for the question. His own faith had been crushed out of him long ago by the events which had taken his son's life and almost destroyed him as well as Aileen. As far as he knew Laura had never been to church in her life except for weddings and funerals.

"And my grandchildren? Will they be little heathens too?" Joe spat the words out and both Thackeray and Rafferty flinched. Thackeray got to his feet.

"I'm sorry this is so hard for you," he said. "But I thought I should tell you myself. It's the best I can do." Rafferty got to his feet and put a hand on his shoulder while Joe remained gazing into the simulacrum of a fire which was all that warmed the bleak little room.

"Let us know when the arrangements are made," he said quietly as they made their way to the door. "I'll talk to him. He'll come round, you'll see. Especially if you're blessed with children."

"You can't imagine how that terrifies me," Thackeray said quietly.

"Oh, I think I can, Michael. I think I can."

From behind them there was a final thrust from Joe which Thackeray only half caught. He turned back reluctantly.

"Go and tell Aileen's parents what you're doing," Joe said. "See what they think about it."

Chapter Ten

Laura sat at her desk the next morning poring over a file of newspaper cuttings which filled her with a mixture of dread and anger. The *Gazette*'s library was not an extensive one, but even so it had accumulated a large enough bundle of articles on the problems of young Muslim girls caught between the traditional demands of their families and the customs of the western society they lived in to make her wonder if Saira Khan was safe. She knew that most of the towns around Bradfield had refuges for the handful of Asian girls who ran away from home each year, usually to escape the marriages their families wished to impose on them or, more rarely, to pursue relationships outside their community. She knew that in many cases these disputes were eventually resolved amicably enough.

But it was also clear from what she was reading that if they were not resolved – if for instance a Muslim girl ran away with an 'unsuitable' boyfriend – then there were groups of young men in the shadows who would seek out the offending couple and a few fathers and brothers who were happier to see a young woman dead than living in a relationship they disapproved of. It was, she thought, a culture clash of immense proportions, rare maybe, but devastating for all involved when it got out of hand. She had written about it before and would no doubt write about it again and she was still hoping that she would be able to set up some sort of discussion for her radio programmes if she could persuade someone in the Muslim community to break the code of silence which surrounded these issues for most of the time.

What Laura was seeking as she riffled through the cuttings

was information about young men willing to hunt down those who ran away. But their activities were both illegal and often violent and few reporters had got anywhere near them. The only cases that had got into the newspapers were the most extreme: the mother and father who had murdered their adulterous daughter, the rebellious girl who had been deliberately run down by a car full of young men, the couple who had changed their names and gone into hiding because they had fallen in love across the religious and racial divide and were convinced, even years later, that those bent on retribution would never call off the hunt.

She shuddered and closed the file. She knew she was wandering into dangerous territory but she was sure she had met enough sympathetic Muslims during her career to be able to persuade at least some of them to talk to her about the sensitive issues of culture and tradition she wanted to explore. But first, she thought, she had better not jump the gun. It was quite possible that Saira Khan had returned home by now, or had at least made contact with the friends who were concerned about her. This time she would tackle her brother the lawyer, in the hope that he might be a bit more forthcoming than his sister Amina had been.

Sayeed Khan had agreed to see Laura readily enough, but when she was shown into his office later that morning she soon discovered that the last thing Khan proposed to do was give her information about his missing sister. That, she soon discovered, was a wishful thought too far.

"My sister Amina's already told me about the insinuations you're making about Saira," he said after he had waved Laura into a chair and refused point blank to allow her to tape-record their discussion.

"I don't remember making any insinuations," Laura said, trying to keep her temper with this overbearing young man in his smart suit and Armani tie. "I was merely trying to find out if she was safe because her friends at the university seemed to be very worried about her."

"They don't need to worry," Khan said, leaning back in his leather executive chair. "There's no need for anyone to worry. Saira is quite safe."

"You know where she is then?"

"You know, Miss Ackroyd, I don't think that is any of your or your newspaper's business. No business at all."

"Has she gone to Pakistan to be married?" Laura persisted, even as Khan's face flushed above his neatly trimmed beard and his eyes hardened.

"You know, you are like most white British people," he said. "You have this stereotypical image of Muslims. We are either ill-treating our women or threatening to blow up the world. It's extremely offensive to people like me and my father and ninety-nine per cent of the rest of us who do neither of these things."

"I'm sure it must be," Laura said. "But if Saira's Muslim friends are worried enough about her to contact me in the first place it really isn't my role to tell them that they're wrong. They evidently have some grounds for their concern as they've not been able to contact her by phone."

"In my experience mobile telephones are not a very reliable means of communication. The batteries go flat," Khan said dismissively. "And there are places where they simply don't work."

"Like Pakistan, for instance," Laura suggested.

"Miss Ackroyd, I'm not going to tell you anything about my sister. I've told you, it's none of your business. And I would really like you to leave the subject alone."

"Saira's friends thought it might be my business," Laura said, her face hardening into a determination which her friends would have warned Khan to avoid if they had been there. "I'd never heard of your sister until they called me."

"Saira's friends should have known better. If there are problems in our community, we deal with them ourselves. We don't need to involve outsiders, especially not outsiders who are racist and prejudiced and ignorant of our customs."

Laura felt her colour rise.

"You're a lawyer, Mr. Khan, and no doubt know very well that the law applies to your community just as much as it does to mine."

"And do you have a shred of evidence that the law has been broken here?" Khan snapped back.

"Not yet," Laura said. "But I'd feel much happier about it if you could arrange for me to speak to Saira, wherever she is. Mobile phones may be unreliable but on the whole conventional phones work pretty well anywhere in the world, if a little slowly. Can I speak to her? Then you can set my mind at rest, I'll know she's safe and I'll pass on the message to her college friends if you won't."

"I'll discuss the matter with my father…"

"You see, if no one can make any contact at all with Saira, then inevitably they're going to draw the wrong conclusions, and maybe very nasty conclusions at that," Laura pressed on, speaking quickly now and with increasing force. "You know how imaginative people can be, especially if they start from a basis of prejudice and suspicion. I'm not saying I'm like that, Mr. Khan, but I know my editor certainly is, and he's only one…"

"Are you threatening me?" Khan asked angrily.

"Not at all," Laura said reverting to her most reasonable smile. "I'm just suggesting that the people who are already worried about Saira may take their worries elsewhere if I don't succeed in setting their minds at rest. To the police,

140

perhaps, or to some newspapers very much nastier than the *Gazette*."

Khan banged his fist on the desk.

"Is it too difficult for you to understand?" he asked. "The most precious thing a Muslim girl has is her honour. If any scandal damages that she has no future, she'll not be able to marry – no man will have her. To suggest in public that she is missing is to suggest the worst. There is no half-way house, don't you see?"

"So she is missing?" Laura asked quietly.

"I didn't say that," Khan came back quickly.

"Talk to your father, Mr. Khan," Laura said. "You know as well as I do that if a young woman is missing, whatever her race or her religion, she may be in danger. I know your community tries to find people who step out of line…"

"No, nothing like that," Khan said, his voice hoarse now.

"One way or another she may be in danger," Laura said. "You need the police to help you."

"No, not that either," Khan said. "Please leave us alone, Miss Ackroyd. I assure you we can handle this ourselves. Saira will be home safely very soon, I promise you. Very soon."

The next stop on Laura's roller-coaster ride of a day took her to the farther extreme of Bradfield opinion and one which she hoped Sayeed Khan might believe she disliked intensely. Ted Grant had evidently been surprised when she had volunteered promptly when he sought out a reporter to get a quote from Ricky Pickles about the rising tide of racist incidents which looked set to destabilise the town. She had already asked the police Press Office about the abortive inquiries into the British Patriotic Party which David Mendelson had mentioned and they had been more than usually dismissive. All incidents were taken seriously, she had been told with bland assurance, but there was no evidence of a concerted campaign in Bradfield or that things were getting worse. Laura did not believe a word of it but when she asked for statistics she was assured that they would take time to assemble and that the Press Office would get back to her. She would not hold her breath, she had thought as she hung up angrily.

But by the time she had driven up to the BPP's office and persuaded the heavyweight doorkeeper that she was from the *Gazette* and had an appointment she did not have high hopes of fighting her way any further through the blanket of cotton-wool which seemed to surround the subject.

Pickles leaned back in his chair easily as he faced Laura with a complacent smile.

"Our view is quite simple," he said. "If you put two incompatible groups of people together, you're bound to get trouble. That's what I'll be telling the electorate in May when we'll be putting up ten candidates for the council. And I'm sure we'll get massive support."

"We're getting quite serious violence on the streets, Mr. Pickles," Laura said carefully. "Some of it aimed at women and children. What's your party's view on that?"

"We condemn violence on any side," Pickles said easily. "It's not one-sided, this violence, you know. There's gangs of Paki youths giving as good as they get..."

"Throwing acid at school-girls?" Laura snapped. "I don't think so."

"A nasty business," Pickles conceded, without warmth. "A pity resentment is running so high."

"And you've no idea who might be behind that sort of campaign? There's no connection between your party and street attacks, graffiti at the synagogue, all the rest of it?"

"As I say, we're a legitimate political party…"

"With many members with a history of violence," Laura hazarded, knowing she was pushing her luck and going much further than Ted Grant wanted her to go.

"Not to my knowledge," Pickles said, an edge to his voice now. He glanced at his watch. "Now you'll have to excuse me, I've an election campaign meeting to go to at the community centre on the Heights." Where no doubt, Laura thought, he would do his best to fight fire with torrents of inflammatory abuse.

But with that, as Pickles stood up and put on his jacket, she had to be content.

Laura had fallen asleep on the sofa in front of the television by the time Michael Thackeray got home that night. She woke with a start when she heard his key in the lock and was surprised by his appearance as he came into the living room, pulling his coat off wearily.

"What happened?" she said. "You look as if you've been down a coal mine. You're filthy."

Thackeray ran a hand across his face which merely smeared the dirt more effectively across his brow and into his untidy dark hair.

"Just rummaging around the site of a fire," he said. "A nasty bit of arson."

"Don't you have minions to deal with that sort of thing?" Laura asked lightly. "You don't actually have to go digging in the ashes yourself, do you?"

"I do when the building belongs to the local trade union in Aysgarth Lane just at the moment they're planning a strike at Earnshaws mill. Coincidence, d'you think, or what?"

Laura sat up suddenly at that, her mind swinging sharply back into gear. She had come home bubbling with anger at the end of her frustrating day at work, and suddenly all her rage returned.

"Oh shit," she said. "That sounds as if it could set light to half the town."

"The Muslim half, which may be exactly what the arsonists intended," Thackeray said grimly. "Fortunately the fire brigade was very prompt and the damage isn't too bad. They managed to save most of the papers and files, which was a miracle considering the bastards had poured accelerant through the letter box. And thankfully, Mohamed Iqbal, the convenor at Earnshaws, keeps most of his paperwork locked in metal filing cabinets so it survived – just a bit smoky round the edges. But they've lost a computer and other equipment and they're pretty angry. "

Anger, Thackeray thought, was an under-estimate of the cold fury with which Iqbal had greeted him when he had arrived to meet the police at the smoke-blackened ruin of his office, where water flowed from the doorway into the gutter and firemen were still working to damp down whatever was still smouldering inside the dark interior.

"I suppose it's a stupid question to ask whether you have enemies, Mr. Iqbal," Thackeray had said after he and the convenor had taken a cursory glance around the offices.

"Where do you want me to start, Mr. Thackeray?" Iqbal had asked derisively. "You know as well as I do who's creating mayhem around here. I'm just waiting for you to arrest them." Behind him the crowd of young Muslim men who had gathered overheard his words and murmured their agreement.

"I can't arrest anyone without evidence," Thackeray had said.

"Well, perhaps we'll get you your evidence," Iqbal had promised in a lower voice. "If you can't protect us maybe we'll have to protect ourselves." Thackeray had ignored this threat and changed tack.

"Do you think this could have any connection with your dispute at Earnshaws?" he asked.

"D'you mean is Frank Earnshaw resorting to fire-bombing?" Iqbal had asked. "I doubt it. I think if he wants to get rough he'll use the courts, not this sort of crude assault. But you never know. His father was always accusing us of getting 'uppity' – isn't that the word they used to use about black slaves?"

"So, what have we got? Some sort of race war?" Laura asked after listening to a summary of all this. "I've been up to my neck in it myself today, what with sexist Muslims and butter-wouldn't melt neo-Nazis. You don't really think Earnshaws could be getting up to dirty tricks themselves, do you? The last thing they want at the moment is a strike, that was very obvious when Frank Earnshaw came to talk to us at the *Gazette*. I think it would put a very large spoke into his plans."

"I wish I knew," Thackeray said. "I know I'm in for a long session with Jack Longley in the morning to work out how to investigate all this on top of the murder of Simon Earnshaw. It's going to be a bit like disarming a time-bomb in the middle of an ammunition dump."

"My father's pretty annoyed about the strike threat too, though he's hardly likely to be pouring petrol through letter-boxes," Laura said. "I had a quick drink with him at the Clarendon on the way home. I don't think things are going his way. I know he was hoping to have wrapped up whatever it is he's planning by now but he says he's off to London tomorrow for meetings and then back here by the weekend. I'd dearly love to know what he's plotting."

"Well, I may need to have a word with him when he

comes back. I hope whatever he's up to is something which will keep Earnshaws going," Thackeray said. "If all those jobs go down the tubes it will just crank up the tension another notch. The hotheads on both sides are just itching for an excuse to let rip."

"I've stumbled on another story that won't help race relations either," Laura said thoughtfully and told Thackeray about the missing student Saira Khan. "Whether the family's shipped her off to Pakistan, which is what her friends believe, or whether she's run off with an unsuitable boyfriend, which is what I suspect, people are going to get upset if I use Saira's story. Her brother was absolutely furious that the *Gazette* was asking questions."

"I know Sayeed Khan," Thackeray said. "He's a popular defence lawyer in his community, always keen to find excuses for some of the less reputable Muslims who find themselves in court."

"Isn't that his job if he's defending them? Or are you turning into one of those coppers who believes if you charge someone they must be guilty?" Laura asked, tartly. "Anyway, it's not only the disreputable ones he's helping. He was advising the Malik family when I went to interview them the other day."

"Yes, he would be. He doesn't let us get away with much, doesn't Mr. Khan."

"As I say, it's his job," Laura said sweetly.

"Just as yours is to poke around where you're not wanted, I suppose," Thackeray said, though without much heat. "I wish you'd be careful, Laura."

"Can you investigate Saira Khan's disappearance if her friends lodge a complaint?" Laura asked.

"Difficult if her family don't report her missing," Thackeray said. "It's not illegal to drop out of your university

146

course, is it? Her friends' only worry seems to be that she's not answering her phone."

"I'm not sure I believe her brother," Laura said.

"That's as maybe, but we're not exactly underwhelmed with investigations at the moment. We're working flat out, Laura. I'd need a bit more to go on than feminine intuition, yours or Saira's friends," Thackeray said with a faint smile, knowing he would annoy her.

"Oh, of course, Chief Inspector," Laura mocked. "Don't let's have intuition getting in the way. Seriously though, I thought you had a Muslim DC on the strength now. Couldn't he make some discreet inquiries about this girl?"

Thackeray sighed, serious now and his weariness showing.

"Laura, before you take over CID completely, can I just remind you that I have a murder inquiry on my hands, a vicious attack on a young girl, which incidentally has outraged the Muslim community, and now an arson attack which could be racially motivated as well. Don't you think all my DCs are fully occupied?"

"Sorry," Laura said. "Sorry, sorry, sorry. It's just that I got really bad vibes from Sayeed Khan. Nothing he said sounded quite right."

"And I've no doubt you'll burrow around until you find out why," Thackeray said, his expression a mixture of worry and amusement. "But I'm serious, Laura. Do be careful. There's a lot of tension around and extremists on both sides just waiting their chance to whip up a riot or worse."

"It's not the West Bank out there, you know," Laura complained.

"No, but there are times when I think it's going that way. What's all this about neo-Nazis?"

"Oh, I just needed a quote from that bastard Ricky

Pickles," she said airily. "He behaved like a pussy cat, don't worry. It's just what he's thinking that's so alarming. He doesn't succeed in hiding where he's really coming from."

"Please be careful, Laura," he said quietly. "I mean it."

"Fine," she said. "Have a shower and I'll sort you out something to eat. I'm sure your colleagues in uniform have the like of Pickles under control."

Later, when they had eaten and Laura had treated herself to a couple of glasses of wine, she luxuriated for a moment in domestic contentment as they sat watching the late night news, but she sensed that Thackeray was edgy and she wondered if it were just the pressures of work bothering him, or something else. In the end he turned and put his arm around her.

"I went to see my father last night," he said.

"Ah," she breathed. "I wondered why you were so silent when you came back yesterday. And how was he?"

"As unforgiving as ever. It would be nice to think that after the hard life he's had he could enjoy his retirement, but he's eaten up with resentment. He never wanted to retire. I think he hoped he'd end his life out on the fells one day with his dogs and his sheep, not sitting like this, waiting for death to creep up on him while he could still be active and working if things had turned out differently."

"Joyce finds it hard too," Laura said. "Her mind is still sharp but her body won't let her do what she wants to do any more. It's very frustrating."

"And then I go blundering in, reopening old wounds," Thackeray said.

"You told him what we're planning?"

"He has a right to know, though I'm sure he didn't want to. Frank Rafferty was there and he was more sympathetic than my father was."

"I met him once," Laura said. "He seemed a reasonable man, for a Catholic priest. Perhaps they're getting more tolerant of human frailty at last."

"The Church may be, but not my father."

"You must do what you think is right," Laura said, tentative now. "I can live with it."

"I think it's right to make an honest woman of you," Thackeray said firmly, tightening his grip on Laura. "I've got a lot of things wrong in my life, but I'll not get this wrong. My father can go to hell, though I'm sure he thinks that's the last place he'll end up. He's got a place there reserved for me."

Laura turned her face up to kiss Thackeray and was infuriated when his mobile phone rang. He pulled away and listened to the call impatiently, but as Laura watched him his expression became grim.

"Right, thanks for calling, even if somewhat late in the day," he said at last. "I'll get one of my officers to come to see you in the morning to take a statement."

"Bad news?" Laura asked.

"That was Simon Earnshaw's tutor. Calls himself his friend, though in the circumstances I have my doubts. This is strictly off the record as far as the *Gazette* is concerned, of course, but he says that he's discovered who Earnshaw's girlfriend is – by putting two and two together he claims, but I wonder if he knew all along. She's Muslim, her name is Saira and she's a student at the university."

"And she's gone missing?" Laura breathed.

"She's not been seen at the university, apparently, since Simon was killed."

"Of course she hasn't," Laura said, her stomach tightening with fear. "But the question's not just where she is, Michael, is it, but what she is? Is she your murderer or is she another victim? I think she's probably dead."

Chapter Eleven

DCI Thackeray could feel the tension in the cramped interview room as soon as he walked in. Sayeed Khan, smartly dressed in a dark suit and silk tie sat behind his father, who wore a dark jacket over white shalwar kameez, and was puffing heavily on a cheroot which had filled the stuffy room with acrid smoke. Sergeant Kevin Mower, who was sitting across the table from the older Khan, glanced up as the senior officer came in and shrugged almost imperceptibly. The fourth man in the room, DC "Omar" Sharif, was leaning against the wall opposite the door and continued to stare down at his shoes, evidently happier to allow events to proceed without his direct participation.

"Mr. Khan asked if he could talk to you personally, sir," Mower said, not making much effort to disguise his displeasure with this turn of events. "I told him you were extremely busy…"

"Not too busy, surely, given the delicate nature of this inquiry, Chief Inspector," Sayeed Khan said smoothly, directing his remark exclusively to Thackeray. "I don't think you've met my father, Chief Inspector. There's never been any reason why you should. My father, Imran, like the cricketer, though sadly not so famous. Merely a businessman in this country although in Pakistan his family is distantly related to the other Imran."

Thackeray nodded in the direction of the older man without enthusiasm. In spite of his credentials as a Yorkshireman, cricket was not his game and he was aware he was being humoured and not very skilfully at that.

"I see nothing particularly delicate in trying to trace

someone who seems very likely to be a material witness in a murder inquiry, Mr. Khan," he said. "And my officers are entirely competent to talk to you and your father and, I would hope, as an officer of the court, you are entirely ready to help us with our inquiries."

"Of course," Sayeed Khan said, with only the briefest of glances at his father who remained grim-faced. "But I think what my father and I need to discuss is your basic premise. As a family we have no evidence at all that Saira knew Simon Earnshaw. She has never mentioned his name at home to any of us, not even to her sister, Amina, who is her closest friend. As I understand it, Mr. Earnshaw was a post-graduate student in another department at the university. We have no reason to suppose that they've ever even met."

"And if Saira was having a relationship with Simon Earnshaw would she be likely to tell you, or her sister?" Kevin Mower broke in sharply. "Do us a favour, Sayeed."

Imran Khan began to speak to his son quickly in Punjabi, but then with a glance at Sharif, who had begun to pay attention now, he switched to English.

"I have given my daughters a great deal of freedom and encouragement to pursue their education," he said. "But I know my daughter would not have a relationship with a man who is not a Muslim. She would not have a relationship with anyone who was not known to me and my family and who met my approval. Saira is a good Muslim and an obedient daughter. Whoever is suggesting otherwise is slandering her name and dishonouring my family."

Thackeray sighed and sat down beside Mower at the table.

"Then when we speak to her she will be able to confirm all this," he said.

"Who is making these allegations about Saira, Chief Inspector?" Sayeed Khan asked quickly.

151

"You know I can't discuss that," Thackeray said. "Let's just say that whoever it may be is in a position to know. He's sufficiently reliable for us to feel the need to speak to Saira urgently. So if you will just tell us where she is…?"

"Not the gossip of girlfriends then?"

"Not the gossip of girlfriends," Thackeray said. "But it was her girlfriends at the university who alerted us to Saira's unexplained absence. They were worried about her and I believe someone in your family told them that she was safe and that they didn't need to be concerned."

"I'm not aware of that," Sayeed Khan said, glancing at his father again.

"Is Saira in Pakistan, Mr. Khan?" Thackeray asked, not disguising his anger. "This is what her friends seem to think. Have you sent her abroad for some reason? Any reason."

The Khans, father and son, seemed disinclined to answer this direct challenge, and Thackeray's face hardened perceptibly.

"Mr. Khan," he snapped, addressing himself to the younger man. "You're a practising solicitor and I'm engaged in investigating a murder case in which your sister appears to be involved in some way with the victim. I want to know where Saira is. If she's in this country I need to see her, and if she is out of the country I need to speak to her on the phone. I can arrange to interview her wherever she is – in Pakistan if necessary."

Khan senior spoke rapidly to his son again in Punjabi and Thackeray turned quickly to Sharif.

"Translate, please." Sharif looked uncomfortable but did as he was asked.

"Mr. Khan says how strange it is that English men only become very interested in women's rights when they can use it against Muslims." An image of Laura flashed briefly in front of Thackeray's eyes and he allowed himself a half smile.

"If that's a convoluted way of calling me a racist, Mr. Khan, I assure you it's unjustified," Thackeray said. "I'm not accusing you of harming Saira in any way. But there is a possibility which I am surprised hasn't struck you. It's what suggests to me that you really do know exactly where Saira is and that she is probably quite safe. From where I'm sitting, it's conceivable that Saira herself could also be a victim of whoever killed Simon Earnshaw."

Saira's father and brother both drew sharp breaths at that but still neither of them spoke. Thackeray's face darkened again.

"Mr. Khan, there is an offence of perverting the course of justice, as I am sure you're very aware, and if you refuse to help us find Saira I think it could be argued that you are coming dangerously close to committing it. I doubt very much if the Law Society, as your professional body, would be much impressed with that."

Sayeed Khan turned to his father and said something in Punjabi. Thackeray swung round to DC Sharif again.

"Mr. Sayeed Khan said to his father that he has no choice but to answer our questions," Sharif mumbled.

"That's the first sensible thing I've heard since I came into this room," Thackeray said. "Is Saira in Pakistan, Mr. Khan?"

"No, she's not," Sayeed Khan said. "We didn't know about this alleged relationship. As my father said, we believed Saira to be a devout young woman, like her sister."

"It is a slander," the older Khan said bitterly. "Saira would not be seduced by your western so-called morality." Thackeray was checked for a second by that. This man could be his own father in shalwar kameez, he thought. So much for cultural differences. But he knew he had to press on now he had started this interrogation.

"So where is she?" he persisted.

Sayeed Khan shrugged wearily.

"We don't know," he said. "We haven't seen her since last Saturday, more than a week ago now. We've been worried sick."

"So why the hell didn't you report her missing?" Kevin Mower asked explosively.

"We preferred to make our own inquiries first," Khan said. "As my father said, there is great shame in admitting that a young woman has run away, particularly for the older generation. My father didn't want it widely known. He preferred to make inquiries within the community first…"

"So that's what you thought, is it?" Thackeray's voice was full of scepticism. "Isn't that just a little contradictory? You say you knew nothing about the relationship with Earnshaw, but when Saira fails to come home you assume she's run away, presumably with a man."

"What else could we assume?" Khan said.

"Well, most families might be afraid she had come to some harm, had an accident, been attacked or worse. Most families might have contacted not only the police, but hospitals, her university, anyone who might know anything. Is this shame you talk about so profound that you can't make the most obvious efforts to find a daughter who goes missing?"

"Yes," Imran Khan said explosively. His son put a restraining hand on his arm.

"We have been looking for Saira," he said. "In our own way, in our own community."

"Making use of the young men who allegedly seek out errant daughters?" Thackeray asked, stony faced. "Who will allegedly kill rather than allow a family's honour to be blemished?" He heard Sharif draw a sharp breath behind him and the two Khans flushed darkly but this was a gauntlet he was determined to run to the end.

"I know of no such young men," Sayeed Khan said, his voice thick with emotion.

"I'm pleased to hear it," Thackeray said. "Because as a lawyer you know as well as I do that what such young men do is illegal in this country, that we do not hound and harass young adults who choose to marry or live together, regardless of their religion or their ethnic background."

"If Saira was having such a relationship, and I don't believe it, we knew nothing of it," Sayeed Khan said, his face set and his eyes angry.

"Which leaves us with the evident fact that she is missing and I need to speak to her on the assumption she may have been deceiving you," Thackeray said flatly. "So I'll tell you what will happen next. We will report her missing and put out a national call for her to be traced urgently. We'll also need to carry out a search at your home. Our forensic people will no doubt be able to obtain DNA samples from Saira's room which may match samples found at Simon Earnshaw's flat. That should prove pretty definitively whether there was a relationship between the two of them or not."

"Not publicity in the newspapers," Sayeed Khan objected. "Her photograph, all that?" Beside him, his father groaned.

"It may well be necessary," Thackeray said. "I think you're still not quite appreciating the seriousness of my interest in your sister, Mr. Khan. She's a possible suspect in a murder inquiry. And if she had nothing to do with Simon Earnshaw's death herself it seems at least possible that she has been killed as well. Do I need to make myself any clearer than that?"

Laura had been surprised that morning when she got to the office to find an urgent message from Radio Bradfield asking her to find time to go in to see the station manager some time that day. She called Kelly Sullivan but she was not available, so Laura arranged to walk across town to the station during her lunch hour, wondering just what might have gone wrong with the plans for her to fill in for Kelly while she was away. She was kept waiting ten minutes in the reception area, surrounded by potted plants, copies of what's-on leaflets and a feed of the local lunchtime radio news, before she was allowed through the security doors and shown into the station manager's office. It was immediately obvious from the slightly cool handshake Steve Denham offered across his desk that this would not be as cosy a chat as they had had last time she had been there. Kelly Sullivan, who was one of two other people waiting for her in the office, half-smiled as she came in and Denham introduced the man sitting next to her as his "legal adviser" Colin Makin.

"Thanks for coming, Laura," Denham said. "I just wanted another chat before you go ahead with these interviews you're planning for when Kelly's away. To be perfectly honest, and on reflection, with what's going on in the town at the moment, we're beginning to have second thoughts about the wisdom of such controversial subject matter just now."

"Controversial?" Laura said, feeling stupid because for a second or two she simply did not understand what Denham meant. "I didn't think I was doing anything particularly controversial." Denham raised an eyebrow at that.

"With the state of race relations at the moment, with the attack on the young Malik girl, I think you have to admit that raising the issue of women's rights in the Muslim community could be construed as – how shall we put it – a tad provocative."

"On the contrary," Laura said angrily. "If the Muslims are closing ranks and being defensive about their women and girls, I think that's just the moment to raise the issues I want to talk about. That's certainly what some of the Asian women I've been talking to think. As they put it, they're worried about being set back a generation by what's happening."

"It's a subject we ought to explore – with some sensitivity," Denham conceded. "But I think not now. It's too inflammatory."

"You obviously haven't heard the latest news here at Radio Bradfield," Laura said waspishly. "It'll be in the first edition of the *Gazette*, of course. The police are looking for a young Asian woman who seems to have run away because she was having a relationship with Simon Earnshaw."

This was clearly news to Denham and Kelly Sullivan worked hard to stifle a smile at her boss's discomfiture.

"Of course that raises even more issues worth discussing," Laura went on. "Why did she feel it necessary to conceal her relationship? Will she be pursued by her family? Or has she already been bundled off to Pakistan to get her out of the way? Or, worst of all, has she been killed as well?"

Radio Bradfield's lawyer flinched visibly at that list of questions and made to object but Steve Denham raised a hand impatiently.

"I'm sure Laura is experienced enough to know the risks of defamation," he said.

"All to be discussed in general terms," Laura said innocently. "Obviously we can't comment on a police investigation." Me less than most, she thought to herself wryly.

"But most urgent of all perhaps, as a topic," she went on, "is the fact that there are young Muslim men who will try to hunt down girls and young women who step out of line. That's illegal, and if no one talks about it they'll continue to get away with it."

"The same young men who'll be ready with their petrol

bombs if tension rises any higher," the lawyer, Colin Makin, got in quickly this time with a sour look in Laura's direction. "I wouldn't recommend that sort of debate at any time, but especially not now."

"I thought this was a news station," Laura said sweetly.

"Laura," Kelly Sullivan broke in. "I think all Steve is suggesting is that we postpone this particular set of interviews for now. I'd certainly like to follow the idea up myself, when things are a bit calmer." She flashed a glance at her boss. "But perhaps you could come up with something a bit less, well, difficult this time?"

Less difficult and more boring, Laura thought but this time she kept her temper in check.

"Don't you think that half the problems in this town could be resolved if we didn't keep on dodging the difficult questions?" she asked, far more calmly than she felt. "You know what they say? The communities are living parallel lives? But on the fringes there are people who want to get closer together, young women in particular, who want to integrate, become more Westernised if you like, leave behind some Muslim traditions which they find oppressive, and isn't that their right if they've been born and brought up here? In a free country it's their choice. And in a free country their voices should be heard. What you're saying is that we close off a debate about that so we can all have a quiet life and don't get accused of racism by the men at the mosque."

"This is all a bit heavy for me at this time in the morning," Steve Denham said, with an attempt at lightness. "Let's call this a postponement of the issue, shall we? I wouldn't want the research you've already done to go to waste, Laura, so you and Kelly can certainly come back to it in calmer times. But for now I want you to come up with something less inflammatory. OK?"

"OK," Kelly said, glancing at Laura, who sighed and nodded ungraciously. She knew she could not defy the station manager and as an outside contributor she was in an uniquely weak position. If she wanted to maintain any sort of toehold at the station, which she did, she would have to acquiesce, however unwillingly.

"Thanks for coming in, Laura," Denham said. "I was sure we could work something out. Talk to Kelly about a different topic and I'll look forward to your interviews. You've got a good voice for radio. You never know. There might be a good career move in this direction some day."

Laura did not believe him for a moment. Her chances here were almost certainly blown.

Sergeant Kevin Mower sat in the same cramped space he had occupied last time he had visited Dr. Stephen McKenna and the scientist gazed back at him across the equally cluttered desk with the same mournful expression.

"So how come you're now sure Simon Earnshaw was having a relationship with Saira Khan when the last time we spoke you were adamant you didn't know who the girl was?" Mower asked. DC "Omar" Sharif perched against the cluttered windowsill watching the proceedings with dark, unreadable eyes.

"I told you I thought the girl was Asian. Simon was being so cagey that it had to be something like that. Obviously she wouldn't want her family to know." McKenna glanced at Sharif, who scowled at him. "I'm not being racist," McKenna said fiercely. "You must know how it is. We have lots of Asian women students here. The families are thankfully becoming really ambitious for their children now. But some of the young women are brought here every day by minibus and picked up again in the evening. The traditions about what women can do run very deep, as you must know very well."

"So?" Mower pressed. "How did Saira's name crop up. Was she one who came in the minibus, or what?"

"No, I don't think so. You need to talk to her tutor as well to find out more. That's Olive Makepiece in the pharmacy department. She was the one who told me one of her Asian students had not come back this term and she was wondering if she'd gone off to Pakistan or something." Another glance at Sharif. "It happens sometimes. Anyway, I began to wonder, put two and two together and maybe make five or six, but I thought I'd check it out. Simon was a good man, a good friend, and I want his killer found, and it seemed to me not impossible that his love life had something to do with what happened. I couldn't think of any other reason why he should be killed."

Stephen McKenna shuffled the papers in front of him on his desk for a moment, evidently needing time before he felt able to continue.

"Anyway, I waylaid some of the students coming out of their pharmacy lectures yesterday," he said. "Eventually I pinned down a girl called Fatima Achmed who everyone said was Saira Khan's best friend and it all came out. She was frightened to death for Saira. She hasn't seen her for more than a week, her family has told her to mind her own business and she suspects – well, I think she knows really, but she says she only suspects – that Saira was in a relationship with an older student that she didn't dare tell her family about. It has to be Simon, doesn't it?"

McKenna hesitated again for a moment and Mower waited patiently. It was obvious that there was more to come.

"What puzzled me is why he never told me about Saira," he said slowly. "He knew very well I wouldn't mind who his

160

girlfriend was. But he said something odd once. We were talking about the city, and regeneration and all that, and he said the problem with Bradfield and the immigrant community was that neither side wanted to know the other, both communities wanted to keep themselves to themselves. I got the feeling he was talking personally somehow, that he wouldn't have wanted his own family to know he was going out with an Asian girl any more than she would want it known by her parents. It was just an impression, you understand, but it might be relevant."

By the end of the afternoon Mower and Sharif had questioned Saira Khan's tutor and more than a dozen of her friends and acquaintances on her course, but without being offered anything more than vague speculation about her private life and her likely whereabouts since she had last been seen by Fatima Achmed on a cinema trip just before the start of the university term. As the two officers joined the stream of young people flooding out of the university buildings at the end of the day and made their way the short distance down the hill to the town centre and the main police station, Mower glanced at his companion, who had said little all afternoon.

"Come on, Omar," he said. "What do you really think about all this? Are we looking for another body?"

The younger man shrugged.

"It's possible, sarge," he said. "Don't imagine I don't think that, and wouldn't work as hard as anyone to find out who did it."

"I wasn't suggesting that you wouldn't," Mower said. "But watch yourself. If we get into investigating the dark side of Muslim traditions, runaway girls and family honour and all that stuff, you'll have a crucial part to play, and they'll be watching you from on high, believe me."

161

"You mean they don't trust me because I'm a Paki?" Sharif asked, letting his anger gleam for a moment in his eyes.

"I mean you'll have to prove you can be trusted," Mower said. "D'you think the family will be trying to hunt her down, however much they deny it?"

"Quite possibly," Sharif said uneasily.

"Can we find out who does the hunting? We need to know. Will people know at the mosque, the community centre? Or do you know yourself?"

"No I don't," Sharif said, struggling not very successfully to hide his discomfort.

"So you'll make inquiries, then?"

Sharif shrugged.

"If that's what you want, sarge," he said. Mower glanced at him curiously, taking in the angry eyes and frozen expression on his colleague's face.

"Surely you're not into all this tradition yourself, are you? Are you going to let your parents choose your wife for you, for God's sake?"

"Maybe," Sharif said. "And if I do it'll be no one's business at work, will it? What gives you, or anyone else, the right to criticise?"

Mower sighed.

"You're going to make life difficult for yourself," he said. "That's all I'm saying. You know what the job's like. They play all the right tunes on equality but there's plenty still resent it and they can make your life a misery if they think you're stepping out of line. Believe me. I know. See what you can find out about what the Khan family is up to, right?"

"Right," Sharif said.

Chapter Twelve

Earnshaws mill had stood four-square on the hill above Aysgarth Lane for more than a century, a great looming stone battleship of a building, its towering chimney dominating the hills of Victorian terraced cottages for miles around. But where once the structure had shaken daily with the deafening clatter of a thousand looms, large sections of the four-storey building were now closed off, some of them structurally unsafe, and the huge cobbled yard, where as little as twenty years earlier the bulging hessian bales of British and Australian wool had been stacked several stories high waiting to be winched to the upper floors, was now often deserted. Thackeray drove in past a couple of desultory security guards and parked next to the handful of staff cars which used the yard as a car-park. He glanced up curiously at the decaying, blank-windowed relic of the industrial age. It was, he thought, quite ostentatiously ornate, a florid symbol of a confidence long dissipated and a wealth now only a fading memory in these steep Yorkshire valleys. He did not see how Earnshaws could survive. The world was moving on at a frantic and accelerating pace, leaving it high and dry.

But that was not a thought which he wished to share with Frank Earnshaw, into whose wood-panelled office he was ushered by a secretary five minutes later. The room shuddered slightly to the rhythm of the few machines which were still active in the cavernous depths of the mill. Thackeray had come to see the mill's managing director alone and in person in deference to his superiors' sensitivities. He did not at this stage want to interview Earnshaw again in any formal way, but he thought there were some aspects of the case that the dead man's father might illuminate for him one-to-one, without the presence of officers taking notes or tape-recorders inhibiting every word they exchanged.

"Have you got any news, Mr. Thackeray?" Earnshaw asked, his face more grey and lined than the last time Thackeray had seen him. "My wife's finding this very hard." And you too, Thackeray thought, his sympathy automatically with any bereaved father. He knew every bitter step of that road only too well.

"I'm sorry," he said. "But not news in the sense you mean it. We're no further forward in the main part of our investigation. If you asked me who the prime suspect is I'd have to tell you that I've no idea yet."

Earnshaw nodded, and gazed out of the office's tall window over the roofs of the little houses which snaked down the hill below the mill towards the town centre. They had been built for Earnshaws workers and still housed most of them, although a whole history of failing industry and lost Empire had intervened.

"I wanted to talk to you a bit less formally than last time about your family as a whole, about how they got on." Earnshaw looked wary but nodded.

"For instance, you've just the two sons – were they friends?" Thackeray asked.

Earnshaw turned his now bleak gaze onto the policeman and shrugged.

"More Cain and Abel than David and Jonathan? Is that what you're thinking, Chief Inspector? Well, in one sense I suppose you're right. They weren't great friends, no. They never were, really, not even when they were little lads. They were always very different and Matt was always jealous of Simon. I think he thought that I approved of Simon more than I approved of him, and he was right of course. Matt's been nowt but trouble in many ways, at school, at college. The drink started early on, his marriage never looked as if it would work – and it didn't. When Simon left the company I was deeply disappointed. My father was appalled. I don't think he's seen Simon since, cut him out of his life completely…I'd always regarded Simon as my successor as well…"

"So Simon was the blue-eyed boy?"

"Aye, I suppose you could say that. Not only mine, his grandfather's too. My father wanted to fire Matt more than once. I have to confess that I couldn't ever bring myself to that point but he was – is – a disappointment."

"Your father is still actively involved in running the company then?" Thackeray asked.

"Not active in the day-to-day running, no," Earnshaw said. "He's not fit enough for that now. But he's still a director and he makes his views known." Earnshaw shrugged ruefully and Thackeray, thinking of the tall gaunt old man in his cluttered, empty house, guessed that George made his views known pretty forcefully on occasion.

"It's a difficult time right now, as you probably know. We need to make changes here but it's proving very hard to get the directors to agree. You could say my father heads the status quo party. He believes that trade will pick up and Earnshaws will be restored to its former glory. He's living in cloud cuckoo land, to be honest. The textile industry in this country is as good as dead. There are only two options for this place. We go bust and someone else acquires the site dirt cheap and redevelops, or we try to diversify and regenerate ourselves, which means bringing in some extra capital. In the meantime we're making economies and trying to hang on. That's what all the trouble with the union is about."

"And that's the line you're pursuing personally? Hanging on until you can negotiate a rescue package?" Thackeray asked carefully, not wanting to let Earnshaw know of his contact with Jack Ackroyd and his apparent interest in the future of the mill.

"Right, but it's complicated," Earnshaw said. "The way the company is structured, deliberately structured by my father, I may say, three out of four of the family directors have to agree to any major strategy. With my father and I at loggerheads the two boys' shareholdings are crucial. I think I've persuaded Matt that my proposals make sense, although he tells me that his grandfather's been trying to persuade him different. But that still leaves Simon's shares. That's what Matt wanted to discuss the night we realised Simon was missing, when he didn't turn up at the Clarendon. I'd already talked to Simon by phone and I really thought I'd got him on side but last week he seemed to be backing off again, making difficulties... His priority seemed to be getting some community benefit out of any changes which were made – which wasn't impossible. There's all sorts of ways you can develop a property like this."

"But if you can't get an agreement...?

"We carry on as we are, and eventually we go bust – sooner rather than later, I'd say," Earnshaw said harshly. "My father can't see that but it's inevitable."

"Do you know who'll inherit Simon's shares?"

"I don't even know if he's made a will," Frank Earnshaw said. "If he hasn't I suppose they come back to the family. I'm not sure what the legal position would be."

"That's something we'll have to investigate. You do understand that," Thackeray said.

"Good God, man, d'you think one of us killed Simon for his shares? The idea's bizarre." Earnshaw looked genuinely shocked.

"I don't think anything at this stage, Mr. Earnshaw,"

Thackeray said. "But you have to appreciate that in a murder investigation nothing's sacred, nothing's off-limits. It's not a pleasant process for the victim's family, even if they're as innocent as the driven snow."

"Not innocent till proved guilty then? More possibly guilty till proved innocent?"

"That's about it," Thackeray admitted.

"Did you track down Simon's alleged girlfriend?" Earnshaw asked.

"We think we may have identified her although we haven't actually found her yet," Thackeray said. "But we've some more inquiries to make before we can be sure." Thackeray did not want to broach the subject of Saira Khan with Simon Earnshaw's family until he had a clearer idea of whether she had been spirited out of Bradfield by her own family, in spite of their denials, or indeed whether she was dead or alive.

"It does seem possible that she may be of Asian origin," he conceded, not averse to watching Earnshaw's reaction to that piece of information.

"Asian?" Earnshaw said, visibly surprised. "We had no idea."

"Would it have caused you and your family a problem, if you'd known? Was that why Simon didn't tell you about her?"

"Not me, or Simon's mother," Earnshaw said, quickly enough to be convincing. "If she was fond of Simon I'd like to meet her. But my father wouldn't have been too happy about it. I think it'd be fair to say he's had more difficulty than most in coming to terms with immigration to Bradfield. He wouldn't employ Asian workers when they first began to come over. Brute economics forced his hand in the end, but he didn't like it. He spent some time in India just after the war when he was in the RAF. Came back after independence. He never talked about it at all but I think he saw things there that shocked him. It was pretty bloody business, wasn't it, the partition of India? Whatever happened out there, when Pakistanis turned up here in the 1960s it seemed to upset him more than most."

"You're sure your father hasn't seen Simon recently? Had a row with him, perhaps?"

"Obviously I can't be absolutely sure, but I don't think he's seen him for a long while," Earnshaw said. "But if you're thinking what I think you're thinking, Chief Inspector, you must realise that he's an unlikely murder suspect even if he is a bit of a racist. You may not know that my father has prostate cancer. It's a slow disease but it's killing him. His doctors don't reckon he has much more than six months to live. Unfortunately, to put it brutally, we can't wait for him to go before we tackle the problems of the mill. We've got to move faster than that."

"I'm sorry to hear that," Thackeray said. "But I may need to talk to him again."

"I'm sure there's nothing I can do to stop you," Earnshaw said, his face suddenly drawn with weariness.

Amina Khan, in a long grey coat and hijab, caused a slight rustle of interest amongst the mainly young, white and well-dressed clientele as she came into the café bar to meet Laura Ackroyd that lunchtime. It was not an environment much frequented by evidently devout Muslim women on their own and the fact that she was momentarily the focus of attention might have explained the look of anxiety with which she scanned the tables in search of Laura.

"What can I get you?" Laura asked when Amina eventually eased her way between the crowded tables and sat down.

"Coffee?" Amina nodded and Laura realised just how strained she looked beneath the severe head-covering.

"Is there still no news of your sister?" Laura asked when she had dealt with the waitress. Amina's eyes filled with tears which she dashed away impatiently.

"I do know she's actually missing," Laura went on. "I know, even though your brother tried to deny it when I went to see him. Did he tell you that?"

Amina shook her head.

"I didn't know you'd seen Sayeed," she said. "My father and my brother are saying very little, although I can see they're worried." She doesn't know yet what the police suspect, Laura thought, and wondered as she stirred her own latte whether she should tell her.

"So how can I help?" Laura asked eventually, deciding for the moment to keep her counsel about what she had learned from Michael Thackeray.

"I know where she is now and it's not good news," Amina said. "I had a letter. It was sent to the school, no doubt so that my father wouldn't see it."

"So she's alive?" Laura said quietly, filled with relief at that.

"When she wrote it, at least," Amina said. "But she's run away with a man."

"Ah," Laura said cautiously. "So why are you telling me all this now?"

"Because you've discovered she's missing, and now I want you to forget all that. I don't want anyone else to know about what's happened, especially my father and brother. I want you to stop asking questions about my sister."

"Don't you think your father will try to find her?"

"They'll be furious, and they may try. Though I don't think it will be that easy. The letter was posted in Paris. She seems to have gone abroad."

"Can I see it?" Laura asked, wondering where this conversation would leave her in relation to the police inquiry. Amina took a tightly folded envelope from the small black bag she had placed on the table in front of her and passed it to Laura who glanced at the handwritten address and French stamp before unfolding the letter and beginning to read.

My dearest sister,

By the time you read this I'll have gone away. Already I feel like something out of one of those classic novels that we used to read at school. I know you'll think I've dishonoured our family and you'll never want to see me again, like poor Kitty in "Pride and Prejudice". Do you remember? I know you'll think I am weak and treacherous which is why I want you to have this letter to remember me by, so that you'll know that I did try to live by the rules you believe in and that I've been taught too. But in the end it didn't make sense for me and I've made my own decisions. I hope one day you and the rest of the family will be able to forgive me.

You see, I've met someone I love very much. There's no reason why we shouldn't marry and that's what we intend to do. You've been so busy with your work, which I admire, that I don't think you've noticed how much Father has been pressuring me to go home with him when I graduate and marry our cousin Ahmed. But even before I met the man I love I'd decided I didn't want that. It's difficult enough to live in two cultures without constantly being pulled back into the old one by traditions that my English friends regard as unacceptable. I know you'll think I'm very wrong but I want an English marriage between equals. I've thought and thought about this, and can't accept anything else. I don't believe any more that this is immoral. I don't believe I've been immodest in getting to know my lover, although I know you'll think that. I do admire your decision to live a more traditional life, but I can't do that.

*I won't tell you where I am going, and I won't contact you. I
know Papa and Sayeed will want to seek me out and punish me and
I hope we'll be far enough away to prevent that.*

*Don't think too badly of me, my dearest sister. I wish we could
have stayed close together for the rest of our lives as we always
imagined we would when we were little girls.*

Your loving sister,

Saira

"I suppose you sympathise," Amina said angrily when she
saw that Laura had finished reading and was staring into her
coffee cup.

"I sympathise with you both," Laura said. "I think trying
to live in one culture while surrounded by a quite different
one must be incredibly hard."

"Not if you live according to our faith," Amina said. "But I
didn't come here to talk about that. I just wanted to ask you to
forget that we ever talked about Saira. I've talked to her friends
at college and we all agree that it's best if our parents, the
mosque, the rest of them, don't know anything about all this.
It's safer that way. Let them go and never be found. That's all."

"There's just one problem with that," Laura said. "You
obviously don't know, but I'm afraid the police are looking
for Saira too. I'm surprised they haven't been to see you by
now."

"But why?" Amina protested. "Did you tell them about
her? How can they be looking for her when no one has
reported her missing? What have you done?"

Laura took hold of the agitated young woman's hand.

"It wasn't me," she said. "And it's worse than you think.
Far worse. The police have discovered that Saira's boyfriend
was Simon Earnshaw, the student who was found dead in
Broadley a few days ago. They want to talk to Saira and I
don't think they're going to take no for an answer."

171

"He's dead?" Amina said, almost to herself, but the horror stark in her face. "What will she do now? Whatever will she do now?"

"If she's any sense she'll come back to Bradfield and talk to the police," Laura said.

"You don't understand," Amina said. "You don't understand anything. You liberals think you do, but you don't."

"So tell me," Laura said more gently.

"She can't come back here – ever. She's had a love affair and the family is dishonoured. She has no future here now. She's on her own. She'll never be forgiven. And it may be even worse than that. There'll be people who will want her punished. She can never never come back."

"Do you know how to contact her?" Laura asked.

"You've seen the letter. There's no address." Amina's face was pale and closed now, as if the news Laura had given her had sealed her own fate in some way as well as her sister's.

"No mobile phone number?"

"No."

Laura signalled to the waitress for a bill for their coffees and her lunch.

"You know you'll have to show the letter to the police, don't you?" she said.

"No, I can't," Amina said, her voice determined.

"You must, Amina. If you don't go to them yourself, I'll have to tell them what's happened. This is a murder they're investigating. You could get into a lot of trouble if you don't pass on information."

"No," Amina said again.

"Look, I'll give you twenty-four hours to talk to DCI Thackeray. After that, I'll have to tell him myself."

Amina shrugged, pushed back her chair with a noisy scrape on the tiled floor and stood up, which Laura could

172

only interpret as another no. She took a two pound coin from her bag and put it on the table.

"For my coffee," she said, and walked out of the café without a backward glance.

As Laura was driving home that evening along Aysgarth Lane, the busy heart of Bradfield's Asian community, she was startled to be overtaken by four or five powerful motorbikes with riders in full black leathers moving fast round the slow stream of traffic making its way out of town towards the suburbs.

"Idiots," she muttered to herself as the last of the convoy squeezed between her car and an on-coming van, forcing her towards the kerb and an Asian family innocently doing their shopping at one of the greengrocers which had spread its wares across the pavement. A man in shalwar kameez stepped back from the edge of the road and shouted a protest at Laura which she could not hear. She raised her hands to indicate her helplessness and glared ahead at the motorbikes which seemed to have caused more mayhem further up the road by unexpectedly swinging right into one of the tightly packed sidestreets leading up the hill towards Earnshaws mill. There had been something menacing about the string of heavy bikes and their presence had evidently been noted by some of the Asian men who tended to gather in Aysgarth Lane to chat at the end of the working day. Laura watched for a moment as the traffic inched slowly forward, and saw several groups of bystanders gesticulating angrily and a number of younger men beginning to run in the direction of the bikes – up streets almost exclusively occupied by Asian families.

Spurred on by curiosity and a sense that something bad was about to happen, Laura flicked on her indicator and took the same right turn that the bikes had done, although the traffic jam meant that she was now some five minutes behind them. She glanced at the passenger seat where her mobile phone lay beside her handbag and pushed the door locks on with her elbow as she noticed more young men running along the pavement beside the car. She accelerated slightly to outpace them but as she reached a crossroads just a street away from the tall brick façade of the mill, she had to brake hard as the bikes cut across the car and swung away down the hill again the way they had come.

Cautiously she glanced down the street to her left before deciding whether or not to turn into it and quickly realised that it was already blocked by a crowd of people which was growing by the minute as front doors opened and more of the residents looked cautiously in both directions before venturing out. She did a U-turn and parked on the opposite side of the road she was in, locked her bag in the glove-box and with her mobile phone firmly clutched in her pocket, got out of the car and began to walk towards the centre of the disturbance, one of only a handful of white faces amongst the growing throng of brown.

By the time Laura had wormed her way to the front of the crowd, the mood was already becoming angry and in the distance she could hear the sound of approaching sirens. It was obvious that someone had been hurt but she was unable to get close enough to see who the victim was or exactly what had happened. Within minutes an ambulance with blue lights flashing began inching its way through the press of people. From the excited chatter, some in English and some in Punjabi, she gathered that the motorcyclists were being held responsible for whatever had gone wrong and that the victim was a man, but whether what had happened was an accident or an assault was impossible to glean. She caught no more than a glimpse of paramedics in green coveralls leaping out of their cab to be greeted by angry shouts before deciding that she had seen as much as it was safe to see. She edged her way back to her car, through the shoving, jostling crowd which grew with alarming speed as men and boys came racing from surrounding streets. Slamming and locking the doors, she pulled out her mobile and called her editor and then Michael Thackeray. Even as she spoke she could see the outrage growing in the street around her and she pulled very cautiously away from the kerb, attracting angry glances as she went. It was not until she had driven safely home that Michael called her back, by which time he already knew that the man lying in intensive care in Bradfield Infirmary with his life in the balance was the trade union convenor from Earnshaws, Mohammed Iqbal, and that in Aysgarth Lane the petrol bombs had begun to fly.

"I saw the bikes go up there," Laura said. There was a long silence at the other end of the phone.

"And you followed them?" Thackeray asked, his voice chilly.

"I was curious," Laura said. "It's my job to be curious."

"You were lucky not to be hurt."

"I know," Laura conceded and realised that her hands were still trembling.

"I won't be home for a while," Thackeray said. "There's all hell broken loose up there. Could you identify any of the riders, or the bikes?"

"No," Laura said. "Not with their big helmets, and it all happened too quickly to catch number plates or anything like that. Will this man Iqbal survive?"

"Unlikely," Thackeray said flatly. "It looks like another murder. And a race-related one at that. I have to go, Laura. I'll see you when I see you, and Laura…"

"Michael?" she said.

"Don't do anything silly."

"I'll try not to," she said soberly.

Chapter Thirteen

Superintendent Jack Longley thumped his fist on his desk and glared at his assembled senior officers.

"I'll not have no-go areas in this town," he said. "I don't give a damn who's at death's door and how strongly the Muslim community feels about it. The streets will be policed and people will walk in them without any hindrance from vigilantes of any colour. You'll make that clear at your community relations meeting this afternoon, Brian?"

Chief Inspector Brian Butler, in charge of Bradfield's uniformed officers, nodded, his dour expression giving nothing away.

"Any progress on tracing the bikes?" Longley asked but Butler, always a man of few words, shrugged slightly.

"Nowt," he said. "No one's come up with registration numbers. Witnesses say that when the gang got back down to Aysgarth Lane they peeled off and went their separate ways. After about five minutes from the assault I've had no sightings. We may get more when the *Gazette* comes out with an appeal for witnesses later on."

"And how's Iqbal?" Longley asked, offering Michael Thackeray the same fierce glare that he had bestowed on Butler.

"I've got Mower waiting for a call to his bedside on the off-chance he comes round," DCI Michael Thackeray said. "But the doctors aren't hopeful. He suffered a massive head injury and he's on life-support."

"Wonderful," Longley said. "You know what sort of conspiracy theories that'll have whizzing around Aysgarth Lane, don't you? Earnshaws can't afford a strike so they put this gang up to attacking Iqbal after the fire-bombing of the union offices didn't scare the union off. Anything in that for a line of inquiry, do you think, Michael?"

It was Thackeray's turn to shrug and look slightly blank.

"It's worth giving some thought," he said doubtfully. "It's pretty clear from the witness statements we've been able to get overnight – which is not a lot because of the rioting – that the gang were intent on finding Iqbal in particular. They went straight to his house and unfortunately he was outside on the street talking to some of his union members. They were pushed aside and they set on Iqbal with iron bars. He was obviously the target, but it may be very difficult to prove they were put up to it by anything other than sheer bloody malevolence. It could just be that the local Nazis have worked themselves up because of the strike threat. Ricky Pickles is at the top of my interview list and anyone else on the loony racist fringes, so we'll take it from there."

"But you'll talk to the Earnshaws?"

"If you say so, sir," Thackeray said cautiously.

"I bloody say so," Longley said. "You don't pussyfoot around in this situation whatever ACC Ellison suggests."

"Sir," Thackeray said, wondering if Longley's dislike of Ellison was affecting his judgement, but Longley had already switched his attention back to Butler.

"So how many casualties last night?" he asked.

"Two officers with minor burns," Butler said. "About a dozen Asian lads treated at the Infirmary, two detained overnight with burns, half a dozen white lads, none detained."

"Where the hell did they come from?" Longley asked.

"Oh, I think they heard there was a bit of a rumble going down and thought they'd join in," Butler said sourly. "Most were from Wuthering and reckoned they were on our side when we interviewed a couple we arrested. Bloody fools."

178

"And how many arrests altogether?"

"Fourteen – ten Asian, four white. I doubt we'll be able to make charges stick. They'll all have mothers who'll swear they just slipped out for five minutes to see what all the fuss was about. The Fire Brigade reckons the damage to the car showrooms at the bottom of Market Street alone'll be about half a million. Then there's the Lamb pub burned out and a couple of houses next to it badly damaged. Fire engines couldn't get near for about an hour."

"So what happens if Iqbal snuffs it?" Longley asked no one in particular.

"Take to the lifeboats," Butler said. "I think I'll put in for a spot of leave."

"You'll do nothing of the sort," Longley growled. "In fact you'd best cancel all leave for the duration. If Michael's right and this Iqbal lad's on his way out, we're going to need every officer we've got on duty twenty-four-seven."

"My little joke, sir," Butler said, but neither Longley nor Thackeray smiled.

While the police were assessing the damage to people and property caused by the previous night's riot around Aysgarth Lane, Frank Earnshaw and his father were engaged in a similar stock-taking at the family mill. Frank had been only slightly surprised when his father had appeared at eight that morning and presented himself in the office looking haggard and leaning heavily on a stick. George had evidently been even less surprised by the news that the vast majority of the mill workers had failed to turn up at all for work that morning.

"There's nothing you can do here, Dad," Earnshaw said eventually in exasperation as the two men stood at the office window and gazed down at the empty yard and the slate roofs of tightly packed terraced houses gleaming almost black in the morning drizzle. "When I get through to Jim Watson I may be able to make some progress but as things stand the beggars are on unofficial strike and we'll get no production today, and maybe not for some while."

"Is Watson even in bloody Bradfield?" George asked, stepping away and sinking into the single comfortable chair in the managing director's office with what sounded to his son more like a groan rather than a grunt.

"You shouldn't have come," Frank said, glancing at George's stick-thin frame which was hunched over his knees, head down. "You're not well enough to be driving, let alone worrying about this mess. You're retired, for God's sake, and you're not a fit man. Why don't you bugger off and get some rest."

George glanced up at his son and although his face was grey and deeply lined his eyes were still bright and very angry.

"This mess would never have happened if I'd been fit," he said. "Where's bloody Watson? Why isn't he here sorting these Paki beggars out?"

"He's not likely to be in Bradfield with the union office burned out, is he?" Frank said. "I've got Rita trying his mobile every fifteen minutes, we've left messages at his regional office and on his voicemail. There's nowt else I can do. No one seems to know where he is."

"Rita's not out on bloody strike then?" George asked. "More sense, has she?"

"No, the office staff are all in. Of course, they're not in a union."

"And most of them are white," George said. "Just goes to show."

Frank sighed and returned to his vantage point. The

180

streets leading down to Aysgarth Lane appeared deserted this morning, but a haze of smoke still hung over the cluster of buildings on the major junction close to the town centre which had been the focal point of the wrath of the crowd of young Asians who had run amok within minutes of the attack on Mohammed Iqbal the night before, taking the police and emergency services completely by surprise. He could see blue lights still flashing through the gloom.

"We should never have let the union back in. We never had all this trouble when Maggie gave us the option," George said.

"Yes, well you know there's no possibility of that now. We'll sink or swim together with the men," Frank said. "And if this stoppage goes on long we'll be sunk by the end of next week."

"Bloody nonsense," George said, consumed by his anger again. "We'll be nowt of the sort. They'll come crawling back to work as soon as they realise there'll be no wage packets if they don't. You'll see. It's all hot air, this sort of wild cat strike. Watson'll sort them out."

"I hope so," Frank said. "This looks like his car coming into the yard now. He must have got one of my messages after all."

But if the Earnshaws had hoped for reassuring news from the union's regional officer they were to be quickly disappointed.

"I was at the Infirmary," Watson said, breathing heavily from the climb up stone stairs to the top floor as soon as the usual pleasantries were over. "Had to turn my mobile off. I came as quick as I could."

"How's Iqbal?" Frank Earnshaw asked.

"Critical," Watson said, his voice flat and unemotional. "You think you've got problems now, Frank, but I tell you, if

Iqbal snuffs it there'll be all hell let loose. I should think the last thing on anyone's mind will be getting production here up and running again."

"The attack on Iqbal was nowt to do with us," Frank Earnshaw said angrily.

"That's not how the Asian lads see it," Watson said. "A fire bomb at t'union office and a vicious attack on their convenor just at the moment when you're trying to cut wages and possibly lay people off? Come off it, Frank. Who the hell d'you think they'll blame?"

"Well, they'll be wrong. We need the unions on side if we're to get any sort of restructuring plan through. I need bolshie workers and inexperienced convenors like I need a hole in the head. This is all part of some neo-Nazi campaign that's been going on a while now. Christ, some little lass had acid thrown at her in the street only the other day. They don't think we organised that an'all, do they? It's politics they want to blame, not us. You know as well as I do that the right wingers are planning to stand in the local elections. That's what all this is about: show the Pakis up as trouble-makers, get the police to crack a few heads, put them in their place and win a few votes up on Wuthering Heights."

"Nice try, Frank, but I don't reckon there's a man down there'll believe you," Jim Watson said, nodding at the tightly packed streets below the mill. "They know you've been pushing Mohammed Iqbal to deliver what he can't possibly deliver and now he's out of it they'll put two and two together and make a hundred and five – in petrol bombs, most like – and there's nowt I can do to make them think any different."

"Well, you're a great help. I must say," Frank said while George mumbled something incomprehensible as he lay back in his chair with his eyes half closed.

"Is your dad all right?" Watson asked. "I heard he weren't so good…"

"I'll run him home in a bit," Frank said dismissively. "He's no right to be out of his bed. So what do you propose to do about your members, then, Jim? They're out of order walking out without a ballot, you know that. I could take you to court, you know."

"And that'd cost you," Jim Watson said easily. "I'll read them t'riot act, though I'm not sure it'll do much more good today than it did last night when a lot of them were out on t'streets. But I'll give it a go. I'll call a meeting this afternoon if we can use t'yard."

"Use anything you want if you can get them back for tomorrow morning," Frank Earnshaw said. "If this goes on any longer it'll put all our plans for this place back to square one, or scupper them altogether. I don't think you realise quite what a knife-edge we're on here."

"Flaming nonsense," George Earnshaw said, half-opening his eyes.

"Aye, well, we'll see about that," Frank said. As father and son glared at each other there was a knock on the door and the young receptionist put her head round.

"There's Chief Inspector Thackeray to see you, sir," she said. All three men glanced at each other.

"He chooses his moments," Frank Earnshaw said at last. "I suppose you'd better show him in. Let us know what goes off at the meeting, will you, Jim?"

The union official nodded and left the office as Michael Thackeray came in. If he was surprised to find George Earnshaw there as well as his son he disguised it well.

"Good morning, gentlemen," he said quietly. "I'm sorry to bother you when I know you've got other things on your mind but there's a couple of things I need to discuss with you."

"You've made some progress?" Frank Earnshaw asked quickly. "Have you found out who killed Simon?" Thackeray was conscious of the old man's eyes glittering from beneath half-closed lids.

"No, I'm afraid we haven't," he said. "There's still a lot of routine work to do before we even have a clear picture of who the likely suspects might be. But we have confirmed the identity of his elusive girlfriend. He's apparently had a fairly long-standing relationship with a young woman called Saira Khan. She's a fellow student at the university and, as I suggested might be the case last time I saw you, she's an Asian Muslim. Did either of you have any idea that Simon had an Asian girlfriend?"

George Earnshaw was wide awake now, leaning forward in his chair, his cheeks flushed, but it was his son who spoke first.

"We had no idea," Frank Earnshaw said.

"I don't believe it," his father added angrily.

"Would it have bothered you?" Thackeray asked, knowing the answer already but wanting to hear it confirmed by George Earnshaw in person. "Would that be why he didn't introduce her to the family?"

"As I told you, it'd not bother me. His mother and I take as we find," Frank Earnshaw said quickly, but he glanced sideways at his father as he spoke and Thackeray caught a glimpse of something more than anger in George Earnshaw's eyes, something closer to hatred.

"And you, Mr. Earnshaw?" Thackeray faced the old man squarely. "Would you have objected to a Muslim coming into the family? Was it on your account that Simon kept his relationship with Saira quiet?"

"How do I know?" George Earnshaw shot back with surprising venom for one so frail. "I've not seen him for years and I've certainly heard nowt about it from anyone else. But then anyone who knows me knows I don't like Pakis. It's no secret in this town. I'd not have given them the time of day in the mill if I hadn't been pushed into it by Frank so it doesn't take a degree in bloody detection to work out I'd not want them in the family. So I'd not expect Simon to tell me if he was carrying on with one of them, would I? What do her family make of it any road? They're not keen on mixed marriages, any more than I am. It's not a crime, is it? There's good reasons to stick to what you know in this world."

"The world's changing, Dad," Frank Earnshaw said, glancing at Thackeray as if to seek sympathy which he certainly didn't find in the policeman's chilly eyes.

"Do you have something specific against Muslims, or is it just a general dislike of immigrants?" Thackeray asked George.

"Saw too much of the beggars when I was in the RAF at the end of the war," Earnshaw said. "They should have stayed at home. They went to enough trouble to get their bloody independence."

"Then it looks as if Simon and Saira deliberately kept both families in the dark about their relationship," Thackeray said quietly.

"If there was a bloody relationship," the older Earnshaw put in, his face flushed again. "Who says there was? I don't believe Simon would get serious with any lass without telling the family – his mother and father at least, even if he wouldn't tell me. He was a good lad, was Simon, worth ten of that shiftless brother of his."

"Simon was always my father's favourite," Frank Earnshaw said. "Matt never got much of a look in there."

"So let me get this straight," Thackeray said. "None of the family knew about Saira? Simon hadn't told anyone and no one had seen them together and mentioned it to any of you? As you say, Mr. Earnshaw, the world is changing but not so fast that people who knew Simon might not comment if they saw him out with an Asian girl. You know as well as I do that we're not as liberal in Bradfield as they are in Leeds and London yet."

"We didn't know," Frank Earnshaw said flatly.

"If it happened at all," his father added. "Are you sure it's not just some little gold-digger looking for the main chance? He'd be a catch in the long run, would our Simon."

"I doubt it, Mr. Earnshaw," Thackeray said sharply. "Saira Khan is a very bright girl who was expected to get a good degree. But she hasn't been seen herself since Simon was killed. We're looking for her urgently."

Simon Earnshaw's father and grandfather looked at Thackeray silently for a moment.

"She killed him?" Frank asked eventually, his face grey. The old man merely leaned back in his chair, eyes closed and a single tear creeping down his cheek.

"I've absolutely no evidence for that," Thackeray said. "But obviously I need to speak to her. So if you know anything about what was going on I must know. And I'll be asking your wife and your other son the same question. Did they know about Saira Khan, and if so do they know where she is now?"

"You said there were a couple of things, Chief Inspector," Frank Earnshaw said irritably, as if trying to throw off whatever images of the missing girl had taken root in his mind. "We've a lot on our plates this morning as you can imagine. There's not a production worker on the premises. They've all walked out on unofficial strike."

"That was the other thing I wanted to raise," Thackeray said, his face grim. "It's pretty common knowledge that

Mohammed Iqbal is a bit of a thorn in your side. Have you any idea who might have assaulted him last night and put him on a life support machine?"

"You mean did we put someone up to it?" Frank Earnshaw snapped back, furious now. "We don't conduct business with baseball bats and iron bars, Mr. Thackeray. We're in negotiation with the union and I've no doubt we'll continue to be, although obviously not with Iqbal himself for a while. Considering our workers have walked out this morning it would've been a particularly stupid move to get ourselves involved in that sort of violence, wouldn't it? Any fool could see it would be self-defeating."

"Maybe someone thought they were doing you a favour?" Thackeray persisted. "Following on the fire-bomb attack on Iqbal's office, this looks as if it's anti-union as much as racist violence."

"I'd like to meet the idiot who thought they were helping Earnshaws," Frank Earnshaw said. "I think you're looking for racist thugs, Mr. Thackeray, and there's plenty of them about. But those aren't the circles we move in. I know nothing about the attack on Iqbal, or the union office, and I don't know anyone who might."

"Town's like a bloody tinder-box," George Earnshaw said unexpectedly. "Stands to reason someone'll get hurt. Bloody multi-racial society my backside."

"It's all right, Dad," Frank Earnshaw said. "I think Mr. Thackeray's on a fishing trip and that we can do without. If you've nothing else to ask us, Chief Inspector, I think we'd like to get on. We've enough problems here without you inventing any more for us."

Chapter Fourteen

It was halfway through the afternoon, when thoughts of home were distracting Laura from her computer screen, that she heard her name bawled raucously across the newsroom by Ted Grant. She glanced up and saw the editor peering out of his glass-walled lair at the far end of the open plan room, caught a few sympathetic glances from colleagues whose eyes quickly shifted back to their work, and got slightly wearily to her feet in response to the summons.

Grant closed the door ostentatiously behind her and then settled himself back in his black leather chair. He did not invite Laura to sit down. When did he ever, she thought to herself and she took a hard chair opposite the editor anyway.

"So what's your dad doing in Bradfield?" Grant asked, bristling.

"He's not. He's in London as far as I know," Laura said quickly, wondering if that were still true. It was quite possible that Jack Ackroyd had come back to Bradfield without telling her or his mother.

"But as I understand it, it's Bradfield he's interested in, isn't it?"

"I really don't know what he's up to," Laura said, putting all her not inconsiderable acting skills into looking innocent and slightly bored at the same time. "He's still got business interests in this country but he doesn't confide in me."

"Pull the other one, girl, it's got bells on it," Grant said. "Someone I know saw you having dinner with him in the Clarendon the other night. You and your grandma. Don't tell me he didn't let on what he was here for."

"He didn't, as it goes," Laura said. "We had a pleasant

family reunion, that was all. He went back to London the next day." She saw no reason to tell Grant any more than that, and certainly not the vague hints Jack had offered her on his discussions with Frank Earnshaw. The *Gazette* employed Bill Wrigley, an industrial specialist, whose job it was to ferret out this sort of information and Laura guessed it had possibly been Bill who had spotted her and her father at the Clarendon, which was one of his favourite haunts for chatting up his more prosperous contacts.

"Is he here to help Frank Earnshaw out?" Grant persisted. "Bill Wrigley says they go way back, those two."

"Well, you'd best get Bill to check it out, then," Laura said sweetly. "I told you. I don't know anything about his business affairs. I'd be the last person he'd confide in."

"What about your granny? Would she know?"

"You must be joking," Laura said with a genuine grin of relief as well as amusement. "She thinks my dad sold his soul to the devil years ago. Apparently she had dreams of him becoming a Labour MP in Harold Wilson's time. She's never forgiven him for going into business instead."

"Can you get him on the phone?" Grant asked. "See if you can find out anything about contacts with Earnshaws and a bloke called Firoz Kamal. Rumour has it they're in some sort of rescue package together but the murder may have put the kibosh on the whole thing."

"Who's Firoz Kamal?" Laura asked, playing for time.

"He's another millionaire who specialises in buying up property and redeveloping it into leisure centres and shopping malls and the rest of it. This could be the biggest financial story Bradfield's seen for years if what Bill's heard is true. Now come on, girl, don't piss me about. Get your finger out and use the contacts you've been blessed with. Do you know where your father's staying in London?"

189

"He left me a number," Laura said reluctantly. "But I've no idea whether he's still there or not."

"Try him," Grant instructed, his bulging eyes cold. "We want this story."

Laura shrugged, feeling trapped.

"Try him," Grant repeated. "He's much more likely to talk to you than to Bill. Stands to reason."

"I'll give it a try," she said. "But don't be surprised if I get a flea in my ear."

She walked slowly back to her desk, dug in her bag and found the London number Jack had given her the last time she had spoken to him. By the time she had dialled she was conscious of Ted Grant standing behind her, a looming presence, his heavy breathing lifting the hair on the back of her neck, listening to every word she said. But when the hotel in Mayfair responded it was only to tell her that Mr. Ackroyd had checked out the day before and had left no address apart from that of his home near Lisbon. She spun round in her chair to relay this to Grant who scowled.

"Hasn't he got a mobile?"

"He doesn't use one in Portugal," she said. "And if he's rented one for this trip he hasn't given me the number."

"Bugger," Grant said. "I suppose we'll have to wait until he gets in touch with you then."

"He's quite capable of flying home without telling me," Laura said truthfully. "He didn't tell me he was coming over till he got to Heathrow. It's not as if we're close."

"Find out what you can," Grant said. "I'll get Bill to dig around the Kamal lead. You can see who comes up with summat usable first." Grant was a devoted practitioner of the fear and loathing school of management and saw nothing wrong with setting one of his staff against the other.

Laura sighed as Grant stalked back to his office and

slammed the door. After a decent interval she made her way to the women's cloakroom and made sure that there was no one in any of the cubicles before using her mobile to contact the Clarendon hotel where she was not entirely surprised to discover that her father had checked back in the previous evening.

"Dad," she said when she was connected to his room. "You're getting me into all sorts of difficulties here. The industrial man has discovered you're involved with Earnshaws in some way and he'll be snooping around again as soon as he finds out you're back in Bradfield. You promised me this story. What exactly is going on?"

"Nowt," Jack Ackroyd snapped, at the other end of the phone. "It's all set up on our side but bloody Frank Earnshaw still doesn't know whether he has the shares he needs to go ahead. This murder's buggered the whole thing up because the lad Simon's shares seem to be floating around in limbo. No one knows whether he's left a will, where it is or who the beneficiaries are. It's possible he's left his property to some-one outside the family entirely."

"His girlfriend maybe," Laura said thoughtfully.

"Did he have one?" her father snapped.

"Oh yes, he had one. But no one knows where she is," Laura lied, wondering whether by now Amina Khan had told the police at least roughly where to look for her sister.

"Will you let me know if anything develops?" she asked her father.

"I told you. You'll be the first to know," Jack said. "But it could muck everything up if word gets out now. Can't you get Ted Grant to hold his horses?"

"Fat chance, so watch out for Bill Wrigley," Laura said. "And make sure any colleagues you've got called Kamal are careful too. It's a name that's being bandied about."

She heard her father draw a sharp breath at the other end of the line but at that moment one of her colleagues flung the door of the cloakroom open and went rather quickly into one of the cubicles where she was unable to stifle her sobs completely.

"I've got to go," Laura said quickly and cut the connection. Ted Grant, she thought, seemed to be having a vintage morning tormenting his female staff.

Mohammed Sharif hesitated outside Superintendent Longley's door and took a deep breath. Summonses from superintendents to lowly detective constables were rare and he suspected that nothing but trouble lay behind the panelled wood. He knocked and responded to the muffled summons to find both Longley and DCI Thackeray bent over the conference table with a number of maps spread out in front of them.

"Come in, Omàr," Longley said with what Sharif interpreted as a moderately friendly if harassed expression. "We need the benefit of a bit of inside knowledge here." Thackeray moved slightly to make space for the slim young DC at the table and he slid into the space between the tall, burly DCI and the short fat superintendent to get a view of their map of Bradfield, where a crooked line had been drawn in red marker pen across the town centre between the Heights and Aysgarth Lane.

"The British Patriotic Party have helpfully decided they want to stage a march next weekend," Thackeray explained. "Part of their build-up for the local elections, they claim. We wondered what you thought the reaction would be on the Asian side of town?"

"Depends how close to Aysgarth Lane they want to come," Sharif said, his voice as unemotional as he could make it.

"Oh, right down the length of Aysgarth – naturally," Longley said. "There'd be no bloody point in it from their point of view if they didn't, would there? They seem to regard it as their own personal Garvaghy Road."

"Well, if you want a few more business premises burnt down, let them march," Sharif said, not bothering to disguise his anger now. "The community's seething as it is, what with the attacks on the little Malik girl and now Mohammed Iqbal in hospital half-dead. A gang of racists marching past the end of their streets is just what you need to set a match to the place again."

"We have the option of banning it," Thackeray said. "They've applied for permission late, in any case, so we can get them on a technicality. Or so the lawyers at County claim."

"Then ban it," Sharif said. "You'll get nowt but trouble if you don't."

"Then we'll get complaints about tolerating no-go areas," Longley said, resuming his normal place behind his desk. "I don't want that."

"It is a no-go area at the moment," Sharif said. "And it'll get worse if this strike carries on. Even I'm keeping my head down up there and uniformed are still going around in vans. They cracked too many heads the other night for comfort. You'd better believe it."

Longley glanced at Thackeray and grunted in frustration.

"I'll talk to Brian Butler again and to County about banning the BPP," he said reluctantly. "It's Brian's officers who'll bear the brunt of any trouble, but personally I think Omar's right. It's too big a risk. We'd need a bloody army to keep the two sides apart. It'd be like Belfast at the height of the troubles."

"You'll get a furious reaction from Ricky Pickles and his

mates," Thackeray said. "But I agree. It's too risky to let them loose on Aysgarth Lane. You could suggest they parade around the other side of town, but that's not what they want, is it? Far too tame."

"I need to talk to you about Pickles, sir," Sharif said to Thackeray.

"I'll see you in my office in fifteen minutes," Thackeray said. "And ask Kevin Mower to be there as well, will you?"

"We're going for a ban on the march," Thackeray told Sharif and Mower fifteen minutes later when he returned to find both younger men standing waiting for him outside his office door.

"Good," Sharif said. He and Mower followed Thackeray in.

"Right," the DCI said. "We can't go on like this. Let's look at progress to see if we can help calm things down a bit in Aysgarth Lane. Kevin, any developments with the Malik girl?"

"Not a lot, guv," Mower said. "House-to-house inquiries have turned up one witness prepared to say she saw the boys running away and she's sure they weren't Asian, which isn't much of a surprise. She says their hoods had slipped back a bit as they ran past her, but apart from revealing a bit of white skin she couldn't see their faces properly even then. But she's given us some details of clothes, height, that sort of thing."

"There's a lot of white youths hang around the BPP offices," Sharif said. "I think they've had some sort of recruiting drive amongst unemployed teenagers up on the Heights. I'd put money on the attackers coming from there."

"I'll see what the word is on the street up there," Mower said. "We may pick up a whisper from informants in the Grenadier."

"And Mohammed Iqbal? What's the latest from the Infirmary?"

"Still critical, guv," Mower said. "Still unconscious. I've got lads checking motorbikes registered in Bradfield and the surrounding area to see if that throws up anyone of interest. What information we've been able to glean – which isn't a lot with all the mayhem that's been going on up there – says that they were heavy bikes, dark coloured, probably black, with riders in full leathers. One lad who saw them on Aysgarth Lane says that one was a Kawasaki and one a Harley, and there can't be many of those about. So if they're local we may be able to pin them down."

"Someone at Ricky Pickles' place rides a big bike," Sharif said. "I've seen it parked at the back of the offices."

Thackeray's eyes brightened at that.

"That might just justify us paying him a visit and asking him who it belongs to and where the owner was when Iqbal was attacked," he said. "But if I know Pickles himself, he'll have a cast iron alibi in a tea-shop in Harrogate with his great-auntie at the relevant time. He's not a man to take risks when someone else can take them for him. You've not seen anyone riding the bike then?"

"No," Sharif admitted. "I can't be there all the time. But the bike's definitely been there once or twice when I've been there myself. I'll make sure I get the registration number next time I'm up there."

"Maybe we should step up the surveillance on Pickles, guv?" Mower suggested but Thackeray shook his head.

"I can't justify the overtime," he said. "Wait and see what the bike checks turn up, if anything. Now, next – and biggest – problem. Where are we with the Simon Earnshaw murder? I saw his father this morning and he's not a happy man. He and the grandfather were there and they claim they know nothing about Simon's relationship with Saira Khan. Kevin, I want you to catch up with Mrs Earnshaw and Matthew, and ask them the same question – urgently before the family's had time to close ranks. Did they know about Saira Khan? I think both of them may have been in closer contact with Simon than Frank and George imagine. I also want to find out whether Simon Earnshaw left a will and if so what's in it."

"Nothing like that turned up when we searched the flat," Mower said.

"There must be a family solicitor," Thackeray said. "Track him down and ask him. And his bank. People sometimes store important documents with their banks."

"Right, guv," Mower said.

"Now, Omar, have you unearthed anything about Saira we need to know."

Sharif hesitated for no more than a second although both his colleagues noticed the pause.

"According to one of my mates who's close to the mosque, Sayeed Khan was worried about his sister," he said. "Before she disappeared, I mean."

"Was he now? And do you think that worry might be about a white boyfriend?"

"Could have been. Or perhaps not as serious as a boyfriend – just getting too friendly with someone at uni. Something like that."

"And how did your friend know that?" Thackeray pressed.

"He knew Sayeed had been talking to the imam," Sharif said, with obvious reluctance.

"About what?"

"About talking to Saira and persuading her it wasn't a good idea," Sharif said.

196

"So we need another chat with Sayeed Khan," Thackeray said, glancing at Mower again. He turned back to Sharif.

"Do you think there's any possibility that the Khan family have sent anyone looking for Saira? Could she be in danger from her own family?"

Sharif shook his head uncomfortably.

"I've not heard anything like that," he said. "The Khans are highly respected in the community but regarded as fairly liberal. Everyone seems surprised she's gone missing."

"Could you find out who might be looking for her, if anyone was?" Mower asked. Sharif shrugged.

"Not one name?" Mower persisted.

"I know what you're suggesting, and I don't know the answer, any more than you do. And after what happened last night it's getting harder and harder to ask anyone up Aysgarth anything at all if you're a copper, even if your skin is the right colour."

"Right, well, we'll have to ask Sayeed Khan himself to tell us a bit more about what he thought his sister was up to. You can go with Kevin to check that out later," Thackeray said.

"And Ricky Pickles?" Sharif said, his face tense.

"Leave Pickles for the moment until we've talked to him again," Thackeray said, dismissing Sharif with a nod. When the young DC had left, Thackeray glanced at Mower.

"Do you believe him?" he said. "About people who might hunt Saira down for the Khans, I mean?"

"Not really," Mower said. "I think that information is something the Asian community doesn't want to talk about to us or anyone else. And in this case the community includes Omar. When things have calmed down a bit I'll go up to the mosque myself and see what I can dig up."

"I think that would be a good idea," Thackeray said.

Michael Thackeray finished work late that evening and stepped from police HQ into a drizzle which drifted down from the hills to the west and brushed chilly wet fingers against eyes and ears and down the back of his neck as he hurried across the car-park. He had already told Laura that he would be even later home than usual that evening, although he had not volunteered a reason. He did not really want to admit to himself that he was at last about to make a visit which he had been putting off for weeks, ever since he had finally decided to go ahead with a divorce.

He drove slowly out of town, up the steep road towards Lancashire, a quiet route ever since the opening of the motorway to Manchester, and then turnèd down a country lane which was as familiar to him as the lane to his parents' farm had once been. But this was a road which promised no happy memories of a solitary but contented boyhood spent running wild over the moorland he still loved. The lane to Long Moor was shadowed not just by overhanging trees and the drifting rain but by a pervading sense of guilt, which he had begun to hope had left him as he inched towards an acceptance that Laura's presence in his life might become permanent. But he could not break free of years of depression here it seemed, as he took the bends marginally too fast and had to brake hard to avoid an on-coming van whose headlights dazzled him through the wet windscreen. Heart thumping, he slowed down, content to put off the object of his journey for as long as possible the nearer he got to it.

Long Moor Hospital was ablaze with lights as he pulled up in the visitors' car-park. It was several months since he had been to see his wife and although he knew that the passage of time meant little to someone who seldom seemed to even recognise him when he did visit, that did not lessen his own sense of obligation to the wreck of the woman he had once loved. Sins of omission, he thought grimly as he made his way to the ward where Aileen had been confined for more than twelve years. Well, there had been plenty of those over the years, as well as the sins of commission which had wrecked his marriage in the first place and destroyed his son as well as his wife. The priests knew how to achieve what they set out to achieve, he thought bitterly. Once in their web there was no escape, even after all this time. The mind might make a break for it, a lunge for freedom, but the threads were still ravelled around the heart, the memory, and the dreams that came in the darkest watches of the night. They might translate it into English, damp down the fires of hell, create cuddly confessors to replace the oppressive martinets of so many Catholic childhoods, but the ingrained guilt survived. It would go with him to his grave.

"Mr. Thackeray, nice to see you," said the middle-aged woman seated at the nurses' station at the entrance to the ward who buzzed open the locked door for him. "You're late tonight. I think your wife may already be asleep."

"How is she?" Thackeray asked, his voice curt with suppressed tension. The nurse gazed up at him with mild, sympathetic eyes.

"There's never much change, is there, dear?" she said. "But I know that the doctor's a bit concerned about her physical health. Did he not contact you?"

Thackeray shook his head dully.

"Well, you know you really need to talk to him, but I know he's been worried about her heart."

"Her heart?"

"Well, it's not surprising really is it? All these years of hospital food and no exercise. She's put on a lot of weight. Even when she's at her best it's very hard to persuade her to leave her room…"

"And she's not often at her best?"

The nurse looked at Thackeray with an expression which made him cringe inside.

"It never gets any easier, does it, dear?" she said, getting to her feet. "Let's see if she's awake, shall we?"

Aileen was not awake, but Thackeray sank into the chair beside her bed anyway, gazing at the bloated figure under the duvet with a mixture of shame and despair. He thought, as he always thought, that not even a vicious pagan deity could have been as cruel as the allegedly kindly One who had allowed Aileen to survive the onslaught of pills she had inflicted on herself, leaving her with her physical self intact but her mind almost totally destroyed. She ate, she drank, she expelled waste products, she even, occasionally, smiled, but the eyes were blank, the will gone, and the only emotion left what appeared to be panic, as she curled in the corner of her bed against the wall, her eyes wide and terrified, and an occasional blind outburst of what looked like rage which threatened the safety of anyone within range of whirling arms and feet and scratching hands. However many times the doctors told him that these wild emotions were not real, that she could not in fact suffer as she appeared to suffer, he did not believe them. He had occasionally sat beside her when she had been subdued with sedatives and wished he had the moral courage to take a pillow and place it over the puffy remnants of a once-beautiful face, a face he had to his bitter shame more than once bloodied and bruised himself.

He had never told Laura any of this. She had been with him to see Aileen once, and found her mercifully, and as most usual, asleep. This evening, too, his wife lay unmoving, impassive, her eyes closed and her breathing regular, as if it would never cease. And yet he knew that one day it would, sooner perhaps rather than later if the doctors' fears for her heart were correct, and he wished for that day with every fibre of his being. Tonight would not be soon enough. It was time, for both of them, that this nightmare was finally over and Aileen laid to rest with her baby son.

Driving back out of the hospital gates half an hour later Thackeray hesitated, looking too long in both directions for traffic he knew was not there.

"God help me," he said, feeling another craving which he had not experienced recently sidle like a crab into his brain. Instead of turning back towards Bradfield, at this distance a mere orange glow in the dark night sky, he swung north and by creeping his way almost instinctively along a series of narrow unlit lanes he found himself within half an hour in Arnedale, where groups of youths and half-clothed girls patrolled the wide main street, staggering their way from pub to pub. He pulled up outside an off-licence which, with old-fashioned rectitude, wrapped his purchase in brown paper. He slung the bottle onto the passenger seat and set off again, this time taking the main road out of the small town and heading west again and then, on a narrow climbing lane, north into the high hills. At the end of the moorland road, which petered out into an unmetalled track beyond the village of High Clough, he pulled the car into a narrow opening blocked by a five-barred gate. He did not bother to pull any further into the farmyard, leaving the car with its boot protruding into the lane, confident that no traffic would be inconvenienced at this time of night.

This was terrain he knew instinctively. The surface of the farmyard underfoot, pitch-black beneath the overhanging hill, felt more overgrown than he remembered but that was only to be expected. And when he reached the back door –

the front only ever being used for weddings and funerals – it was as firm against his thrust as he had expected it to be. His father was a careful man and would not have left the house unsecured even though its only likely future, if he could be persuaded to put it on the market, would be to be gutted to make someone a chilly holiday home. Thackeray applied his shoulder to the door and thought after several assaults that it would defeat him. But eventually there was a sharp crack as the wood around the lock splintered, and after one more shove it swung open in front of him.

He tried the light switch but was not surprised when it failed to produce any effect. He pulled his cigarette lighter out of his pocket and the flickering flame briefly revealed a heart-stopping travesty of the family kitchen. Joe had evidently taken anything of use when he finally closed up the house, and what remained was grimed with several years of dust and bird-droppings. In one corner a crumpled heap of feathers indicated where an owl had starved to death. In another a mound of half demolished newspapers, shredded almost to powder, had made a family of rodents a fine nest.

There used to be candles, Thackeray thought, and to his surprise there were still candles tucked away in a drawer of the huge fitted dresser which dominated one side of the kitchen. Leaving one flickering on the windowsill he carried a second and walked slowly from room to room, tormented by visions of the past so real that he thought he could reach and touch his mother in the wheelchair in which she had spent the last years of her life, so conscious of the presence of one of the many dogs who had served his father that he could almost hear the animal panting behind him, and above all aware of his father's eyes, watching, judging, grieving, condemning in every room, on every stair, in every corner of the house.

Frantic, he flung himself into the one intact chair in what had been the parlour, unwrapped his bottle of whisky and cried out in pain. But instead of opening the bottle he eventually placed it on the floor in front of him and stared at it intently. When he had first begun to recover from his drinking, he had had a mentor whom he could call on at any time when the temptation to open a bottle or order a drink in a bar became too great. He had long ago passed beyond that stage, gained enough control to survive, ceased to need a liquid crutch to lean on. Or so he thought. But tonight he longed for the comfortable voice of his friend Geoff, long departed now for a new life in Australia and never replaced, to tell him just how unwise it would be to unscrew that bottle top.

He wanted Laura, too, here, in this bleak and dingy room, with a naked physical desire which hurt. But the very thought of Laura tormented him in other ways. He had desired Aileen too, and they had enjoyed a passionate physical relationship before they began to tear each other apart. Could he, he wondered now, his eyes fixed unblinkingly on the seductive gold of the spirit, have the one without the other? Or would he ultimately and inevitably destroy Laura too?

Holy Mary, Mother of God. The old familiar words sprang into his mind unbidden, along with an image of his mother as he had last seen her, barely conscious but with her rosary twined around her fingers in the huge white bed in his parents' room upstairs. But as tears began to run down his cheeks he knew that neither Mother nor Holy Mother would help him. This was a battle he had to win or lose alone. Convulsively he picked up his bottle and hurled it across the room, where it smashed into fragments and the spirit ran in glittering rivers through the dust and filled the air with sharp vapours as he cursed and swore against the unfairness of life.

And when his mind finally ran out of obscenities he buried his face in his hands and took a deep breath as he faced the inevitable, knowing that he had to carry on without any guarantees that he could succeed.

"I love you Laura," he told the dark shadows which surrounded him. "But I don't know if I can do marriage and children again."

Chapter Fifteen

It was a moot point whether Laura Ackroyd or Vicky Mendelson looked most distraught the next morning when Vicky opened the front door in a dressing gown and with a red-faced baby daughter in her arms.

"Your night looks as if it was as bad as mine," Laura said as she kissed Naomi's hot damp hair and brushed her lips against her mother's cheek.

"At least Naomi can't help having a cold," Vicky muttered as she led Laura into the kitchen where the wreckage of a family breakfast lay scattered across the table. "Can you hold her while I make coffee?" she asked, thrusting the grizzling child onto Laura's lap. "This is the down-side of family life. She kept us all awake most of the night. Thank God David had time to take the boys to school." Naomi for her part took one look at Laura and began to howl in full-throated protest.

"She sounds the way I feel," Laura said, putting the child onto her shoulder and trying to soothe her. She wondered just when the paracetamol she'd taken for her dull headache would kick in.

"Have you made contact with that bastard Michael yet?" Vicky asked. Laura had rung her at seven that morning, just as an extremely unwelcome alarm turned on the bedside radio. She had been close to tears as she explained that Michael Thackeray had failed to return home that night.

"Nope. He's still not answering his mobile. I've left text messages, voicemail, but nothing." She shrugged wearily.

"He couldn't have had an accident?"

"Someone would have let me know. He is a bloody policeman," Laura said angrily. "He said he'd be late home but there was no hint he'd be out all night. Kevin Mower says he doesn't know where he went after work and I'm sure I don't."

Vicky brought the cafetiere to the table and rinsed two mugs under the tap.

"What time does he usually get to his office?"

Laura glanced at her watch.

"About now," she said. "I'll try again in a minute but it's often difficult to get him at work."

"But at least if he's there you'll know he's OK," Vicky said.

"I suppose," Laura said, her voice dull and her eyes full of tears.

"Here, give me Naomi," Vicky said, taking her daughter from Laura. The child buried her head in her mother's neck which muffled her sobs although it did not calm them. Vicky sat down and filled mugs with coffee and shoved a milk bottle across the table towards Laura. "Do you think this has got anything to do with the divorce?"

"Probably. I think perhaps he went to see his father last night, or maybe his wife. Kevin said he seemed edgy all day yesterday so maybe that was why. I know he's worried about how his family will react. Which is crazy after all this time."

"Once a Catholic…" Vicky said.

"Tell me about it. Do you think I'm going over the top, Vicky?"

"No, I don't. I'd be furious if David sloped off for a night without telling me." She bit back what she was about to say next but Laura could supply the script without even thinking about it.

"But David wouldn't, would he?"

"I don't think so. We got all the religious stuff out of the way before the wedding and his parents have been wonderful ever since, even though the kids technically aren't Jewish

206

at all," Vicky said, attempting to spoon cereal into her daughter's mouth without much success. She wiped the mess off Naomi's chin and sighed. "Men," she said.

"No, not men in general, just this man in particular," Laura said. "He's impossible."

"You don't mean that," Vicky said. "I've seen you together."

"It's been going on too long, Vicky," Laura said quietly. "I thought that at last he was going to commit himself, but now I don't know. Where did he go last night? What happened? Why couldn't he call?"

"Maybe he was in a dead spot for the mobile," Vicky said. "It happens."

"Then why didn't he drive out of the dead spot?" Laura was clearly not to be placated. She glanced at her watch again. "I've got to work," she said wearily. "Though my brain feels like cotton wool."

"Join the club," Vicky said without too much sympathy. "I'd almost forgotten what it's like to have a broken night like that, Naomi was such a good baby. Can't you take a sickie?"

"Not really. I'm already in Ted Grant's bad books because I can't tell him what my father's up to in Bradfield."

"And what is he up to?" Vicky asked, her curiosity stirred by that unexpected remark.

"I think he's trying to rescue Earnshaws mill. But knowing my father it's just as likely he's trying to buy them out before turning the place into a call-centre or a supermarket."

"Just what Bradfield's crying out for, more dead-end jobs," Vicky said. "So you're going to work then?"

Laura nodded and drained her coffee.

"I must. I promised I'd go up to my grandmother's. She says she's got someone she wants me to meet with something interesting to discuss about Earnshaws, so I'm hoping that'll get me some Brownie points with Ted. My father's refusing point blank to say anything at all to me or anyone else."

"Let me know what happens with Michael. I still feel responsible, you know, seeing as we introduced you."

Laura smiled faintly.

"I think if we're in a mess it's of our own making," she said. "I've let him get away with it for too long. I think it's make or break this time. We have to resolve it."

Half an hour later Laura pulled up outside her grandmother's tiny bungalow in the shadow of the Wuthering tower blocks. She parked behind a dark blue Rover and realised that Joyce's visitor must already have arrived. Battling against a knife-edged wind from the Pennines, she found Joyce's door ajar and a burly, bull-necked middle-aged man sitting close to the gas fire opposite Joyce herself and making the living room seem even smaller and more claustrophobic than usual.

"This is Jim Watson, regional organiser for the textile workers union and an old friend," Joyce said, trying with difficulty to get up from her own chair until Laura waved her back. Watson offered his hand and crushed hers in a over-firm grip.

"A chip off the old block, are you, Laura?"

Laura shrugged as she picked up the teapot from the coffee table and poured herself a cup. She would soon be awash, she thought, and the headache showed no signs of improvement.

"I'm not sure about that," she said. "I keep an open mind in my job."

"That's what reporters call it, is it?" Watson's eyes were not friendly and Laura did not warm to him.

"My grandmother tells me you've got a story you think the *Gazette* might be interested in," she said.

"I'm damn sure you will," Watson said. "It'll be the biggest thing to hit Bradfield for a generation if it goes ahead. Right? In outline, what we've got is a financial consortium ready to buy out the Earnshaw family and redevelop the mill. What they've got in mind seems to be luxury apartments, a built-in health club with swimming pool, squash courts, secure parking, a few luxury shops, the bloody lot. They've been down south to some development in an old mill in Oxfordshire and are basing it on that, right down to t'lift-shaft running up the effing mill chimney. Can you believe it?"

"So the end of Earnshaws then, as a textile mill?" Laura asked.

"Oh, aye, there'll be nowt in this for the folk who live around Aysgarth – no jobs, no housing, no amenities. And that'll be the end of what used to be the biggest mill in town. Yuppified to destruction."

"It's a disgrace, Laura," Joyce said, her face creased with anxiety. "It'll cause nothing but trouble."

"Can they get planning permission?" Laura asked.

"If the consortium's bought the place up what's the alternative for the planning committee? Let the place rot? They can't force anyone to run a business there, can they?" Watson said. "We'll be fighting it, of course, on behalf of our members. Which is why we want the whole scheme out in the open as soon as. But I have to say I'm not bloody optimistic. We've not saved a textile mill yet, any more than old Arthur Scargill ever saved a coal mine, not when they've claimed they're broke. In the end the jobs go, and that's that."

"D'you think there's a connection between this and the attacks on your colleague and the office?" Laura asked anxiously. "Are you in touch with the police on this?"

"Word is the neo-Nazis are behind that, as far as I know," Watson said. "I've not got a lot of time for bosses but I'd be surprised to find one into that sort of aggro."

"So do you know who's behind the redevelopment scheme?" Laura asked carefully.

"A man called Firoz Kamal, apparently," Watson said. "Based in London but he's got connections here and he's been involved in similar developments up and down t'country. Made a packet out of property. Ironic really when you think how many of his own kind he'll be putting out of work in Aysgarth."

"Can you substantiate all this?" Laura asked, ignoring the racist tone of the last remark. "We can't use it if it's just a rumour. We need something concrete to go on."

"Colleague o'mine got it from someone in t'City of London," Watson said. "Someone's drumming up investment cash for the redevelopment before the agreement's even signed, apparently. I've no reason to doubt it, given how slippery Frank Earnshaw's been lately. I doubt the old boy's in on it, though. Reckon he'll do his nut just as much as the workforce will when they find out. I'll put you in touch with our source any road, and you can take it from there. This is what we know so far." He got to his feet and handed Laura a file of papers.

"Right," Laura said. "I'll see what I can confirm. I'll be in touch if I get to the stage of writing something. OK?"

"Anything I can do to help," Watson said benevolently, heading for the door. "Quotes, owt like that, you've only to ask, love."

Laura sat for a moment looking at her grandmother, who looked grey with fatigue, her fingers picking aimlessly at the material of her skirt.

"So there you have it," Laura said, knowing exactly why

Joyce was so upset. "I already knew Dad had some link with this man Kamal. He must be in this scheme up to his neck. He'll be the one who's been drumming up support in the City."

"I don't know where I went wrong with that lad," Joyce said. "Of course he'll be in it. He's in for anything that'll line his pocket, is our Jack. And Frank Earnshaw's an old friend of his."

Laura flicked through Watson's file quickly.

"It says here that the consortium's had talks with all the family shareholders, though not who they've reached agreement with," she said. "But what puzzles me is how they thought they could persuade Simon Earnshaw to go along with something like this. As I understand it, he was some sort of environmentalist, went back to university to find out how to save the planet, that sort of thing. You'd think he'd have wanted something a bit more constructive done with the old mill."

Joyce ran a hand across her face wearily.

"I'm getting too old for all this, pet," she said.

"You look as if you need a holiday. Why don't you go back with Dad to Portugal when he goes. The change would do you good."

"And wrangle with him for a couple of weeks," Joyce said. "I don't think so, love. I'll have a holiday in this country when the weather gets a bit better." She cast a sharp eye over her granddaughter, taking in the untidy copper hair and the purple shadows under her eyes. "You don't look too bright yourself this morning, any road. Is everything all right with that man of yours? Not been quarrelling, have you?"

Laura smiled faintly at her grandmother's all-too-accurate perception, but she did not want to burden her with her own troubles.

"We're fine," she said shortly. "Work's a bit heavy at the moment, but it'll pass."

"But you said you were taking on extra work, this radio programme?

"Yes, well, that's still up in the air," Laura said, unable to disguise her annoyance. "I wanted to do something about the problems of young Asian women but apparently that's too controversial to tackle on local radio just now."

Joyce's eyes sparkled angrily.

"They'll all try to keep the lid on these problems until they blow up in their faces," she said. "They're all as bad: the council, the police, the media. Pretend it's all sweetness and light until we get trouble like we had the other night. If you've got one lot of young men furious because they're unemployed and discriminated against and another lot unemployed and blaming the first lot you're bound to get clashes. This so-called Labour party's just ignored poverty and frustration amongst young people and now they wonder why lads are throwing petrol bombs. The tragedy is they're throwing them at each other instead of at the folk who are really to blame in Westminster."

"Still the revolutionary, Nan," Laura said tiredly.

"Aye, well, leopards as old as me don't change their spots," Joyce said.

But Laura's mind was already elsewhere. Ted Grant would be pleased with the information she had gained from Jim Watson, she thought, but she knew that the police would be interested in it too, and that meant talking to Michael Thackeray urgently, something which she had so far signally failed to do for twenty-four hours. She guessed that she now had more than personal reasons for trying again.

As far as Ted Grant was concerned, Christmas had arrived

212

gratifyingly early and if it seemed a bit unusual to find Santa disguised as a red-headed and somewhat truculent reporter, he was not in a mood to argue. He leafed through the file that Jim Watson had given Laura with the expression of a very satisfied cat in front of a bowl licked very clean.

"Bloody luxury apartments," he said incredulously. "They'll never sell, mind. Folk in Bradfield've got more sense than those silly beggars in Leeds who think it's smart to live in drafty old warehouses tarted up with a bit of red paint. Any road, it's not a bad story. Brief Bill Bradley and tell him to get on to this fellow Kamal's company. If they won't confirm what's going on I'm sure he'll have some contacts who will. You'll need to talk to the Earnshaws an'all. You can take charge of that side of things. In the circumstances, with the grandson dead and all that, a woman's touch might go down well. Get out and see the old boy. He'll be sick as a parrot if this scheme goes through. You can bet your life he's not sold his shares to Mr. Kamal. You'll get some good quotes there."

Laura did as she was told and by lunchtime she was out of the office and free to pursue her inquiries with the Earnshaw family for the rest of the day. But as she sat in the *Gazette* reporters' favourite pub over a mineral water and a salad sandwich, she was only too aware that there were several things she had to do first. She had not told her editor that she was almost certain that her father was involved in Firoz Kamal's consortium. Nor had she so far managed to make contact with Jack, on her own or her editor's behalf, as her father had apparently left the Clarendon Hotel early that morning, according to the receptionist, and would not be back until late afternoon.

And behind all the urgency of working on what would undoubtedly become the front page story of the next day's paper, if the details could be confirmed, loomed the shadow of Michael Thackeray who had still not contacted her, and whose silence cut into her like a knife every time she allowed herself to think of him. But she knew she must contact the police in some shape or form. Finishing her sandwich she pulled out her mobile and called the central police station, only to discover from a harassed-sounding Sergeant Kevin Mower that the DCI was at county headquarters.

"Can I help?" Mower asked, not altogether enthusiastically.

"Come and have a quick drink," Laura said. "I'm in the Lamb." Mower had hesitated before agreeing and it was twenty minutes before he turned up, by which time the tension in Laura's stomach had increased by several notches. But when Mower's swarthy features appeared through the lunchtime crush around the bar, and he dumped a pint of lager, a vodka and tonic and a damp-looking baguette on the table in front of her, his smile had its usual warmth.

"You look as if you've lost a tenner and picked up a bent rouble," he said as he settled himself in his seat. "I got you your usual. Is that really water you're drinking?"

Laura grinned in spite of herself.

"I've got to drive this afternoon," she said.

"And who am I to ply you with alcohol?" Mower said. "You'll be OK on one. But why so glum? My sainted boss playing up?" The question was too close to home for Laura's quick shake of the head to carry much conviction, but Mower did not dare pursue it. There was a depth to Laura's obvious distress that he did not feel strong enough to probe. But if this relationship broke up, he feared for both sides of it. Laura sipped her vodka and tonic, squared her shoulders and seemed to snap out of her depression.

"Something's come up at the office this morning I thought CID ought to know about," she said quickly. "Well, two things really." She filled him in with what Jim Watson had told the *Gazette* about the secret plans for Earnshaws mill, not leaving out her conviction that her father was involved in the scheme. Mower's eyebrows shot up.

"Your dad didn't confide in you then?"

"He refused to tell me anything much. I don't think Michael's going to be too enchanted when he hears."

"You may be right," Mower said fervently. "It can only make a fraught situation worse. And what was the second thing?"

"Have you heard from Amina Khan, Saira's sister?" Laura asked cautiously.

"I don't think so," Mower said, equally carefully. "Should we have done?"

"I wanted to give her the chance to tell you herself, but she's had a letter from Saira. I don't think it'll be an enormous help, but it was postmarked Paris."

"Well, well," Mower said. "That's interesting. I don't suppose there was an address and a phone number, was there?"

Laura shook her head, smiling weakly.

"No, I didn't think so," Mower said.

"Do you think she killed Simon Earnshaw? It didn't sound like it in the letter. She said she was in love with someone and they wanted to marry. If that's the truth, she'll be devastated when she discovers he's dead. She obviously didn't know when she wrote to Amina."

"There's forensic evidence she was in Simon's flat. Fingerprints all over the place...And I never told you that," Mower said.

"Oh God," Laura said, looking stricken. "So he was definitely her boyfriend then?"

"I'll have to get back," Mower said, finishing his pint and not answering her question. "I'll have to follow up on all this sharpish. Shall I get the boss to call you when he gets back?"

"Yes, fine," Laura said, hoping that Mower would not notice any sign of the lurch her stomach gave at that innocuous remark. "Tell him I may be late home tonight."

In the event Laura fell out of Ted Grant's good books as swiftly as she had gained entry to them that morning because she completely failed to gain any useful information from any of the surviving Earnshaw men. Matthew, she discovered, was away in London, Frank refused point blank to speak to her on the telephone when it emerged that she had uncovered plans to redevelop the mill, and when in desperation she drove out to Broadley to try to interview old George Earnshaw, he slammed the front door in her face. Admitting all this slightly apologetically in Grant's office she was not surprised to see his face darken.

"You should still be out there on the bloody doorstep, not back here whinging," he exclaimed. "When I was your age I once doorstepped some dodgy trader for a day and a night without a break in pouring rain – and Annie Freeman – you won't remember her but she was a famous singer in her day – I was outside her fancy pad in Mayfair for three days looking for a quote when her boyfriend topped himself. You don't know what getting a story's all about, you youngsters."

"Well, if you give me a nice waterproof tent I'll go and camp out on the Earnshaws' front lawn," Laura said. "But I don't think it'll do you any good. They've closed up as tight as clams, and with all this violence going on with the union, I'm not surprised. Letting on they're definitely planning to close the place down will be like pouring petrol on the flames."

"Aye, well, we'll have to run with what we've got. Call it discussions instead of a plan, summat of that sort, if they won't confirm or deny. We've got more than enough evidence

216

for that. We'll lead with it on Monday. It's not the sort of thing we want to be bothering with on a Saturday with the big match on for United. We'll leave the sports lads the front page tomorrow."

"You're the editor," Laura said.

"Aye, and don't you forget it."

Chapter Sixteen

DC Mohammed Sharif, dressed in white shalwar kameez under his navy anorak, and with a lace cap clinging slightly precariously to his short cropped hair, stood outside the Aysgarth Lane mosque after Friday prayers watching the small groups of men wriggling their feet into their shoes and following him out. The Punjabi conversation was animated, and amongst more than one group, obviously angry. Sharif still regarded himself as very much part of this community and yet he was acutely aware that his job as well as his flat on the other side of town placed him apart. Some of the anger swirling around Aysgarth Lane – with its network of tightly packed Asian streets, and Pakistani butchers and groceries which served as meeting points for the many men who wanted to keep abreast of events – would be shared with a detective, but much of it would not. He watched a group of young bearded men gesticulating wildly a little further down the street. He could almost guess what they were saying, but if he went any closer he knew that the conversation would stop and wary glances would flicker in his direction from under hooded eyes. Two white men had been attacked on the Heights estate the previous night and Sharif guessed that there were youths here who knew who had wielded those baseball bats, even if they had not done so themselves. But an almost Sicilian *omerta* ruled. He would never be told. And if he would not, then the chances of any white police officer infiltrating the gangs, criminal or religious, which had sprung up within the community recently, were minimal.

What he was hoping to glean from his unaccustomed observances at the mosque that morning was the latest gossip about the murderous attack on the union official, Mohammed Iqbal, who was still lying in a coma in the Infirmary. Nothing so far had linked the assault to Ricky Pickles and his racist friends in the British Patriotic Party, even though Sharif had now established, to his mind much too late in the day, that the motorbike frequently parked at the back of the BPP offices belonged to Pickles himself. But no hint of a recognisable registration number had emerged from witnesses to the attack on Iqbal by the heavily leathered bike-riders, and Pickles had provided what looked like a solid alibi at the relevant time, not with an auntie in Harrogate but at a garage on the other side of town, just as DCI Thackeray had predicted he would. Sharif's schedule for the day included an unauthorised and surreptitious snoop around that garage too.

But before he could insinuate himself casually into the group of men he knew were union associates of Iqbal's, he felt a hand on his shoulder.

"We don't often see you here for prayers," Sayeed Khan said softly. "Perhaps you're like me? Living away but felt a bit of solidarity was called for?"

"I'm still trying to get a lead on the pigs who almost killed Mohammed Iqbal," Sharif told the solicitor with a shrug.

"No progress there then?"

Sharif shook his head.

"Nor with the kids who attacked the Malik girl," he said. "If this goes on we're going to have to persuade people to be more watchful up here. You'd think someone would have got a number from one of the bikes."

"Most of the time people feel safe enough," Khan said. "That's why they live here and are so reluctant to move out. I know what it's like. We were the first Muslim family to move into suburban Eckersley. People didn't like it. You feel exposed if you're on your own, in the street, at school – praying instead of drinking, being different in ways which irritate people, making them feel it's a reflection on their morals and way of life."

"Tell me about it," said Sharif who knew all about exposure in a largely white organisation, but Khan shook his head angrily.

"But it won't do, will it, in the long run? We have to get closer. We can't go on living parallel lives. And there's no sense in clinging onto the security blanket of Muslim areas if people aren't even aware enough to notice when they're being attacked. Rather defeats the object, don't you think?"

"I don't live up here any more either," Sharif said. "But to be fair, the bikers and the muggers seem to have been well covered up. They're not stupid, whoever they are."

"Oh no, they're not stupid," Khan agreed. "And what worries me is how well-funded they seem to be. I wouldn't be surprised if Ricky Pickles doesn't get onto the council in the next elections. He's making a big thing about his publicity, getting quoted in the *Gazette*, sounding reasonable though I shouldn't think for a moment he's changed his spots."

"We'll have to make sure we lock him up first," Sharif said, only half joking.

Khan glanced around at the lingering worshippers and drew Sharif away slightly so that they could not be overheard.

"There's one thing you can do for me," he said. "We've still heard nothing from Saira. Have you made any progress in tracing her?"

Sharif shrugged.

"You know I can't tell you about on-going investigations…"

"This is my sister we're talking about," Sayeed Khan

whispered angrily. "There is talk in the community. My family is frantic with worry. My father's threatening to use informal channels to try to find her and you know what that means. I don't want that. It's very dangerous for Saira. I really need to know what's going on."

"DCI Thackeray…"

"…will tell me nothing," Khan interrupted again sharply. "But you could. You owe the community that at least."

"From what I hear there'll be no love lost between Saira and the rest of the community now," Sharif objected. "The further away from Aysgarth she's gone the safer she'll be, I reckon."

"And you think that's right? A young unmarried woman?"

"You know the law, Mr. Khan. She's a free agent. She can do what she chooses to do, and nothing you or I might think about her morals has any bearing on anything."

Khan's face darkened in anger but Sharif stood his ground, aware of other eyes watching the exchange between him and the solicitor. Suddenly Khan seemed to come to some conclusion.

"It might be different, if I could tell you something of interest in return, perhaps?"

"Like what?" Sharif asked cautiously.

"Like give you a lead to Iqbal's attackers."

"And how could you do that?" Sharif asked. "And why wouldn't you come forward with that information anyway. As a lawyer?"

"Because I heard it in confidence, as a lawyer," Khan said so quietly that Sharif could hardly hear him. "I was duty solicitor the other night, and picked up a client who really didn't want a 'Paki' brief but he had to put up with it or do without. He let something slip that might be relevant to your inquiries – and earn you some credit with Mr. Thackeray."

"OK," Sharif said. "It's a deal. Not that I can tell you much about Saira, because there's not much to tell that you don't know already. But we've confirmed that she was having a relationship with Simon Earnshaw."

"You're sure?"

"Her fingerprints are all over the flat. Her voice is on the answerphone. Her friends identified it. There's no doubt."

Khan groaned slightly at that.

"So where is she now?" he asked.

"We have no idea," Sharif said. "She's not been seen since his body was found. And according to our latest information we suspect she might have gone abroad."

"Abroad?" Sayeed Khan was evidently stunned by that. "Does that mean you think she killed this Earnshaw fellow? Is she a suspect? Are you going to Interpol and all that stuff to find her?"

"Let's just say that DCI Thackeray is very anxious to have her help us with our inquiries," Sharif said quite formally, aware that if he said much more he would almost certainly unleash a fury in the Muslim community that might be difficult to contain. The Khan family might be liberal in the way that they had educated their daughters but he could see from Sayeed's expression that there might well be limits to their tolerance.

"Don't let your father do anything stupid about Saira," he said.

"I don't know what you mean," Khan said.

"You're a lawyer. Leave it to the law," Sharif came back sharply. "You do know what I mean."

"I love my sister," Khan muttered. "But this…?" He was obviously stunned by what Sharif had told him.

"So what can you tell me about this client of yours?" Sharif changed the subject quickly. "What makes you think he might be involved in the attacks on the textile workers' union?"

"Talk to him yourselves," Khan said, his voice thick with emotion. "You took him in after a fight outside the Grenadier pub last evening. You know there was some trouble on the Heights last night. Not content with his fists, he'd hit someone with an iron bar. But what seemed to be bothering him more than anything when I spoke to him was that his motorbike had been damaged in the mayhem, and no one seemed to know what had happened to it. It was a large powerful Kawasaki. A coincidence maybe, but one you might like to investigate, Detective Constable. It wouldn't do your reputation any harm, would it, either up here with your brothers or down there with your boss?"

Sharif shivered and pulled his jacket tighter around himself. The line he walked had never seemed fainter and more difficult to follow. Khan turned away dismissively to join another group and Sharif glanced around for the Earnshaws workers he had been seeking but they seemed to have drifted away. Yet the gesticulating bearded youths were still there, and he noticed that one of them had a heavily bandaged hand. He walked over to them slowly and, as he expected, the conversation petered out and he was faced with a sullen silence and half-a-dozen pairs of deeply suspicious dark eyes. He greeted them in Punjabi.

"I hear some of our people went up to the Heights last night," he said conversationally. "It's not my job to track down people looking for a fight, though my uniformed friends might be trying to find out who they were. What I'm concentrating on is much more important and that's the people who come up here looking for much worse. People throwing acid at our children, people on motorbikes thrashing our brothers almost to death. You know the sort of people."

The silence continued though one of the young men spat in the gutter and Sharif thought the unfriendly eyes became just marginally less unfriendly. He was, he guessed, pressing the right buttons though not hard enough yet.

"One of the thugs who uses the Grenadier is complaining that his motorbike has been stolen," he said. "Pity that, because it just might be one of the bikes that came up here when Mohammed Iqbal was attacked. It might give us some forensic evidence…" He wondered if he imagined the faintest flicker of interest in one pair of eyes but still the young men said nothing.

"Iqbal is still in a coma," he said. "The doctors aren't hopeful he'll recover." He said no more, hoping his words would ease open a crack in the young men's hostility, but still no one spoke and the silence lengthened. Eventually he shrugged.

"We need something on the bikes. We need something on the men riding them. We need forensic evidence," he said. "This may turn into a murder inquiry and if it does I won't be asking for information nicely; my bosses will be up here demanding it. And so will everyone who lives up here and works at Earnshaws and is furious at what's happened to Iqbal. You may think you can deal with this yourselves, but you're wrong. So get in touch, why don't you, when you've anything to tell me. You know where to find me."

Sharif turned on his heel and walked quickly back to his car. When he glanced back as he unlocked the driver's door the group of young men had disappeared into the side streets leading up the hill to the mill.

"Stupid idiots," he said to himself in English. "Stupid, stupid idiots."

Kevin Mower was surprised at how curtly DCI Thackeray greeted the two men who were already sitting in the largest of the police headquarters' interview rooms that afternoon. He was very aware that Thackeray knew both of them well enough to offer more than the nod he gave Jack Ackroyd and his solicitor, who turned out to be Victor Mendelson, the doyen of legal practice in Bradfield and the father of one of Thackeray's closest friends. Both men were formally dressed in dark suits and silk ties, both responded only minimally to the DCI's greeting.

"Thank you for coming," Thackeray said as he let Mower and DC Val Ridley settle themselves on the other side of the table. "I think you probably know why I asked you to come in and the sort of questions I need answered to assist my inquiries into the murder of Simon Earnshaw. But I won't be staying myself while you talk."

Jack Ackroyd raised an eyebrow.

"Too close to home, lad?"

"Victor would have every reason to object," Thackeray said, and Mendelson nodded imperceptibly in agreement.

"There is such a thing as commercial confidentiality, you know," Ackroyd offered, aiming the remark at no one in particular but evidently very angry beneath the apparently urbane facade.

"I'm sure there is," Thackeray said. "But there's no confidentiality at all when a young man's lying dead and no one is willing to discuss what the motive behind his killing might be. That comes close to obstructing the police, Jack, and I'm sure you wouldn't want to be involved in anything like that." And with that he turned and left the four of them, closing the door very carefully behind him.

Sergeant Mower glanced down at the file he had opened on the table in front of him which contained little more than the list of questions which he and Thackeray had decided needed answering the night before. He drummed his fingers briefly on the papers before meeting Ackroyd's deeply suspicious blue eyes and offering him what he hoped was a disarming smile.

"Tell me about your relationship with Frank Earnshaw, sir," he said. "I'm told you and he go way back."

Ackroyd shrugged.

"Nothing secret about that, but there's not much to tell. In the early seventies when I was setting up in business on my own I rented accommodation at the mill from the Earnshaws. They were running at less than full capacity even then. There was a bit of a recession on and of course it got worse with the three day week and all that crap. Nearly finished me off before I'd barely got started, Ted Heath did. Any road, Frank and I got on well enough. Had the odd meal together, played a bit of golf, that sort of thing. Then when my business took off I moved into bigger premises and I saw less of Frank after that. We were both busy – him trying to survive, me expanding as fast as I could, both with young families – you know how it is? I was onto a winner in plastics at the time, he was in a dying industry even then. No contest. I suppose he resented it. Who wouldn't?"

"So the friendship lapsed?"

"You could say that, aye. It lapsed."

"And when exactly did your interest in Earnshaws' fortunes revive?"

"Six months ago. Summat like that. I've still got investments in this country and contacts in Bradfield. I got a call from a friend in the City who said he'd heard that Firoz Kamal, who's got connections in Yorkshire like I have, was looking to get hold of the Earnshaws site for redevelopment and might find my local knowledge useful. To cut a long story short, we cut a deal, the three of us, and we've been working on the Earnshaw family ever since. We need – or

226

needed, until Simon was killed – agreement with three of them for a buy-out."

"And did you get it?" Mower asked sharply.

"We thought we had up till a week or so ago. And then Simon began to get a bit iffy. Tried to push the price up. I was surprised, to be honest. My impression was that it was the other brother who might stick and try to up the ante. By all accounts he's up the creek financially, but he seemed to be going for the quick sale at any price last time I spoke to him. Seemed a bit desperate. Simon was the one who'd decided to play hard to get. Bloody annoying. I had to go running down to London to see our backers and tell them we weren't likely to get an agreement this week as I'd anticipated."

"But you still thought you could close the deal?"

"Oh, aye," Ackroyd said expansively. "I think we could have gone high enough to satisfy young Simon. But you don't want to give that impression too soon, do you, when you're having a bit of a haggle? Make them think they might not get owt at all, and then they generally come running back to settle, in my experience."

"So where exactly were you with the four Earnshaw directors when Simon died?" Mower pressed.

Jack took a moment before replying, turning to Victor Mendelson as if for reassurance but Mendelson merely nodded him on.

"Well, George was against a sale from the off – nowt surprising there. He's stuck in the 1930s is old George, so apart from a formal letter, which he never replied to, we wasted no time on him. Frank was keen on our ideas from the start and as I say Matthew seemed keen an'all, and began to press for a quick decision. Simon was the one who made difficulties all along, firstly because he wanted us to make guarantees about the use of the site that my backers weren't too keen on

227

– community use, the bloody environment, as if the environment up Aysgarth Lane has got anything worth preserving in it. All a load of cobblers but we humoured him, of course. Kept him sweet. And then, the last time I spoke to him he tried to push the price up, which shook me, to be honest, because of all three of them he was the one I thought was least anxious about the price."

"Did you meet him face-to-face?"

"No, I spoke to him on t'phone when I arrived in England, that's all, and I called Frank when I realised things were going pear-shaped. Frank said he'd get Matthew to talk to Simon and get him back on board but of course as it turned out, that never happened, did it? He were dead before owt was settled. Pity that."

"Mr. Frank Earnshaw doesn't seem at all sure whether or not Simon had made a will," Mower said thoughtfully. "Do you know what happens if he hasn't?"

Ackroyd glanced at his solicitor again and in the end it was Victor Mendelson who replied.

"Normally I would regard this information as confidential but Mr. Frank Earnshaw has asked me to be as helpful to the police inquiry as possible," he said. "If there's no will there's a clause in a family trust to ensure that the shares are divided equally between the surviving shareholders. So Frank, Matthew and old Mr. Earnshaw will each inherit a third of the holding."

"And Frank and Matthew can force the sale through?" Mower asked, his eyes suddenly sharper than before.

"Indeed," Mendelson said.

"Can I ask you, Mr. Mendelson, then, whether this was a piece of information which could have reached Mr. Ackroyd and his colleagues..."

"Absolutely not," Mendelson said sharply. "I wasn't aware

of the arrangement myself until yesterday when Frank Earnshaw told me. I'm not professionally involved with the company, or with any of the Earnshaws individually, but it so happened that Frank Earnshaw rang me, as I think he has rung a number of solicitors, to ask whether we were holding a will on behalf of Mr. Simon Earnshaw. We were not. And nor, as I understand it, have the family discovered anyone who is."

"I knew nowt about it," Jack Ackroyd said angrily. "If that's the way you're thinking, sergeant, you're on a hiding to nothing. This was a reputable business deal we were negotiating. If it fell through it fell through, no skin off my nose or my colleagues', for that matter. There's plenty more redevelopment opportunities on the cards. No one's dependent on Earnshaws mill falling into their hands, least of all me. If anyone's desperate enough to commit murder in this business you can draw your own conclusions about who it might be. But it's certainly no one on my side of the deal. You can be bloody certain of that."

Mower was very tempted to believe him, although he knew that DCI Thackeray would make no allowances for sentiment when considering Jack Ackroyd's statement. The reverse, in fact. Mower hoped for Thackeray's sake, and Laura Ackroyd's, that Jack was as squeaky clean as he professed to be.

Chapter Seventeen

Mohammed Iqbal was pronounced brain-dead at 5.42 that evening. The news was relayed to DCI Thackeray by the young uniformed constable who had been watching over the union man's fight for life alongside the attentive medics and distraught members of his family. Even before the life-sustaining tubes had been removed from his body, and the dead man had been wheeled to the mortuary in the basement of the Infirmary, news of his death was racing out around the town, raising emotions of very different kinds as it electrified almost everyone who had had contact with the determined young official.

At police HQ Thackeray and Longley, summoned by an urgent phone call from his early evening golf practice session, listened grim-faced as Chief Inspector Brian Butler outlined how he had deployed his uniformed forces around Aysgarth Lane in the hope of preventing any violent reaction to news of Iqbal's death.

"I've got more officers off sick after last night's bit of mayhem on the Heights," Butler complained. "At the moment all we've got is a crowd around the mosque, calm enough so far but you can't rely on that for long."

"You know we want words with the lad from Wuthering you've charged with GBH, don't you?" Thackeray said. "DC Sharif reckons that he could be one of the ones we want for the attack on Iqbal. What's his name?"

"Craig Porter. We could oppose bail," Butler offered. "Should be able to swing that in the circumstances. Their worships aren't going to want anyone with a history of violence let out into this atmosphere."

"That would be handy, now we're talking murder," Thackeray said.

"Coming up with summat useful, young Mohammed, is he?" Longley asked.

"Maybe," Thackeray said. "He's certainly trying hard."

"Aye, well, we're all going to have to try hard," Longley said. "The Asian community leaders are going to be clamouring for a result on this one and I've already had the ACC on the blower asking how this will affect the Earnshaw case. What am I supposed to tell him, for Christ's sake, Michael?"

"I'm interviewing Matthew Earnshaw formally tomorrow," Thackeray said quietly. "I think at last I've pinned down a motive for Simon Earnshaw's death, and I reckon, looking through his brother's first statement, that he had the opportunity as well. My rough scenario is that he did meet Simon, either the evening he says he was supposed to, or perhaps earlier, had a row over the redevelopment, which it turns out Simon was holding up, and killed him. With Simon dead, he and his father can go ahead with the scheme regardless of old George's wishes. I'll ask Matthew's permission to look at his mobile phone records tomorrow and if he refuses I'll be asking you for permission to check them out anyway. Simon's own mobile still hasn't turned up. It wasn't at his flat or on the body. I reckon he left it in his car, or someone left it there for him, so we're still relying on the car turning up somewhere. We need to know who he was talking to before he died. The phone at the flat's been no help. There's a pay-as-you-talk mobile coming up regularly so I guess that's Saira Khan's, but apart from that nothing. No calls from the rest of the family at all."

"The car's probably at the bottom of Gawstone reservoir," Longley said gloomily. "Or any one of a dozen others. It's not hard to lose a car up the Dales if you really want to."

"So why not dump the body in the reservoir as well?" Thackeray said. "It makes no sense. The only reason I can think of is that whoever killed him wanted it known that he was definitely dead, not just missing, and that would fit with it being a family member."

"Whoever dumped the body must have been convinced the death would be taken for an accident," Butler offered.

"And it very nearly was," Thackeray said. "He died of head injuries and head injuries consistent entirely with a fall from the crag are what we found. We're just lucky the old boy who found him admitted moving the body and Amos Atherton picked up on the implications – eventually."

"Not like Amos to make a mistake," Longley said. "Mind, he must be coming up to retirement, must Amos. He's a sight longer in the tooth than I am. I'll tell Peter Ellison that there's some progress being made, then, shall I? Though he'll be appalled if that's the direction you're heading in. It's not the sort of progress Frank Earnshaw's going to like much, is it, if you've got a Cain and Abel situation here?"

"I'd tell the ACC nothing," Thackeray objected. "I don't want any of this filtering back to Frank Earnshaw, or any other members of the family, for that matter."

Longley looked at him thoughtfully for a moment and then nodded.

"Happen you're right," he said. "I think I'll get back out onto the golf course for the weekend and inadvertently switch my mobile off. You two can send someone to find me if you really need me, but otherwise I'm incommunicado."

"Right," Thackeray said. Incommunicado was the way he had hoped to spend his own weekend, but there seemed little chance of that now. Agonising over his future with Laura would have to wait – and he was not at all sure that she was prepared to wait much longer.

* * *

Laura herself heard the news of Mohammed Iqbal's deathfrom her grandmother who had called her as she was eating a microwaved Thai meal in front of the television that evening and feeling distinctly sorry for herself.

"Are you sure?" she asked her grandmother somewhat tetchily. "It wasn't on the local TV news."

"I don't suppose it's got out to the media yet, love," Joyce said with a touch of satisfaction in her voice. "I still have some contacts, you know. He died at tea-time, apparently."

"They may be keeping it under wraps," Laura said. "There'll be trouble again up Aysgarth Lane when people find out."

"What sort of country are we living in?" Joyce asked. "It's getting like some banana republic, union officials being attacked and murdered, folk rioting every night. I hope your Michael is going to get the thumbscrews out for Frank Earnshaw over this. I wouldn't be at all surprised if he didn't set it up. Old George was always anti-union. They had to fight him every inch of the way to get decent pay and conditions when he was running that mill. I can remember standing on more than one picket line up there."

"I think this has more to do with racism than the Earnshaws' plans for the mill," Laura said, trying to keep the irritation out of her voice. As conspiracy theories went, she thought, this was one of Joyce's wilder examples. Industrialists might still have bloody talons, but on the whole they concealed them pretty effectively these days in the velvet gloves of legal sanctions and redundancy packages generous enough to persuade most sacked workers bought off with a few thousand pounds that they were being well treated. Street violence, she guessed, was unlikely to be

233

part of the Earnshaws' armoury, however keen they were to cut costs or close the mill.

After doing her best to reassure Joyce, who sounded almost as deeply depressed as she felt herself, Laura reluctantly called her father at the Clarendon Hotel. He had not heard the news and after Laura told him what had happened he lapsed into a long silence.

"Dad?" Laura said anxiously at last. "Are you still there?"

"Aye, I'm here," Jack Ackroyd said. "But I'm increasingly thinking I ought not to be. What sort of a redevelopment are we going to end up with if this carries on? No beggar's going to want to live anywhere near Aysgarth Lane, are they, let alone the young yuppies we had in mind. There'll soon be no one left in Bradfield wi'tuppence to rub together. They'll all have buggered off to Harrogate."

"I think maybe you got a bit carried away on this one, Dad," Laura said, trying hard not to add 'I told you so'.

"I should know better than to get involved with old acquaintances like Frank Earnshaw," Jack said. "I reckon we've been taken for a right ride here."

"Could well be," Laura said, unsympathetically.

"I really thought we had this one wrapped up, until bloody Simon Earnshaw started upping the ante. I don't know what got into him at the end. Any road, at least that meant that nothing was signed and sealed before these murders, so mebbe we'll slide out of it yet. I'll get onto my partners right away, love. I'll let you know if I'm checking out, though God alone knows when I'll be able to get a flight home. Can you tell your feller what's going off? He seems to be taking an altogether unnecessary interest in my affairs."

"Then you'd better tell him yourself," Laura said sharply, not wanting to go down that avenue. She hung up without waiting for a response and flung herself back onto the sofa, gazing unseeing at the latest make-over programme in which a young couple appeared to be staring in blank disbelief at their new bedroom apparently modelled on an illustration out of the *Arabian Nights*.

"Bloody fools," Laura muttered to herself, an all-embracing comment which encompassed her father and his colleagues, the credulous couple on TV, and herself and Thackeray, thoughts of whom still boiled at the back of her mind like a tropical storm about to break. She zapped fruitlessly between programmes, trying to find something which would take her mind off the decision she knew Thackeray would make over the weekend, wondering for the thousandth time whether he would in the end find it impossible to make the commitment he had promised. In that event, she thought, she would hand in her resignation to the *Gazette* on Monday and leave Bradfield for good as soon as she could. Her beloved Joyce could come with her, she thought, if she was still reluctant to take up Jack's offer of a home in the sun. What she could not face was a situation where she risked meeting Michael Thackeray again and again, as inevitably she would in a small town, after their affair was over. Her body still craved for him however sternly she told it not to, and she knew that meeting him casually with composure would be more than she could bear.

The curry was cold by now and she pushed it aside irritably. She still did not know whether Michael Thackeray would be coming home that night and as she sat watching television, trying to distract herself from the leaden lump of anxiety which threatened to overwhelm her, her mobile rang. She put the TV on mute.

"Michael," she said, as levelly as she could.

"I'm sorry," Thackeray said. "You can curse and swear if you like. I know you must want to."

"We have to talk," Laura said, although very tempted by his invitation.

"I know, but first I need some time to think."

"So you're still not coming home?"

"Not tonight. I'll go back to my place when I've finished here. But I'll be up to my eyes for hours yet. We banned the BPP march this morning, so there's a high risk there'll be trouble on the Heights tonight. Enough of them live up there to cause some serious aggro. And Mohammed Iqbal has died so I now have to launch another murder investigation."

Laura was tempted to cut the connection but after a long silence she succeeded in controlling her voice enough to speak again.

"We can't go on like this, Michael," she said.

"I know."

The silence lengthened again. It was Thackeray who broke it this time.

"There was another reason for calling," he said. "After what you told Kevin, we interviewed your father this afternoon. With his solicitor. He's been holding out on us, Laura. There are things he knows about the Earnshaws and their finances that I needed to know days ago. Not to put to fine a point on it, I'm not very happy with Jack."

"Amaze me," Laura said unsympathetically. "My grandmother's been unhappy with Jack for the last forty years or so, and I'm not too sure my mother's always over the moon with him. I've no doubt you found him as charming as a talkshow host and as slippery as an eel. I hope you didn't hesitate to give him a hard time on my account."

"You know I wouldn't do that," Thackeray said drily.

"Will I see you tomorrow then?" Laura asked.

"I'm going to be working all weekend," Thackeray said. "Give me till Monday? Please, Laura?"

"If I must," she said, breaking the connection with a sigh. She gazed at the silently performing newsreader who had appeared on the TV screen through a blur of tears. If this were really the end of the affair, people would imagine she had been outraged by Thackeray's interrogation of her father, she thought wryly, when in fact she was sure that anything the police dished out to Jack Ackroyd and his city cronies would be no more than they deserved. But no one, except perhaps Vicky, would come close to guessing that the cracks in the relationship had been widened by the still-powerful ghosts of children long dead. She had seldom thought about her own hasty termination when she was a student, a source of relief not guilt at the time, until Thackeray had revived the memory with his fierce opposition to such operations. But she recalled it sometimes now, with a faint but real regret for what might have been. I have a man I love to distraction, Laura thought miserably, and I want to give us both back the children we lost, but especially him, because his child was real, a warm presence in his life and he deserves that again. If only he would dare. By Monday, she thought, she would know the answer.

By ten Laura was dozing, still on the sofa, still with the TV flickering quietly in the corner of the room, with the lump of unresolved foreboding slowing her thoughts and reducing her body to inertia. The shrill of the phone startled her and set her heart thumping in hope that it was Thackeray again. Instead she heard a voice she only half recognised.

"Amina," she said stupidly. "What can I do for you? Have they found your sister?"

"I need you to help me," Amina Khan said, her voice husky and so low that Laura could hardly hear what she was saying.

"If I can," Laura prevaricated.

"Saira rang me. I persuaded her to meet me in Paris. But I want someone to come with me. She's not going to believe me if I tell her Simon Earnshaw is dead. She'll think it's a trick of my father's to get her back home. There are seats on the early flight to Paris in the morning from Manchester. We could be there by eleven, meet her, and be home the same day. Will you come with me? Please?"

Laura was fully awake now, heart beating fast, knowing she was being presented with a story to die for.

"I'd want to write about this, when the time's right," she said, hesitantly. She heard Amina draw a deep breath.

"Saira will never be able to come home," she said at last. "All this will wound my family, whatever happens…"

"Better for me to write about it with some sympathy than for the tabloids in London to get hold of it later," Laura said. "You know the police will find her in the end. It's inevitable."

"She hasn't told me where she's staying. Just where to meet her. If the police, or my brother or anyone else she doesn't want to talk to are visible she won't come near, she says. That's why I thought of you. She won't recognise you or, if we're careful, know you're with me. I can talk to her first and then introduce you. Then you can reassure her that what I'm telling her is true."

"But you'll have to tell the police later. Or I will."

"Maybe," Amina said, her voice faint. "But will you come?"

"Yes," Laura said. "I'll come. Book me a flight." The thought of telling Michael Thackeray in advance where she was going did not even cross her mind.

At midday the next day Laura and Amina Khan came up the steep steps from the Metro on the Left Bank of the Seine at St.

Michel in bright winter sunshine and a sharp wind which was whistling along the river from the east. They did not speak or look at each other. They had made their plans carefully and Laura took up a position close to the Metro entrance while Amina crossed the road onto the river embankment where the green-shuttered bookstalls were just beginning to open up and display their wares. She began to work her way along the stalls slowly, as if browsing, while Laura watched, glancing at her watch occasionally to give the impression that she was meeting someone. Surrounded as she was by swirling groups of students and tourists, heads down against the wind, she doubted that even the keenest-eyed observer would notice her.

Saira has asked Amina to meet her by the bookstalls on the Quai des St Augustins but had made it very clear that before she approached her sister she would watch to make quite sure she was alone. In her long coat and white hijab Amina was noticeable enough amongst the handful of browsers who had arrived almost before the book market came to life. Across the river on the Île de la Cité where the vast bulk of the Conciergerie and the Ste Chapelle loomed over the fast-flowing water, there was scant opportunity for anyone to watch the Quai. But on the Left Bank Laura casually scanned the buildings facing the busy road between the embankment and the river and wondered if Saira was watching from one of the small cafes or the flats rising four or five stories above them. Right up at rooftop level, she thought, there were probably still the little garret apartments occupied by artists and students, amongst the glittering slates and chimney pots. Perhaps Saira had found her French refuge in one of those bohemian eyries in this area of narrow streets and milling young people from dozens of nations where a young Asian woman would not be thought at all remarkable.

Wherever Saira had been concealing herself she took her time to emerge. Laura had turned up the collar of her jacket in an attempt to stop the wind from pinching her ears, and begun to stamp her feet and wish she had chosen practicality rather than an attempt at Parisian elegance in the form of a rose silk shirt and fine wool trouser suit, by the time she noticed that Amina, who had been standing reading at one of the stalls on the opposite side of the road, was no longer alone. In fact she was deep in animated conversation with a tall slim girl in jeans and a duffle coat whose long dark hair was tossing wildly in the wind. Laura took a sharp breath and began to think that perhaps her trip would prove fruitless as the two young women appeared to be arguing fiercely but eventually they turned and began to walk slowly back towards the Metro.

Saira Khan was beautiful, although there was anxiety in her eyes and dark circles beneath them when she acknowledged Laura with a cool curiosity which gave nothing of herself away. She pulled her hair inside her collar and shivered slightly, waiting suspiciously for her sister's next move. But Amina seemed frozen, unsure now that she had achieved half her objective of what to do next.

"Why did you come?" Saira asked Laura. "I asked her to come alone."

"Amina felt she needed a bit of moral support," Laura said. "Let me buy you both lunch," she offered, nodding in the direction of the Boulevard St. Michel and its cafes and bars. "It's too cold to talk out here."

The sisters followed her, both wary and unsmiling, and eventually settled at a table close to the window of a bar and ordered coffee and sandwiches. Saira merely picked at her baguette with long fingers which trembled so much that Laura began to wonder whether Amina had already broken the bad news that she had brought from Bradfield. But it seemed not, as the sisters spoke merely of their family, quietly and mainly in monosyllables until Saira tossed back her coffee and turned on Amina angrily.

"So why have you really come?" she asked. "You know I won't come back. We've made our plans."

Amina covered her mouth with her hand, as if to prevent herself from crying out, and her glance at Laura was so anguished that she felt compelled to take the initiative herself.

"I'm so sorry, Saira, " she said. "Amina really brought me with her to help her tell you some awful news. There's no easy way to say this, I'm afraid. Simon Earnshaw won't be coming to meet you. He's dead. He's been killed. And the police in Bradfield want to talk to you."

Saira flinched and leaned back in her chair as if Laura had struck her physically. Then she fastened dark, stunned eyes on her sister.

"Who did this?" she whispered. "Is this Sayeed and Father? How did they find out? How could they possibly find out? We were so careful, Simon and I. So quiet and so careful." It was interesting, Laura thought, that Saira never for a moment thought that Simon had died accidentally. She assumed far more quickly than the police had done that her lover had been murdered.

"The family didn't know about Simon. None of us had any idea. But of course the police found out," Amina said, her eyes as full of tears as her sister's. "And they think you did it."

"No," Laura said quickly. "I don't think that's true. But they do need to talk to you, Saira, as a witness. And they suspect you're in France so they'll no doubt ask the police to look for you. The best thing for you to do is to come back

241

with us and talk to them voluntarily. The longer you stay out of sight the more suspicious they're likely to get."

"You don't understand," Saira said contemptuously. "Amina knows I can't come back to Bradfield. Ever. We were going to live here in France, away from it all. I've been trying to contact Simon for days. I couldn't understand why his phone was switched off…" Her voice trailed away and she seemed to shrink in her seat as the full enormity of what had happened began to sink in. Around them the bar began to fill up with chattering, insouciant groups of young people as the Parisian lunch-hour got into full swing while Laura, sitting between the two stricken, silent young women, felt the full weight of the tragedy which had struck them, crushed as they were between the millstones of sudden death and cultural expectations which would not even recognise the relationship let alone the loss.

"I don't know what your plans were," Amina said hesitantly. "But I brought you some money. It's not a lot." She passed an envelope across the table, but Saira thrust it instantly back at her.

"Money's not a problem," she said. "Simon gave me money."

"I got the impression Simon was worried about money," Laura said cautiously. "He seemed to be trying to get a better deal as part of his father's plans for the mill."

"He was keen to buy a house in France, but he didn't discuss finance with me," Saira said. "There was no problem with money as far as he was concerned. He said his grandfather would look after him."

"His grandfather?" Laura began, surprised by that unexpected Earnshaw family revelation. "You really need to talk to the police about all this." But Saira shook her head furiously.

"No," she said. "I can't come back."

"You could come back to England, to London maybe, even if you don't come to Bradfield," Laura said. "It won't be much fun to be arrested and sent back by the French police."

Saira did not answer. She drew patterns on the table in spilt coffee until Amina stopped her, putting a hand over hers. But Saira pulled away impatiently.

"We were going to live in Provence," Saira said. "Simon had been offered a job in Montpellier, at the university there, with an ecology research programme. We were going to fly down and look for a house in the countryside. The climate sounded so marvellous, not like the cold and rain in Yorkshire. We were going to be happy there, where no one would know us or care that we weren't the same race or the same religion. No families to hassle us, his or mine. Then he got worried about something, something about his grandfather and the sale of the mill, so he suggested I come to Paris to wait for him. He wanted to finish the term and get his masters'… He needed that …"

"What about your degree?" Amina asked angrily. "Didn't that count for anything?"

"It did count, but not so much. When I can speak good French I can finish my education here. It was more important for Simon to finish, for the new job. I had what I wanted, Amina, can't you see that? I was happy and I had what I wanted. And now this!"

Laura felt tears sting her own eyes at Saira's distress but she felt that she must persuade the girl to think about her new situation for her own sake.

"Saira, Simon was murdered," she said quietly. "Perhaps because of you, perhaps not, but you must want the police to find out who did it. You must help them."

Tears were flowing freely down Saira's face now and she glanced at Laura without comprehension.

"What does it matter?" she asked, brushing her cheeks angrily with a paper napkin. "I have no future now."

"Of course you have," Laura said sharply, when Amina failed to respond to her sister's evident despair. "You're very young. You'll get over this, truly you will, and you'll be happy again. But the immediate problem is the police. Please come back with us. Please, Saira. You know it makes sense."

But Saira had got to her feet and Amina still sat with her head bowed, ignoring her sister's distress. Saira spoke quietly to Amina in Punjabi and then turned and left the bar without looking back.

"What did she say?" Laura asked, still furious at the older sister's passivity.

But Amina just shrugged.

"She said goodbye," she said. "I don't suppose I'll see her again."

"How can you say that?" Laura cried. "How can you accept that? Run after her quickly. You can't just let her disappear like that. You don't know what she might do."

"I can't help her," Amina said. "She's chosen a path my family will never accept. I might wish it were different, perhaps in another generation it will be different, but not now. I know that, she knew that when she got into a relationship with this man. She knew what she was doing and what the consequences might be. We all know."

"It's an unforgiving religion," Laura said, thinking of another creed in which she had identified similar tendencies. "I thought God was supposed to be merciful."

"That doesn't mean men always are," Amina said and Laura did not dare ask her if that was a gender-specific remark. She just gazed at Amina, silently appalled.

"You think your morality is any better?" Amina asked angrily. "Girls running around half-naked, drinking, prostitution, pornography – do you really think that is better for women?"

Laura could not find the heart to answer. She glanced through the window at the pavement crowds which had swallowed up Saira Khan as if she had never been.

"They'll find her, you know," she said. "The police will find her. She's only postponing the inevitable."

"I hope not," Amina said.

Chapter Eighteen

Matthew Earnshaw was apparently stone cold sober when he presented himself at police headquarters that Saturday morning for an interview with DCI Michael Thackeray. Dressed in jeans and open-necked black polo shirt, he appeared anxious to give the impression of being calm and relaxed, but there were dark circles beneath his brilliant blue eyes, and from time to time he ran his fingers through his hair, as if to brush lingering cobwebs from his brain.

"You don't want a solicitor with you?" Thackeray asked as he ushered Earnshaw into an interview room and Sergeant Kevin Mower dealt with the tape recorder.

"I've got nothing to hide," Earnshaw said, flinging himself into the interviewee's chair and lighting a cigarette. Thackeray noticed that his hands were shaking slightly and he drew the smoke into his lungs as if his life depended on the hit.

"You're entitled to change your mind at any time, Mr. Earnshaw," he said.

Earnshaw scowled and nodded.

"I'm fine," he said.

Thackeray sat down beside Mower and opened a file which contained little more that Matthew Earnshaw's first statement to the police.

"Are you broke, Mr. Earnshaw?" he asked, without preamble. The younger man tensed slightly and then gave a thin smile.

"What makes you ask that, Chief Inspector? And is it any of your business?"

"If I consider it's relevant to my investigation of your brother's death, then it's my business," Thackeray said.

"Then no, I'm not broke," Earnshaw said. "As you know I'm a major shareholder in Earnshaw and Son, which is still a going concern and has valuable property."

"Which we've now learned from Jack Ackroyd was on the market."

"You know about all that now, do you? Well, that wasn't something we wanted trumpeted about to all and sundry. As far as the outside world was concerned we were trying to save the mill not sell it. Anyway, as far as your question is concerned, when the sale goes through I'll have considerable liquid assets."

"But until the sale goes through?" Thackeray pressed.

"Little local difficulties," Earnshaw said. "Nothing I can't cope with."

"Such as?"

"I'm a bit pressed since the divorce settlement, that's all. Nothing I can't handle."

"You kept the house, didn't you?" Thackeray was obviously not going to give in.

"I bought Lizzie out, if that's what you mean. Cost me an arm and a leg, if you really want to know. So I've got a ball-breaking second mortgage."

"And expensive habits?" Thackeray pressed.

"I don't know what you mean," Earnshaw said.

"But you were very keen for the mill to be sold?"

"Yes, I was, I supported my father all the way on that," Earnshaw said. "It was my grandfather who stood out against it. Tried to persuade me to change my mind, but I told him to get stuffed, if you really want all the family dirt. Told him he'd had the best of the business and it had no future now, and I wanted my share before the whole thing went down the pan."

"You had a row with your grandfather?" Thackeray asked.

247

"Several," Earnshaw said.

"And what about your brother?"

"He kept out of the old man's way, as far as I know," Earnshaw said.

"No, you misunderstand me," Thackeray interrupted. "I meant did you row with your brother about the sale. As I understand it, he was never as keen as you were on the deal Jack Ackroyd and his colleagues were offering."

"No he wasn't," Earnshaw said. "There's no secret about that. First of all he wanted all sorts of clauses written in about benefit to the community – blasted hippie – and then he began to haggle about the price. I couldn't understand that. Money didn't seem to be the main issue with him at first."

"But it was always the main issue for you?"

"Bloody right it was, Chief Inspector. I make no apology for that."

"So when did Simon begin to worry about the price?" Thackeray asked. Earnshaw hesitated, as if trying to work out the time scale in his head.

"A couple of weeks ago, I suppose. All of a sudden the deal didn't seem good enough for him, and by that time we'd got it all lined up to meet Ackroyd and his partners and get a quick conclusion. Jack Ackroyd wouldn't have flown up from Portugal if the thing hadn't been pretty well settled, the papers ready to sign, would he?"

"And that's why you were so anxious to meet your brother in the Clarendon Hotel the night you realised he had disappeared?"

"Damn right. I wanted it sorted out." Earnshaw ground out his cigarette in the ashtray on the table in front of him and lit another. "My father and I both wanted it sorted out."

"One thing puzzles me about that meeting, though, Mr.

Earnshaw," Thackeray said. "You say yourself it was important, your father confirms it was important, and yet when you were waiting for your brother everyone who saw you there confirms that you were drinking heavily. Was that the best way to go into an important meeting?"

Earnshaw flushed and he did not answer.

"Please answer the question, Mr. Earnshaw," Thackeray said. "There are two possible interpretations of the state you were in at the Clarendon that evening, when, by the way, the barmaid says she tried to persuade you not have any more to drink…"

"That bitch," Earnshaw said. "Yes, that's right. She almost refused to serve me, the interfering cow."

"So why were you so drunk? Was it because you were worried about the meeting with Simon? Or did you know by that time Simon wasn't going to turn up?"

"What?" Earnshaw said, his surprise apparently genuine. "What the hell are you suggesting now? That I knew he was dead by then?"

"Did you?" Thackeray snapped.

"No, of course I bloody didn't. I got drunk mainly because I'd waited for him so long."

"So tell me again what arrangement you made to meet Simon. When did you call him?"

"On the Sunday, late on. I'd spent the evening at my parents' place and my father and I decided it might be best if I had another go at Simon rather than him. I called him and he made no objection."

"Did you call him at his flat or on his mobile?"

"On the mobile as far as I can remember. I don't call him at the flat much. He's not often there."

"So you made the date on Sunday, and Simon's body was found on Wednesday morning, but according to the pathologist Simon probably died on the Tuesday evening. Did you know your brother went jogging, Mr. Earnshaw?"

"No, I didn't. What are you suggesting now? That I pushed Simon over that bloody cliff? You must be crazy."

"I'm not suggesting anything, Mr. Earnshaw, yet," Thackeray said. "But I'd like you to go over your movements on that Tuesday for me, if you would."

Earnshaw looked mutinous, but eventually pulled out a diary from his jacket pocket and flicked through it until arriving at the right date.

"I was at work that day at the mill until about three in the afternoon," he said. "I had a meeting with my father and the maintenance engineers at two, I remember now. Then I left early and drove over to Leeds, had a few drinks and then went to a casino."

"Can you be a bit more specific, please? Where did you have your drinks? Which casino?"

Earnshaw reeled off the names of a couple of pubs and a casino and Sergeant Mower ostentatiously wrote them down.

"Did you see anyone in Leeds who would know you? Did you go there to meet friends?" Thackeray asked.

Earnshaw shrugged.

"Nope, I was on my own, at a loose end, you might say. I go to the casino quite often, though," he said. "They'd recognise me there."

"And what time did you get home?" Thackeray asked.

"I really don't remember," Earnshaw said. "It was late and I wasn't keeping an eye on the time. No reason why I have to now Lizzie's gone. Back to an empty house, more often than not."

"And of course you'd been drinking," Thackeray said drily.

250

"Too late to effing breathalyse me now," Earnshaw said.

"We'll need to check these details," Thackeray said.

"Check away," Earnshaw snapped back. "I'd nothing to do with Simon's death, I can assure you of that.

"But you have to admit that selling the mill will be easier for you and your father now he's gone and you look like inheriting his shares."

"In the end, maybe," Earnshaw said. "But if that's the tree you're sniffing round you've got it wrong. I was the one who wanted a quick sale, remember. That's exactly what I'm not going to get now. Persuading Simon to cooperate was certainly in my interests, but everything could be buggered up now he's dead. We may not be able to do anything until probate's settled."

"But you and your father can take the decisions? Your grandfather's objections don't hold water any longer."

"That's true," Earnshaw said.

After a few more routine questions, and gaining permission to look at his mobile phone records, they let Earnshaw go. Back in his office Thackeray looked at Mower with a hint of doubt in his eyes.

"What do you reckon?" he asked. "I don't like that young man but is he a killer?"

"He could be," Mower said. "It all depends on the timings, and if and when we can get confirmation he was in Leeds. As alibis go it's all pretty vague. And we've only his word for it that they set up the meeting for Wednesday at the Clarendon. It could just as easily have been fixed for the day before and Wednesday's little performance all be a charade. That might explain why he got pissed out of his head. He knew damn well Simon wasn't going to turn up, and why."

"And if they met and had a blazing row anything could have happened,"

Thackeray said. "He seems to be permanently drunk, that young man, and you can do things when you're drunk that you'd never dream of doing when you're sober." He spoke, Mower knew, with the voice of bitter experience.

"Check his movements for the Tuesday," Thackeray said. "That list he's given us is like a sieve. People may well remember seeing him in Leeds but you can bet their recall of the time and even the day will be vague. We've got no weapon and no forensic evidence to speak of on the killer. A sharp blow to the back of the head too clean, Amos thinks, to have been caused by the fall – plus other bumps and contusions – and a few unidentified fibres clinging to his clothing, probably from an old blanket, according to the lab. We may be lucky with those in the end but I don't think we've got a strong enough case to search Earnshaw's car or house just yet. But I still think he had the motive and the opportunity. We'll have to pin him down more precisely to find the gaps when he could have met Simon the day before he claims he planned to. Given that Simon was dressed for jogging I'd guess early evening on the Tuesday, before he drove to Leeds. That would fit Amos's time of death. Get the team onto it and ask Leeds for some help with the pubs and the casino."

When Mower had gone to pass on these new tasks to the overburdened murder detectives, Thackeray leaned back in his chair, lit a cigarette and allowed himself the luxury of a moment's thought. Laura edged her way into his mind every time he relaxed and he knew that he was doing neither his job nor his lover justice. Endless stress, endless overtime wrecked marriages. They had helped wreck his own. It was certainly arguable that Laura would be better off without him. But without her, he would be adrift again on an endless sea of despair. He did not think he was strong enough to let her go.

DC Omar Sharif was feeling more overburdened than most
as he ploughed through statement after statement on his
computer screen, hoping to pick up the slightest missed clue
from those who had been close enough to see anything of the
assault on Mohammed Iqbal. It was still early on Saturday
morning and he was waiting his chance to claim the attention of Sergeant Kevin Mower to fill him in on what he had
discovered from his freelance activities of the previous day.
But so far Mower had been fully occupied with the DCI and
an interview with Matthew Earnshaw, and Sharif began to
wonder whether the murder of a wealthy young white man
might not be taking too great a priority over the killing of an
Asian union leader from Aysgarth Lane.

"Sarge," Sharif got in at last as Mower passed his desk
with a sheaf of papers in his hand.

"Omar?" Mower said. "Found something?"

"Not in this lot," Sharif said. "But I put out my own feelers
in the community when I went up there yesterday. I'm sure
someone up there knows something about those bikes but
no one's got back to me yet." He felt this sounded inadequate and sensed that Mower's attention was already wandering.

"And then there's Ricky Pickles' garage," he said.

"What garage?" Mower said sharply. "You mean South
Bradfield Autos, his alibi for the attack on Iqbal? That's been
checked out and it stands up. He took his Escort in to have a
new exhaust fitted and was there for at least an hour while it
was done. We've seen the invoice, looked at the car; it's all
above board."

"I went up there last night to have a sniff around, just as
they were closing and there was no one around," Sharif said.

Mower's attention was suddenly fixed on the young DC and he dropped into a chair at the next desk.

"You what?" he said.

"You know as well as I do that Pickles is almost certainly mixed up with this lot, however many alibis he's got. If he didn't do it, he planned it."

"Wishful thinking, Omar?" Mower suggested quietly, but the young DC shook his head fiercely.

"I told you yesterday, according to someone I spoke to up Aysgarth, Craig Porter, the scumbag we've got banged up for GBH after the trouble outside the Grenadier on Thursday night, is involved in this too. Apparently Porter's got a powerful Kawasaki that he's complaining went missing after he was arrested. I checked his registration number and found the bike at SB Autos, right at the back, tucked away out of sight. And so's another bike that I've seen parked at the British Patriotic Party's HQ. I'd already checked with vehicle registration and that one belongs to Pickles himself. Coincidence? I don't think so."

"Pickles claims..." Mower began.

"So what? You may have seen the invoice for the work on his car, but there's nothing to say he didn't take off on the bike while the work was being done. Him, Porter and the rest. Why else would two bikes belonging to two racist thugs be together? It's not as if SB is a bike specialist. They're not."

"So you reckon someone picked up Porter's bike after he was arrested and took it up to SB Autos for safe-keeping?"

"Must have done. Porter apparently doesn't know what's happened to it."

"It could have been nicked," Mower said.

"In which case we've got a reason to give SB Autos a going-over."

Mower hesitated.

"You have to admit it's odd, sarge," Sharif insisted.

"Porter was remanded yesterday and I've told Armley goal that we need to talk to him about another matter. I'll give them a call and find out when we can go over there – today if possible. I take it you'd like to come? You don't have a weekend break in Ibiza planned?"

"Chance would be a fine thing," Sharif said, his dark eyes inscrutable, and Mower wondered, not for the first time, just how far Sharif conformed to his community's expectations in matters of sex and marriage.

But in the end, when Mower and Sharif faced Craig Porter in a bleak interview room at Armley Gaol, it was a forensic report which had arrived at police HQ just before they left which made the difference to the case and brought a faint smile of satisfaction to Sharif's face as they inched their way through the football traffic back to Bradfield.

"Take it slowly," Mower had said quietly as they were escorted through the locked doors and corridors of the gaol. "Don't let him wind you up. Don't rush."

Porter's initial reaction was stormy. He was a heavily built young man in his middle twenties, pasty-skinned and with a shaven skull and an array of nationalistic tattoos on show beneath his black T-shirt. The pale blue eyes which had flickered over Sharif as he came into the room had been filled with dislike.

"How the hell did you know about my bike?" he asked, addressing himself exclusively to Mower, and as Mower did not know the answer to that question and Sharif was not telling, he had to be content with vague suggestions of 'information received'. Eventually he admitted that one of his 'mates' might have delivered his bike to SB Autos for safekeeping, although he had no suggestions as to who that might be or how they might have found an ignition key to fit.

"That would be one of your mates from the British Patriotic Party, would it?" Mower asked.

"Who said anything about them?" Porter countered quickly.

"You had a membership card in your pocket," Mower said. "It's still there, with the other bits and pieces they took from you when you were arrested. A fake, then, is it?"

"Someone's got to stand up for the English," Porter muttered. "He's a good lad is Ricky Pickles. Knows what's what. Any road, it's not a crime to belong to a political party, is it?"

"Certainly not, so long as the party sticks to politics and doesn't take its battles onto the streets," Mower said.

"It isn't us that takes the battles onto t'bloody streets, is it?"

"You were found in possession of an iron bar when you were arrested," Mower said almost casually. "Carry that often, do you, just in case?"

"You need protection from them bastards," Porter said. "They attacked us, remember? They came up to the Grenadier looking for aggro, didn't they? Self defence is what I'll be pleading, don't you worry."

"They?" Mower said.

"Bloody Pakis," Porter spat, with another scowl in Sharif direction.

"The man you hit has a fractured skull," Sharif came back angrily, only subsiding in response to a sharp glance from Mower, who had known this interview would be edgy and hoped that it would not disintegrate.

"So you're not claiming the iron bar was not yours?" Mower said, knowing that it would be difficult for Porter to make that argument as he had been disarmed by two burly officers from the riot squad and the injured man's blood and Porter's fingerprints had been found all over the weapon.

Porter shrugged and lit another cigarette.

"Used it before, have you?" Mower pressed.

"What do you mean?" Porter asked, with just a flicker of anxiety in his eyes.

"I mean we're very interested in people with a history of violence and access to a powerful motorbike, people like you in fact, in connection with the murder of Mohammed Iqbal."

"Snuffed it, has he?" Porter asked, making no pretence of not knowing who they were talking about. "Bloody trouble-maker from what I heard. Nowt to do wi'me, though. One down..." He glanced at Sharif and sneered, not needing to complete the sentence.

"Perhaps you can tell us where you were, then, last Wednesday between five-thirty and six-thirty in the evening," Mower said quickly.

"In t'Grenadier," Porter said quickly. "I'm always in t'Grenadier at that time of day having a game of pool. Anyone'll tell you that."

"And no doubt any number of people can vouch for you?" Mower said. "And you won't be the least bit worried about the fact that our forensic labs have found traces of someone else's blood on that iron bar you were using on Thursday night, will you?

"What do you mean, someone else's?" Porter said. "What are you trying to fit me up with now?"

"You and the four others who rode up to Aysgarth Lane to beat up Mohammed Iqbal," Mower said.

"Bollocks," Porter said. "Ask anyone in t'Grenadier."

"Oh, we'll be doing that, Craig, don't you worry. Our labs will also be doing a DNA analysis of the traces they've found on your vicious little club. And if it matches Iqbal's we'll be back. It may take a little while but it's nice to know that you'll be here waiting for us when we come looking."

Early the following morning, armed with a search warrant,

the police required Ricky Pickles to open the heavily barred doors of the BPP offices and proceeded to remove every computer and paper file inside.

"This is a legitimate political party. I'll have you for this," Pickles vowed as he watched box after box of the party's information being loaded into police vans. "I'll have you for violating my human rights."

"You'll find out what it feels like, then," Omar Sharif responded cheerfully, catching Pickles' remark as he passed him carrying a computer. For a moment the two men's eyes locked in mutual contempt.

"Leave it, Omar," Mower said, catching the moment. "Let him crawl back under his stone, where he belongs."

Chapter Nineteen

Laura Ackroyd woke late that Sunday morning, with a thumping headache and the sudden desolation of finding herself alone again. Michael, where are you when I need you? she thought. The plane back from Paris the previous night had been delayed and she had finally got home at two, listened to her messages, hoping against hope for some word from Thackeray, but had to be content with her father announcing that he was on his way home. Too disappointed by Thackeray's continuing silence to even try to follow up that bit of news, she had drunk two large vodka and tonics and eventually thrown herself into bed in a state of deep depression. The clouds had not lifted when she finally woke at about eleven although even through the curtains she could see that in the world outside the sun was unexpectedly shining and she could hear a full-throated blackbird singing outside the window.

She got out of bed, picked up the Sunday papers and glanced without much interest at the headlines before dumping them on the sofa. She poured herself a large glass of orange juice in the kitchen and went back to bed again, propping herself up on the pillows as she gloomily reviewed the previous day's nerve-wrenching trip to Paris. She and Amina Khan had made their way back to Charles de Gaulle airport in a silence only broken by the most cursory exchanges about Metro tickets and routes. On the plane, Amina appeared to fall asleep although Laura suspected that this was merely a ploy to avoid any further discussion of her sister's plight. She refused the food and drink on offer and slept again in the car as Laura drove her back across the pitch black moors from Manchester to Bradfield.

Laura was almost as deeply upset by their trip as Amina appeared to be. She knew that they had to report what they knew to the police, but when they sat in the car outside the Khan's family home in Eckersley, Amina refused point blank to contemplate calling DCI Thackeray herself.

"You can tell them whatever you like," she said. "And then I suppose they'll come looking for me too. But I can't call them, I really can't. It will cause too much trouble in the family. Tell them to come to talk to me at school on Monday if they must."

"They'll keep what you say confidential if they can," Laura had said, without much conviction. Amina looked at her from beneath her nun-like hijab and smiled as if from a great distance.

"Wishful thinking," she said. "I don't think any of this is going to remain confidential for very long. My father and brother will be furious, my mother will be heart-broken and the community will be scandalised. If the police bring Saira back to Bradfield she won't be safe. She'll have to stay in hiding. Even if my family wish her no harm, someone will take it upon himself to uphold the old ways. You probably know as well as anyone that we're not all medieval fanatics, but there are some, and they're dangerous and unpredictable." She had opened the car door then.

"Thank you for coming with me," she said. "I am grateful, but there's nothing either of us can do for Saira now. It's all over. She will have to make her own way in the world." She closed the door quietly but, Laura thought, with a finality which was chilling.

Which left Laura to face the next day with a thick head and an unwelcome task to perform. She desperately wanted to speak to Michael Thackeray but about matters very far removed from the problems of Saira Khan. Like a child reluctant to get ready for school, she showered and dressed slowly, before making a large pot of strong coffee to help her consider her options. But before she could even begin to sort out her thoughts, the phone rang and she found herself assailed by Jack Ackroyd in full flood.

"Laura? I'm at Heathrow, on my way home. Where the hell were you yesterday? I must have tried your flat a dozen times. And I got nowt out of your mobile. Didn't you get any of my messages? I wanted to tell you I was packing up. I told your grandmother. Whole trip's been a bloody waste of time, it turns out. Backers have turned tail and fled after all this trouble around Aysgarth. Can't say I blame them, really. I think we were flogging a dead horse: luxury apartments in the centre of Bradfield! Best bet is to turn Earnshaws mill into a gaol, if you ask me. Lock all these rioting beggars up, black, white and everything in between. They're wrecking Bradfield between them. Who's going to invest with all that going on in the streets?"

"Dad," Laura said, trying to absorb all this sound and fury through her dulled perceptions. "I'm sorry it's all fallen through, though I always thought you were being a tad optimistic..."

"Now you tell me," her father said.

"You didn't exactly ask my opinion," Laura snapped back.

"Aye, well, I think I'm well out of it," Jack conceded.

"Does anyone know about all this?" Laura asked, her reporter's instincts snapping belatedly into gear. "Has it been announced officially?"

"Firoz Kamal's issuing some sort of statement tomorrow, I think," Ackroyd said. "It's nowt to do with me now. I'm finished with it. Any road, I've got to go. They're calling my

261

flight. Why don't you get your grandmother out to Portugal for some sunshine? And you too, if you like. Always glad to see you." And with that he hung up.

"And goodbye to you too," Laura muttered, staring at the gently purring phone in exasperation, thinking that winter sunshine was very appealing. At least the conversation had penetrated her depression. If she was the only journalist aware of this unexpected reverse for the Earnshaws she could earn a few Brownie points on a quiet Sunday by following it up ready for the next day's paper. For the moment, she thought, she would put the problems of the Khan family on one side and do her job by trying to get comments from the Earnshaw family about the mill's now very uncertain future.

She started with George Earnshaw, partly because she thought his reaction would be the most uninhibited as he saw his son's plans confounded, and partly because she had been intrigued by Saira Khan's revelation that the old man had been willing to help finance his grandson's liaison with the Muslim girl and his move to France. An hour after speaking to her father, Laura, muffled up in a skiing jacket and scarf, was standing on the doorstep of Earnshaw's modest Broadley home, where the pale sunshine glittered on frost-spangled banks of winter heather and the first virginal snow-drops nestled in a rockery of dark millstone grit like a glimpse of dawn at midnight.

The old man was slow to open the door and Laura was shocked to see his hollow cheeks and sunken eyes above a gaunt frame still dressed in grubby-looking pyjamas and dressing gown at midday. This was a man whose son had described him as fighting fit and still working as a director of Earnshaws only a week ago. Frank's efforts to keep his business afloat, she suspected, were as over-optimistic as his view of his father's health.

George Earnshaw was still waiting and as he did not seem to recognise her from her last abortive visit she explained quickly who she was and why she had come, and saw a flicker of satisfaction light up his face. He waved her into the house and through to a cluttered sitting room.

"Fallen through then, has it?" Earnshaw said. "I can't say I'm surprised. Bloody stupid scheme that was. I told them. Stupid and unnecessary. If we make the savings we planned there'll be no need to sell the mill. Trade'll pick up. It always does."

"Can I quote you on that?" Laura asked, pulling her tape recorder from her bag. The room was warm and stuffy and she took off her coat and dropped it onto a chair. She took a seat as far from the gas fire as seemed decent.

"Of course you can quote me, my dear," Earnshaw said. He was clearly delighted with the news she had brought.

"But you're still facing the same problem with the union, aren't you?" Laura asked. "The workers aren't going to be happy to see their pay cut however necessary that is to save the mill."

Earnshaw's face darkened.

"Pity we ever let the blasted union back on the premises," he said. "But they'll come round. They'll see which side their bread's buttered. They always do." Laura nodded and did not argue although she expected to find Frank Earnshaw and his remaining son rather less sanguine about their chance of keeping the mill going. She glanced round the room curiously for a moment, Earnshaw's collection of Indian brasses and bronzes reminding her of the second reason for her visit.

"You seem to have been the only person in the family who knew about Simon and Saira Khan," she said. "I saw her yesterday and she told me you'd agreed to help Simon financially with his move to France."

For a moment she thought that George Earnshaw was having some sort of seizure. His face went into spasm and he clutched the arms of his chair with a white-knuckled grip, gasping for breath.

"Are you all right, Mr. Earnshaw?" she said anxiously. "I didn't mean to upset you. I'm sure Simon's death is still very distressing for you." But the look Earnshaw flashed as he regained his composure was not one of grief but of hatred.

"Help him?" he said, though gritted teeth. "Help him? Are you mad, girl?"

"I'm sorry?" Laura said. "Saira said…"

"Saira? Is that what she's called. As if it wasn't bad enough for Simon and the rest of them to go along with some Muslim chancer's scheme to take over the mill. Then he tells me he wants to marry one of them. I was appalled, do you hear, appalled…"

"But I thought," Laura hesitated, glancing round the room again. "Saira said…You obviously spent some time in India…"

"Do you know what happened in India after the war, girl?" Earnshaw said, almost spitting the words in her face. "I was in the RAF, 31 squadron, ended up airlifting British families out of Kashmir when the balloon went up. Fifteen at a time in Dakotas with no oxygen and fuel turning up in cans if you were lucky. Chaos. Bloody murderous chaos. They were smuggling their Hindu servants out to get them away from the Muslims, while down on the ground village after village was burning and whole trainloads of people were being massacred as they tried to get to the right side of the new borders."

"I knew there was a lot of bloodshed," Laura said. "On both sides, though, wasn't it?"

The old man did not answer. He got to his feet with difficulty and rummaged in a carved wooden box on a side-table

264

which seemed to be full of photographs, most of them old. He handed Laura a tattered and faded black and white snapshot of a young woman in a sari.

"That was the Hindu girl I planned to marry," he said, his face contorted with bitterness. "She was going to Bombay to take a boat to England. I put her on a train which never arrived. Not a single person survived. And then Simon comes to tell me that he'll back me in the dispute with his father if I'll make it worth his while. And what does he want the money for? To set himself up with a bloody Pakistani girl, a Muslim... He couldn't wait for the sale."

"So you turned him down?" Laura said quietly. "You wouldn't help him."

"Of course I wouldn't help him."

"But he wouldn't have known about your experiences in India, would he?" She touched the worn photograph lightly with her finger. "It's so long ago..."

"I never told anyone," Earnshaw said. "That sort of relationship wouldn't have been welcomed by my family in those days. She was killed. Quite possibly burned alive. What good would telling anyone have done?"

More good, perhaps, than burying his bitterness for fifty years had done him, Laura thought, looking at the creased features etched, she now realised, as much by disappointment and despair as by his illness. Evidently his love had faded like the photograph of his lover, but the hatred her death had sparked had survived more than a generation to blight his grandson's life.

"So you turned Simon away when he came to see you?"

"I told him I wouldn't help him," Earnshaw whispered.

"And what was his response to that?" she asked, guessing that Earnshaw could not have been happy with his grandson's reaction.

265

"He said he'd go along with his father's scheme," the old man said. "He'd help them close Earnshaws down. He was furious with me but I wouldn't listen…" He closed his eyes for a moment and Laura thought he had exhausted himself and had fallen asleep. But then he roused himself again and his eyes blazed and Laura guessed he had been reliving the final row with Simon.

"I killed him," he said unexpectedly and very quietly, leaning back in his chair with an almost peaceful expression on his face. "I hit him, I hit with all the strength I had, and he lost his balance and fell, and I couldn't rouse him. He'd caught his head on that table there." He waved vaguely at the heavy glass-topped coffee table. Laura felt a chill grip her stomach and she swallowed hard.

"It was an accident then?" she whispered.

"Oh, no," George Earnshaw said. "I wanted him dead. He was going to become one of them, give me great-grandchildren with murderers' blood in their veins. At that moment I wanted him dead. My own grandson – can you believe that?"

Laura hesitated. Earnshaw was an old man and evidently frail and she did not feel physically threatened but she was still unsure how to handle such a dramatic confession. She glanced at her tape-recorder, still running on the table.

"Are you sure you want to tell me about this?" she said, her mouth dry.

"It makes no odds to me now," Earnshaw said. "I'll not live to stand trial." The admission made, Earnshaw seemed to have shrivelled in his chair until he resembled little more than skin and bone, the only life in him visible in his blue eyes still blazing from deep dark sockets in his grey and haggard face.

"I should call the police," Laura said. The old man shrugged.

"Do as you like," he said listlessly.

But before Laura could pull out her mobile the door-bell rang and she helped the old man up to answer it. She went to the door with him to find a burly figure she recognised and a white Escort parked behind her car on the drive, blocking it in.

"Ricky," Earnshaw said hoarsely. "You'd better come in, lad. I think I may have caused you a bit of a problem here."

In a sudden flash of understanding, Laura knew that the old man could not have disposed of Simon Earnshaw's body alone and that Pickles must have helped him – and she realised then the danger she was in.

At police headquarters a part of the murder team eager to earn overtime on a Sunday had been tasked to go through the documents which had been removed from the British Patriotic Party offices earlier that morning. It was tedious work and it was not until almost midday that Sergeant Kevin Mower looked up and caught DCI Thackeray's eye as he made one of his increasingly impatient visits to the incident room.

"This is interesting, guv," he said, wondering why his boss looked as if he had not slept for a week. Laura must be giving him a hard time, he thought, with a flicker of jealousy. His own recent liaisons had ended in tragedy and he had felt no urge to to take amorous risks for months.

"What's that?" Thackeray asked, making his way through the desks to Mower's side where he looked over the sergeant's shoulder at the accounts he was studying.

"Donations," Mower said. "A surprising number, given the party's reputation for violence. A lot of money given anonymously but some people don't seem to mind their names being recorded, including, it appears, one George

Earnshaw of Broadley, young Simon's grandfather I guess, unless there are two George Earnshaws in Broadley."

"He has the reputation of being a racist old bastard," Thackeray said non-commitally. "Though it's not illegal for people to make donations to political parties, however obnoxious their aims. How much did he give?"

"Twenty grand," Mower said.

"Not insignificant then," Thackeray conceded.

"Not given that BPP members are now prime suspects for the murder of a union activist who was getting in Earnshaw's way."

"We'd best have another word with Mr. Earnshaw senior," Thackeray said. "But it can wait until tomorrow. Let's get the paperwork cleared today and then we'll see where we stand."

"Right, guv," Mower agreed, turning back to his pages of figures.

"Where's Sharif this morning?" Thackeray asked, glancing round the room again with tired eyes. He had slept very little the previous night.

"I told him to keep a discreet eye on Pickles," Mower said. "He's been snooping around off his own bat. I thought it was time to make it official."

"Is he the best person to do it?" Thackeray asked.

"Let's just say he's the best motivated," Mower said. "He won't do anything stupid, guv."

"I hope you're right," Thackeray said gloomily and turned away to make his way back to his own office where he flung himself into his chair with something approaching a groan, lit a cigarette and drew on it deeply. His sleepless night had brought him no closer to a resolution of his indecision over his future with Laura and had fuddled his brain so that he no longer saw clearly enough where the murder investigations might lead him. At least it was Sunday, thankfully, a day when some inquiries would stall as mobile phone officials and forensic scientists pursued the sort of normal lives denied to police officers. Increasingly, the resolution of murder cases depended on science, the tiny droplet of blood or other fluids, the hair or the speck of fibre, which placed a suspect somewhere he had vehemently denied being. In his heart, he still had Matthew Earnshaw down for his brother's murder and he hoped against hope that Ricky Pickles might be implicated in the death of Mohammed Iqbal. But he knew these were irrational responses, unscientific and of no value, and in the case of Matthew Earnshaw a visceral reaction to a young man in whom he saw too many of his own failings at the same sort of age. Prejudice, he thought, came in many forms, and when it came down to it he was no more immune than Pickles himself. He needed Laura, he thought, to keep him sane but when impulsively he tried her mobile number he only got her voicemail.

"I love you," he said softly after the tone. But did he, he still wondered, love her enough.

He was interrupted by a uniformed constable who put his head round the door waving a slip of paper.

"They thought you ought to see this, sir," he said. The message had come from the French police to inform West Yorkshire that the body of a young Asian woman, carrying a passport in the name of Saira Khan, had been recovered from the Seine that morning.

"Hell and damnation," Thackeray said.

Omar Sharif had parked his unmarked car a discreet distance down the road from George Earnshaw's house and watched as Ricky Pickles swung his Escort behind a VW Golf on the drive and went inside. Thoughtfully he called police headquarters and asked the control room to check the ownership of the Golf. The name they came up with meant nothing to him but he asked to be put through to Sergeant Kevin Mower anyway.

"He's driven out to some village in the country," Sharif said. "Broadley." And he relayed the address.

"That's old Earnshaw's house," Mower said. "We've just discovered that the old bastard's a major backer of Pickles's political ambitions."

"They must be having a campaign meeting then," Sharif said. "There's another car there, a Golf belonging to a woman called Ackroyd, Miss Laura Ackroyd. Is anything known about her?"

"Say that again," Mower said, his mouth suddenly dry. It was ten miles to Broadley and there was no permanent police presence in the village. Sharif was effectively on his own. When Sharif had repeated what he had seen Mower knew both their jobs were on the line, not to mention Laura's safety.

"Take this very slowly, Omar," he said. "Very slowly and carefully. Laura Ackroyd is the DCI's girlfriend, and Pickles is at best a violent bastard and at worst a murderer. We need Laura out of there without a hair of her head disturbed. Have you got that?"

"Loud and clear, sarge," Sharif said, his heart suddenly thumping uncomfortably.

"I'm going to transfer this call to the DCI's office. Stay on the line, Omar."

But by the time Mower had barged unceremoniously into Thackeray's office and indicated that he should pick up his phone, Sharif was already talking again, an edge of panic in his voice.

"They're moving, " he said. "Pickles has been fiddling about in the Golf – I can't make out from here what he's been doing but now he's shifted his car off the drive, and moved the Golf onto the road as well to make space for some old boy – Earnshaw presumably – who's getting a red car out of the garage, some sort of old estate."

"A dark red Volvo, an old model?" Mower snapped.

"Could be," Sharif said. "Difficult to tell from here. The red car's driving off now and Pickles is following in the Ford. They've left the Golf behind. Should I follow or try to find Miss Ackroyd in the house."

Mower glanced at Thackeray who was listening in on his extension ashen-faced and shaken, his knuckles white.

"What do you think, guv?" he asked desperately, knowing that whichever decision they made might be the wrong one for Laura. She could be in the Volvo."

"Follow them, Omar," Thackeray said harshly. "We can't afford to lose them. We'll get help to you as quickly as we can. Keep us in touch with where you are."

For a second the two men's eyes locked in mutual fear.

"Get a local car up there fast to search the house," Thackeray said, his voice hoarse. "And see if you can scramble the chopper to catch up with Omar, and get every car in the area out there, though God alone knows what's available on a Sunday morning."

"Guv," Mower said. "And should we get the Super off the golf course."

"You'd better do that too," Thackeray said grimly.

The phone shrilled again and Sharif came back on the line.

"They're heading out of the village towards somewhere called Gawstone, according to the last signpost I passed," he said.

"There's a big reservoir up at Gawstone," Thackeray said. "If that really is Simon Earnshaw's car they're taking up there I guess they plan to dump it. There's plenty of spots secluded enough. Be careful, Omar. We've got help on the way. Don't do anything rash."

Mower could only guess what that injunction cost Thackeray though neither man was willing to put into words what they dreaded most.

"What the hell was she doing at George Earnshaw's house on a Sunday morning?" Thackeray said later as he and Mower left headquarters and began a frantic drive out of town towards Broadley, where they now knew that the old man's house had been found deserted.

"And what was Earnshaw doing concealing his grandson's car?" Mower muttered, glancing left and right very briefly before shooting a red light.

"Get us there in one piece, Kevin, for God's sake," Thackeray said. "Are you sure they'll keep us patched onto Omar's calls?"

"Quite sure, guv," Mower said. "Don't worry." Although as soon as the words left his mouth he realised that was one of the most pointless bits of advice he had ever offered anyone.

DC Omar Sharif followed the two cars at a discreet distance along the narrow winding lane which clung to the side of the river valley to the north of Broadley. There was little traffic on the road which led only to a small hamlet on the banks of Gawstone reservoir and then petered out on the fells beyond. Only twice did he have to brake hard and pull into a passing place to accommodate traffic coming in the opposite direction; most of the time he was unable to see one or other of the cars ahead as the road twisted between dry stone walls and the occasional deserted barn. This was high, wild country much loved by ramblers but of little interest to an urban man like Sharif.

When the Volvo and the following Escort finally turned off, Sharif almost lost them. The road itself took a sharp turn onto a castellated stone bridge across a narrow part of the steeply banked reservoir which had suddenly come into view round one of the many sharp bends, while a narrow track on the left followed the edge of the lake on its southern bank. Sharif had approached the bridge slowly and been horrified to discover that neither car appeared to have crossed it. He braked hard, looking right and then left, and caught just a glimpse of the dark red Volvo's tail-end weaving its way down a section of the track that was visible on the left. He called headquarters again to give them his position and found himself patched through to the DCI.

"We think they plan to dump the Volvo, Omar," Thackeray said.

"Right, guv," Sharif said, knowing without being told that the obvious place to dump a car at Gawstone was in the lake. "If anyone's got a map they could tell me where this track leads. It's very narrow and if it's a dead end they're not going to get out again without running into me."

There was a brief silence before the DCI replied.

"It goes to some sort of pumping station. It's unlikely that there'll be anyone up there on a Sunday morning. Most of these places are run automatically these days. But the chopper's in the air, Omar. The cavalry's on its way."

"Right, guv," Sharif said, realising without being told that this level of mobilisation meant only one thing.

"They haven't found Miss Ackroyd at Broadley, then, sir?"

"No," Thackeray said. "They found her coat and she left her tape-recorder running. We know that George Earnshaw killed his grandson and that Ricky Pickles probably helped him dispose of the body. Don't take any chances, Omar. Pickles is dangerous."

It was impossible to pick up any emotion in Thackeray's voice through the crackle of static on the line but Sharif tightened his grip on the wheel as he realised the full implications of the situation he was going into.

"Did you hear me, Omar?" Thackeray's voice crackled back.

"Yes, sir," Omar said. "Got to go. They're stopped ahead of me."

He slammed the brakes on as he realised the other two cars had pulled up at a point where the track drew close to the edge of the lake at a spot unusually secluded by bushes tumbling down a high bank. He swung his car hard into the undergrowth, hoping, as he got out, that it would remain unnoticed, at least for a time. Moving to the nearside, he eased himself forward until he could see both the stationary cars ahead and the two men who had now got out of them and were deep in conversation at the lake's edge.

Looking back through the slow-motion replay of recollection, Sharif would not have done anything differently but at the time everything happened so quickly that there was no time for thought of any kind. The two men on the edge of the lake evidently became aware of his ill-concealed presence at the same time as he, and they, heard the faint clatter of an approaching helicopter.

"Police," Sharif shouted, hoping against hope that the chopper was in fact his back-up on the way. Pickles, his face dark with fury, ran towards Sharif, who met his bull-like charge full-on, answering force with force and knocking the older man to the ground as he headed towards the Volvo. But he was too late. Earnshaw by then had flung himself back into the driving seat of the estate car, its engine still running, and with a spray of dust and gravel from the wheels, accelerated the battered old car headfirst into the lake where it sank quickly in a swirl of oil and bubbles.

"You old fool," Pickles shouted from behind. Sharif glanced round briefly to see Pickles scrambling into his own car and executing a hasty U-turn before heading off down the track along which they had all arrived. Barely thinking coherently now, Sharif pulled off his anorak and dived into the water where the car had disappeared, while above him the police helicopter approached in a steep dive.

The lake water was bitterly cold and Sharif surfaced after a few moments, his lungs bursting and his heart thumping painfully. The Volvo was no more than ten feet down on the sloping lake bottom but when he had tugged on the driver's door it had failed to budge and he had only been able to watch helplessly as bubbles rose from the George Earnshaw's mouth and eventually ceased. Sharif spat out a mouthful of bitter water and dived again, the helicopter low overhead now and breaking up the surface of the water with the downdraft from its rotor, but the interior of the car had filled up completely by now, and he knew that there was nothing more he could do. He clawed his way back up to the surface, and crawled up the steep bank, to lie spluttering and shivering on the grass for a moment before staggering back to his car where he wrapped himself in his anorak, started the engine and turned the heater full on. Reluctantly he picked up his mobile and called in.

"Do you think there was anyone else in the car?" DCI Thackeray asked, when Sharif had described what had happened.

"I can't be sure, sir," Sharif said, trying to stop his teeth chattering. "But it's an estate, the boot's not completely separate, and I couldn't see anyone..."

Outside, the helicopter had landed, dust swirling and engine roaring, on a level patch of ground about a hundred yards away, and uniformed officers were running in his direction.

"Pickles got away, sir. I'm sorry," Sharif said.

"The road's blocked. He won't get far," Thackeray said. "Get yourself checked out by the medics, Omar. You did well."

"Sir," Sharif said, convinced he had not done well enough.

Six miles away, Mower took the last steep bend on the hill to the centre of Broadley village and glanced cautiously at his companion. Thackeray had not said anything since Omar had signed off and was staring through the windscreen, his jaw clenched.

"Where to, guv?" Mower asked. "Do you want to go straight to the reservoir or to Earnshaw's house?"

Thackeray looked at the sergeant as if he had not heard him.

"Sir?" Mower prompted quietly.

"It'll take them hours to get divers or lifting equipment out there to pull the car out," he said. "To be sure it was just Earnshaw in it."

"The house then? We may get a better idea of what happened there."

Thackeray nodded and five minutes later Mower pulled up behind two police cars which were already parked behind Laura's Golf outside George Earnshaw's house. The two officers were met in the hallway by a uniformed sergeant who had evidently not shaved that morning, and the local constable, John Moody, who looked as though he held Mower personally responsible for this disruption of his weekend.

Thackeray and Mower listened in silence as the uniformed sergeant described what they had found in the house. When they had finished their report the silence lengthened and Mower shrugged slightly, glancing at Thackeray's frozen expression.

"D'you want to have a look round, guv, while I listen to the tape?" Mower said. He could not be sure how the DCI might react to the sound of Laura's recorded voice. Thackeray nodded and allowed two uniformed officers to lead him up the stairs, leaving Mower to step into the front garden with Laura's mini-tape recorder in his hand. He skipped through her interview with Earnshaw, shaken, as she had been, by the depth of the old man's hatred, and then stopped the tape at the point at which the doorbell could be clearly heard chiming in the background. It was clear from the fading sound of their voices that both Earnshaw and Laura had gone to the front door, but after that nothing was clear at all. Frustrated, he turned up the volume but learned little from the muffled voices and what sounded like a single sharp exclamation from Laura. For seconds after that there was nothing but the faint hiss of the recorder itself, and he was about to switch off, frustrated, when his patience was rewarded as Ricky Pickles' voice emerged again, mainly muffled and incomprehensible but with three words distinguishable from some background movement. "…the Golf later," Ricky Pickles had said.

He put his head round the front door.

"Sarge. Have you searched Ms Ackroyd's car?"

"No one told us owt about Miss Ackroyd's car," the sergeant called back, sounding aggrieved. "We didn't know it was here." Any fool, Mower thought angrily, should have worked out that Laura must have arrived by car. And it was Thackeray who, having evidently overheard this exchange, came hurrying down the stairs two at a time even before the sergeant had finished speaking.

"Something?" he asked, just a glimmer of hope in his eyes. Mower shrugged, not daring to hope for anything at all. Together they ran to the gate and out into the road where Laura's car remained parked neatly beside the kerb outside the house next door. They were followed by the local sergeant, looking anxious.

"Open the fucking boot," Mower instructed the sergeant, his face as frozen as Thackeray's. The sergeant obliged with a heavy kick which smashed the lock and sprang the lid up, to reveal the shape of a body, half concealed by a rug, curled awkwardly in a foetal position inside.

"Laura," Thackeray whispered as the sergeant pulled the rug away and loosened the gag which had been tied around her mouth. Her arms were fastened behind her and she did not move, but even as Mower grabbed his boss's arm, half afraid he would fall, Laura's eyes flickered.

"Am I glad to see you?" she said faintly, licking bruised lips.

"Likewise," Mower said drily as Thackeray picked her up and carried her, head bowed, carefully back into Earnshaw's house.

"There are times, Ms Ackroyd," he whispered as he put her down on a sofa, and untied her hands carefully, "when you stray a bit close to the edge."

Standing at the window of Thackeray's office the next day, watching the rain sweep across the town hall square, Laura sighed.

"Did we do Bradfield any favours after all that?" she asked the DCI who had been reading through the long statement she had come to police headquarters to sign after Bradfield Infirmary decided it was safe to discharge her.

He glanced at the dark bruise on her forehead where Pickles had struck her and knocked her unconscious and winced slightly. He had still not recovered from watching her carried away shivering with cold and shock by the paramedics after her ordeal in the car, or from the near certainty he had felt earlier that she had been killed.

"What do you mean?" he asked.

"Apparently Earnshaws is closing at the end of the week," she said. "Joyce rang me this morning to tell me. She's devastated."

"You can't stop these things," Thackeray said. "And at least we've got Pickles off the streets. And one of his biking friends is telling us everything he knows now there are two murder charges involved. Suddenly Mr. Pickles doesn't have nearly as many friends as he did. Omar has persuaded some of the lads in Aysgarth that they can remember far more than they thought they could about the motorbike attack and some very unexpected people are suddenly remembering a lot of things about his activities which should help put him away for a very long time."

"Good," Laura said.

"There is one thing I haven't told you," Thackeray said slowly. "I didn't want to upset you."

Laura wondered what could be more upsetting than being bundled unconscious into the boot of a car and left there for hours not knowing when captors would return to kill her, only that they would. Even when she had finally come to and heard voices outside she had been too terrified to make a sound in case it was Pickles. But Thackeray was looking at her with sombre eyes and she knew that she was going to like what came next even less.

"They found Saira Khan in the Seine," he said. "They've done a post-mortem and found she was pregnant. That must be why she went to France so suddenly, and why Simon Earnshaw started pressing his grandfather for more cash. He was going to be a father and wanted to get Saira away from Bradfield quickly."

Laura thought of the beautiful, vibrant young woman she had met on the banks of the Seine, a girl full of hope and happiness until she and her sister had destroyed it by bringing the worst possible news from Bradfield, and her eyes filled with tears.

"Shit happens," she said bitterly.

Thackeray got up from his desk and came to stand behind her at the rain-streaked window, with his hands on her shoulders, feeling a certainty that had eluded him for months.

"There was one good thing that came out of Sunday," he said quietly. "I thought for an hour or more that I'd lost you, Laura. And I knew I couldn't bear that. I want to marry you more than anything I've ever wanted in my life. Will you have me?"

She turned with a faint smile lighting up her bruised face for a moment.

"Are you sure?" she asked.

"Quite sure," he said.